'Run away, have you?' asked the Captain.

'That is not your business. Now, I think we should rejoin the coach. And please do not concern yourself about me.' Helen stood up and began to walk towards the coach.

He followed. 'Do you think I am the kind of man who can sit back and watch a silly chit get herself into a pickle and not be concerned? Do you not know the ri~~sks~~

'Risks or no

Born in Singapore, **Mary Nichols** came to England when she was three, and has spent most of her life in different parts of East Anglia. She has been a radiographer, school secretary, information officer and industrial editor, as well as a writer. She has three grown-up children and four grandchildren.

Recent titles by the same author:

TO WIN THE LADY
A DANGEROUS UNDERTAKING
DEVIL-MAY-DARE
THE PRICE OF HONOUR
THE DANBURY SCANDALS

THE LAST GAMBLE

Mary Nichols

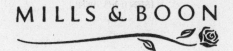

All the characters in this book have no existence outside the imagination of the author, and have no relation whatsoever to anyone bearing the same name or names. They are not even distantly inspired by any individual known or unknown to the author, and all the incidents are pure invention.

MILLS & BOON, the Rose Device and
LEGACY OF LOVE are trademarks of the publisher.
Harlequin Mills & Boon Limited,
Eton House, 18–24 Paradise Road, Richmond, Surrey TW9 1SR

© Mary Nichols 1996

ISBN 0 263 79880 1

Set in 10 on 12 pt Linotron Times
04-9611-82358

Typeset in Great Britain by CentraCet, Cambridge
Printed and bound in Great Britain
by BPC Paperbacks Limited, Aylesbury

CHAPTER ONE

OUTSIDE a watery sun shone in a pale sky and swallows twittered in the eaves, gathering for their autumn migration. Inside it was gloomy because the library curtains had been drawn almost fully across the windows. The only sound was the rhythmic ticking of the clock, even though there were two people in the room, an elderly man and a young lady dressed from head to toe in black crepe.

She was tiny, though perfectly proportioned. Her straight raven-dark hair, topped by a wisp of black lace, was drawn up into a Grecian knot, with one or two tendrils of curl left to frame an oval face which, in the last two weeks, had lost every vestige of colour. The silence seemed to stretch interminably.

'Miss Sanghurst,' he said, at last. 'You do understand what I have been saying?'

'Yes.' She looked up at him, green eyes wide with shock; otherwise, there was no indication of how she felt. Her hands were perfectly still in her lap. 'I think I do. Is there nothing left?'

He hated having to tell her that the father whose death she mourned had gambled away her inheritance and left debts of such magnitude his passing had changed her almost overnight from a pampered, wealthy young lady into nothing short of a pauper. But there had been no point in trying to soften the blow with half-truths and platitudes, she would know the

5

extent of it when his lordship's creditors, hearing of his demise, started knocking on the door. 'Nothing, I am afraid, except the money you inherited from your mother. She made sure he couldn't touch that.'

'She knew then?'

'What he was like? Yes, I am sure she did.'

'And yet she still loved him.' It was a statement, not a question; she knew her mother had adored her father.

'I believe she did, and that he loved her. You know how much her death affected him.'

'Yes.' Papa had shut himself away for days when her mother had died four years before. When he finally emerged, red-eyed and grey-faced, he had been a changed man, broody and curt instead of cheerful and considerate as he had hitherto been. And he started staying out at night, all night sometimes, as if he couldn't bear to be in the house without his wife. Until today Helen had no idea he had spent those nights gambling. How could she have been kept in such ignorance?

She had tried to understand how he felt about losing his wife, tried to make it up to him, and occasionally he would pull himself together and they would laugh and chat together and make plans. Last year they had been planning a European Tour. She had been unusually well-educated for a young lady and had been looking forward to learning more. It was meant to recompense her for her disappointment in not finding a husband.

Her come-out the year before her mother's last illness had been lavish and he could never understand why none of the young eligibles of that year had offered. Several had shown an early interest, but there had been no proposal because Helen herself had not encouraged them to think they would be looked on favourably.

She did not know why she was so particular, except that she had a clear idea of the man she would like to marry and would not accept anything less, and in this she had had the support of her mother. Her father failed to understand that she did not subscribe to the premise that any husband was better than none at all. Now, at four-and-twenty, she was almost an old maid.

In the event, their journey had been postponed because one of Papa's investments had failed. It was something to do with a ship carrying his merchandise which had sunk on its way from the Orient. He had assured her it was only a temporary setback and they would go the following year. Now she never would.

'I wish he had told me the extent of it,' she said. 'I could have made economies.' Her father had never stinted her, never complained when she asked him to buy her a new gown or a bonnet. In truth, he positively encouraged her to have whatever she wanted. Her mother's inheritance, which had been invested to provide her with a tiny monthly allowance, was looked on as pin money; she wasn't expected to use it to clothe herself. 'We could have let some of the staff go. . .' She paused, as the full horror of her circumstances was borne home to her. 'Now, I imagine, they must all go.'

'I'm afraid so.'

'Even Daisy? She's been with me ever since I came out of the schoolroom.'

'I am very sorry,' he said.

'And this house?'

'It will have to be sold to pay his lordship's debts.'

'Oh. Then I shall have to repair to the country. We haven't been there for two or three years, Papa never liked the Peterborough house, he said it was draughty and isolated from Society. And he still thought I would make a match if we stayed in town. . .'

'Miss Sanghurst,' he interrupted before she could be carried away by her plans. 'The Peterborough house was sold last year. His Lordship was hoping the money he realised on that would keep his dunners quiet for several months and pay for your tour but I am afraid he was over-optimistic.'

She looked up at him, her face betraying the horror and grief she had been feeling ever since her father had been discovered in the stables with his brains blown out. It was bad enough to have a father shoot himself, but suddenly to learn that the security you have always enjoyed was no more to be trusted than a puff of wind must be truly terrifying.

He had expected tears and wailing and a refusal to face the truth, but she had been surprisingly strong for one so slight, taking each blow on her pretty little chin and then sticking it out just that bit more. Her head was high and her back straight, but for how long? Surely she must break soon?

'Then I must find employment. I can teach, I love children, you know. Or be a lady's companion. Or perhaps I can be a clerk or a seamstress. . .' Each suggestion was more abhorrent than the last, but she must do something to earn a living and it was no good being top-lofty about it.

'There is one other thing I must mention,' he said,

admiring her courage. 'His Lordship appointed a guardian for you.'

'A guardian?'

'Yes.' He smiled at her astonishment. 'Every young lady, however mature she considers herself to be, needs someone to care for her and protect her if she should be so unlucky as to lose both her parents. Your father made this provision some time ago.'

'Who is he?' Ever since her father's death, she had accepted the fact that she was alone in the world, that she had no relatives, and must fend for herself, even though the full extent of it had only just been communicated to her by the lawyer—she was not only alone but almost penniless.

She had many friends, but none she could call close, so who could possibly have agreed to take her on? It would be a heavy responsibility, especially as she brought nothing with her. Instead of being the considerable heiress everyone believed her to be, she was a nobody, dependent on the charity of her sponsors and everyone would know it. The idea did not appeal to her at all.

'The Earl of Strathrowan.'

'I know no one of that name.'

'I believe he was a great friend of your father's when they served together in India. You were only a baby at the time, so you would not remember.'

'I certainly do not. Is he still out in India? Am I expected to go to him there?' Was there to be no end to the revelations being heaped upon her? She didn't think she could take many more without collapsing under the weight of them. Mourning a father she apparently did not know at all, was bad enough, but how much worse the humiliation of being foisted on a stranger and one that probably wouldn't want her anyway.

Oh, how she wished she were a man, then she could get on with her life. As a man she could find a gainful occupation and make her own way, but as a gentlewoman her hands were tied by convention. She was not expected to work for a living, she could not live alone, she could not even travel unescorted.

'I have discovered he is in Scotland,' Mr Benstead went on. 'He has an estate in the Loch Lomond region. He was a younger son and it was only on the death of his brother, the Viscount, that he became the heir. He succeeded soon after your father returned to England after inheriting his title.'

He might as well have said India, she thought, it was just as wild and inaccessible. 'Does he know that Papa. . .?' She gulped quickly and went on before she could lose her courage altogether. 'Does he know Papa is dead? And how he died?' The manner of her father's death was important too; it was a stigma she would have to carry with her.

'I have written to him and await his reply.' He shuffled the papers on the desk in front of him, drawing the painful interview to an end. 'There is nothing to be done until we hear from him.' He stood up and came round the desk to where she sat and put his hand on her shoulder. She had not moved since first sitting there, it was almost as if she dare not. 'I am deeply sorry to have brought you such distressing news.'

'Did you know how bad it was?' she asked, staring straight ahead. 'Before he died, I mean. Could you not have done something to stop him falling further into debt?'

He allowed himself a tiny smile. 'Your Papa was a very obstinate man, my dear, and if he would not listen to your mother when she was alive, how could I influence him? I tried. I warned him again and again that he was overreaching himself. It wasn't just gambling at the tables, he gambled on the markets, buying commodities and hoping to sell at vast profits. On each occasion he was confident he could recoup his losses. It never worked.'

'No.' She turned her face up to him at last and he noticed that the shock and misery he had seen there had been replaced by determination. There was a light in her luminous green eyes which could almost have been humour. 'If I ever marry,' she said. 'I shall ensure that my husband is not a gambler. I'll have it written into the marriage contract.' The humour spread to her lips in a fleeting smile. 'That is, if I am so fortunate as to find someone to marry me.'

'Of course you will, my dear,' he said. 'You are a handsome young lady, you know, and there must be dozens of young men eager to make your acquaintance.'

'In Scotland?' Now there was a definite twinkle in her eye and he breathed a sigh of relief. Her father had died by his own hand because he could not face up to life in poverty and he had wondered if she might be cast in the same mould, but evidently she was not. She was a fighter.

'We cannot tell what the Earl will decide to do,' he said. 'But as soon as I hear, I shall come and tell you.'

'Is there a Lady Strathrowan?'

'One must presume so.'

'And children? Sons and daughters, grandchildren, perhaps?'

'I have no way of knowing until I hear from him.'

'In the meantime?'

'You may live here until the sale is concluded, of course, but please limit your expenses to the minimum. Do you wish me to inform the servants?'

'No, I'll do it. Is there enough to pay them?'

'No, not until the sale goes through and then. . .' He shrugged. 'There might be something we can give them but if the dunners get there first. . .'

'They must be paid,' she cried. 'It's bad enough losing a position without having to go without the wages owed to you. I shall pay them from my own money.'

'You will need every penny of that for yourself, Miss Sanghurst,' he said. 'And they will soon find other positions.'

'Nevertheless, I shall pay them,' she said firmly.

He sighed as he bowed and took his leave. She was as obstinate as her father had been. He only hoped that her tenacity would stand her in good stead in the future. She would need all her resources, of strength and determination, as well as money, if she were going to survive.

Helen did not rise, knowing that Coster was standing outside the door and would see the lawyer out. But Coster had to be told the news and so did all the other servants. Telling them was to be the first of many unpleasant tasks she was going to have to do and she supposed she had better get on with it.

She rose slowly and smoothed down the skirt of her

mourning gown, reflecting that if she had only known how bad things were she would not have spent so much on it. Then, lifting her chin, she moved over to the door and opened it. The footman was shutting the outer door. 'Coster, will you ask everyone to come here, please. I have something to tell you all.'

'Poor little devil,' he murmured as he made his way to the back regions of the house to convey her orders. All alone in the world and, if the rumours were true, not a feather to fly with. If the old devil hadn't shot himself Coster would have been tempted to do it for him, except that it wouldn't have helped Miss Helen. Nor would it have put bread in his own mouth, not to mention the mouths of all the other servants. He could guess what was coming next. They were all going to be out on their ears.

He was proved right before another ten minutes had passed. The house was being sold and Miss Sanghurst was going to live with her guardian. It was the first any of them had heard of a guardian but they were glad for her sake; she needed someone to look after her. They were very fond of her; not one of them would have hesitated to serve her on half-wages if she had asked it of them, but she didn't.

It was strange how she hadn't shed a tear until Daisy had asked if she could stay on for little more than her keep and then she had run from the room and they could hear her flying up the stairs. The door of her room banged shut and there was nothing any of them dare to do but return to their duties, knowing that the following day, there would be none to do.

* * *

Helen threw herself across her bed and sobbed as if she were trying to cry the Thames dry. She had loved her father dearly, but how could he do this to her? How could he turn his back on her when she needed him so much? How could he have had so little concern for her future as to gamble away every penny and everything they owned and then refuse to face up to what he had done? Why had she never suspected there was something wrong? The questions went round and round in her brain but she had no answers.

His answer had been to end his own life and leave her to a stranger, just as if she were a mongrel dog needing a good home. She hesitated to call his behaviour dishonourable, but she could find no other word for it. He must have known the disgrace would reflect on her, the daughter he professed to love. The tabbies would have a field day and she would be ostracised. It had already begun, for the Dowager Lady Carruther had cut her dead in the lending library two days before and Mrs Courtney had stopped her daughter, whom Helen considered a friend, from speaking to her in the park. Unable to condemn her father, she detested the unknown guardian instead.

She sat up at last and mopped her tears with a face cloth, then rinsed her burning cheeks in cold water from the pitcher on the wash-stand. Crying never achieved anything, except to make her look ugly. She sat at her dressing table and peered into the looking-glass above it. Her eyelids were puffed and red from weeping, and there were two high spots of pink on her cheeks, but otherwise she looked drained of all colour. Her hair, usually so neat, was falling down from its pins.

Was this the picture she was going to present to the Earl? A dishclout full of self-pity? Or someone strong enough to weather life's storms and take whatever was thrown at her right on the chin? She lifted her head and pulled a face at herself in the mirror. 'Now pull yourself together, Miss Helen Sanghurst,' she said. 'No one loves a watering pot, and sitting here feeling sorry for yourself will take you nowhere. Look on it as an adventure, an adventure into the unknown. Are you afraid? Of course you are not, you are your father's daughter...'

And then she began to cry again, but this time not for herself, but for the father she had lost. She had lost him long before that pistol went off; if the truth be known, she had lost him on the day her mother died. But only now could she grieve.

Her sobs subsided at last; she would not cry again. She washed her face, combed her hair and re-pinned it, then went downstairs to give orders for supper, the last orders she would ever give. Tomorrow all the servants except Daisy would leave, each clutching their wages and carrying their personal possessions; Daisy would remain until she herself left. Her maid was more than a servant, she was a friend, and Helen wished she could take her with her wherever she was going, but she had no intention of asking favours of her guardian.

Waiting was irksome, made worse by the fact that no one visited her except her father's creditors who, hearing the news, swooped on her to be first with their claims, and a few prying busy-bodies whose only motive was gathering titbits of gossip to pass on over the tea cups or behind their fans at the latest Society ball. It was easier to say she was not at home to callers.

By the same token, she could not go visiting and so her only recreation was walking in the park, which cost nothing, and sorting her father's books. He had a unique collection of military books and some fine maps; these were expected to fetch a good price. Not that she would see any of the money; Mr Benstead had told her that it was earmarked to pay debts.

The books, the silver and porcelain, the horses and the carriage, even his clothes were all going the same way. The furniture was expected to be sold along with the house; all Helen could call her own were her clothes and the little jewellery she had inherited from her mother. She wondered if some of it might have to be sacrificed.

'No, my dear, there is no call on you personally,' the lawyer assured her when he visited her a few days later. There was no real need to see her, he had no news to convey, but he realised she must be feeling very isolated in that huge house, with only the maid for company, and he wanted her to know she still had a friend, though there was little he could do to help her. 'Your private possessions, clothes, books, jewels are your own. If you choose to sell them, then that is your affair, nothing to do with your father's estate.'

'I have been thinking that it would be foolish to clutter myself up with clothes and jewels I am never likely to wear again,' she said. 'I must dress according to my status.'

'Your status has not altered, my dear,' he said gently.

'You are still the same person, a single young lady, properly brought up. That hasn't changed.'

He was just being kind to her, she knew that. How could she not change? She was going to have to learn to conserve her resources, to watch every penny, to be subservient to those who provided her bread and butter, to be grateful for every morsel. And how she was going to hate it! If she had accepted one of the young men who buzzed around her in her come-out year she might now be married and this whole sorry mess would not be happening, but she had made her choice and now she had to stop thinking of what might have been. 'Have you heard from the Earl?' she asked.

'Not yet. It is a long way to Scotland and back and the mail is not always reliable.'

'Supposing we never hear? Your letter might never reach him. He might have left and returned to India. He might have gone back to his regiment and be serving abroad. He might have died. He might not wish to be associated with me, after what has happened.'

'It is no good meeting trouble halfway, Miss Sanghurst,' he said. 'Let us wait and see, shall we?'

It was a month before he heard, and by that time the new owners of the house were anxious to move in. They pestered him every day, wanting to know when Miss Sanghurst would be vacating the premises. Now he would be able to tell them she would be leaving immediately. The Earl had agreed to take her in, though his letter, if you could call it that, had hardly been welcoming. 'Send her up', was all it said.

Benstead could not tell her that, it would break her

heart all over again; he would simply say his lordship was pleased to comply with his old friend's request and hope she did not ask to see the missive. If he had been anything but a staid old bachelor, he would have taken her in himself rather than let her go where she wasn't welcome. But perhaps he was maligning the Earl; he might simply be a poor letter-writer or had delegated the task to a secretary who did not understand the need for tact. But that didn't account for the fact that he had not even sent the fare, let alone provided an escort, which she might have expected.

'How am I to get there?' she asked, when he told her. 'The carriage and horses have already gone. And I couldn't have afforded to go post chaise even if they had not. I shall have to go by public coach.'

'The mail is by far the most comfortable,' he said. 'They limit the number of passengers, you know, and it's faster than the stage.'

'I am in no hurry, Mr Benstead,' she said, a faint smile on her lips. 'And comfort is not a consideration, but my purse is. I shall travel by stage.'

'Then I shall see if I can find a couple or a matronly lady to chaperone you. . .'

'Mr Benstead, at four-and-twenty I need no chaperone. The pampered daughter of Lord Sanghurst is no more. Hard though it may be, I have to learn to live in the world outside the narrow sphere I was raised in and be self-reliant.'

'You can have no idea of the risks.'

'Then I shall learn by my mistakes. Please do not give me a second thought, Mr Benstead.'

'It is my duty to see that all steps are taken to deliver you safely to your destination.'

'Like a parcel.' For the first time in weeks, she laughed. 'Mr Benstead, you have discharged your duty, more than was called for, considering the circumstances. I imagine you have not been able to pay yourself.'

He neither confirmed nor denied it, but smiled cheerfully; he did not want her to go, thinking he had misgivings. 'Then all I can do now is wish you a pleasant journey. Please write and inform me of your safe arrival.' Oh, how formal he sounded, but he had to remain dignified or he would give way to the urge to take her in his arms as one would a child, and reassure her that she had not been abandoned. He would watch over her somehow. He offered her his hand and she took it firmly.

The following day, he sent round her coach ticket as far as Glasgow, begging to be allowed to pay for it. It was very kind of him and would enable her to spend a little more on accommodation and board on the journey. Looking down at the slip of paper, she felt as if she held her fate in her hand, and she supposed it was true; her destiny was many miles away to the north. But now was no time to mope, now was the time to be positive. She enjoyed good health and, though she was small, she was strong; the journey itself held no terrors for her.

There was consolation in the thought that being so far from the capital, she would not hear the gossip being spread about her and her father and they would soon be forgotten. Besides, the tattle-mongers had more than enough to keep their tongues busy with the antics of the Prince of Wales who, on the death of his mad father, had now become king and was trying to divorce his wife.

Only four months before, Caroline had returned to the capital and demanded to be recognised as queen, and there were many who supported her. The conjecture about what would happen next was likely to go on and on. With such juicy tit-bits, who would be interested in a penniless nobody?

She went up to the attic and pulled out a trunk, bumping it down the stairs to her room, where she packed it, considering each item on the grounds of its necessity before including it, but a miniature portrait of her mother in a silver frame, two or three of her favourite books and writing materials went in along with her clothes.

She had sold all her jewellery with the exception of a diamond clip and her mother's betrothal ring. The brooch she would wear, while the ring in its velvet-lined box went into the very bottom of the trunk. Then she and Daisy manhandled it down the stairs to the hall, after which they ate a frugal, and largely silent, supper in the kitchen before going to bed.

The night seemed long and the old house creaked and groaned as if adding its own protests to the blow fate had dealt it. The wind rose too and a branch of a tree kept banging at her window, so that, even if her mind had not been full of the morrow, sleep would have been impossible.

She rose and sat at the window until the grey light of dawn lightened the roofs and chimney pots and the tops of the trees in the park began to show their branches. Almost overnight they had been stripped of their leaves and she realised that autumn was here and winter not far off. What was winter like in Scotland? Was it true they were often snowed in for weeks on end? Soon she might know.

She dressed in a neat black merino wool gown with a pointed waist and high neck which had a narrow white frill. It was buttoned at the front so that she would not need help with dressing; all her clothes had been chosen with that in mind. Under it she wore two layers of underwear, one flannel and one fine lawn, not only because she expected to be cold but because it had left more room in the trunk for other things. The bonnet she chose was of plain black straw and quite small.

She had never travelled in a public coach before, but she imagined it might be a crush; wide brims and voluminous skirts would hardly endear her to her fellow passengers. Then, feeling decidedly dumpy, she went down to breakfast.

Daisy, who had found a new position with a large family, mostly girls, left immediately afterwards. It was an emotional parting and it took all Helen's resolve to stay dry-eyed, particularly as the maid was making no effort to stem her tears. 'You'll write, won't you, Miss Helen? I shan't rest easy until I know you've arrived safe and well and met your guardian. I pray he is kind to you.'

'Why should he not be kind to me?' she demanded, though the same thought had crossed her mind. 'My father would not have wanted me to live with someone who did not care for me.'

Daisy decided not to say what was in her mind regarding the late Lord Sanghurst. Instead she mopped up her tears and smiled. 'No, course not, Miss Helen, but you know what I mean.'

'Yes. Now off you go and don't worry about me. You mustn't be late on your first day.'

Helen spent the next two hours going round the all the rooms, making sure the dust sheets were in place on the furniture and the curtains were closed to stop the sun fading the carpets. She had lived in this house ever since her parents had returned from India when she was a baby. She had been brought up here knowing nothing of poverty or insecurity or evil, until a month ago when her whole life had been overset. Now it was up to her to make the best of it and not brood.

She went into her mother's boudoir, remembering how it always smelled so fragrant and how her mama's smile lit it, making it seem as though the sun shone even on the dullest day. As a small girl she would be taken onto her lap and would sink her head onto a bosom that was designed for comfort and listen to her telling stories. Story-time before bed was the best part of the day.

She remembered one about a poor little girl who was treated cruelly at the orphanage she was sent to when her mother died, but never gave up hope that one day she would find a loving home and live happily ever after. And she had, of course, when her long-lost uncle turned up. Would the Earl of Strathrowan be her happy ending?

She wondered what he was like to look at. She imagined he must be about the same age as her father if they had served together, but was he tall or short, fat or thin, handsome or plain? And did it matter what he looked like, so long as he genuinely welcomed her?

And if he didn't? Then she would leave, her mind was set on that. She would find work and lodgings and be independent.

She heard the doorbell jangle and for a moment forgot she was the only person in the house to answer it, but when it rang a second time, she hurried downstairs to open the door. A hackney cab stood outside and its driver had his whip raised to bang on the door. 'Thought there weren't no one at 'ome,' he said. 'You ready?'

She had never been spoken to like that before, but she supposed he had taken her for a servant and she could hardly blame him. 'Yes,' she said. 'If you would be so good as to carry my trunk. I can manage the bag.'

She had left a warm cloak on a chair and now she picked it up and put it on, while he half-lifted, half-dragged the heavy trunk down the steps to the cab. 'What you got in 'ere?' he asked. 'The crown jewels?'

She smiled. 'No, only my clothes and one or two books.'

'Books, eh? What d'you want books for? Nothin' good ever come out o' books, tha's wot I allus says.'

Not wanting an argument, she did not reply, but locked the front door, put the key in her bag along with all the others belonging to the house, and waited until the trunk was safely strapped on to the back of the cab before climbing in and directing him to take her to Mr Benstead's office. She had to give him the keys but did not want to stop and talk to him; everything had been said that needed saying.

She had left very little time to get to the Blue Boar at Holborn where she would board the stage for the first part of her journey north. The lawyer was out on business and she left the keys with a clerk and returned to the cab. The past was behind her, all her tears had been shed and the future, whatever it held, was before her; it was up to her to grasp whatever opportunities were offered.

The Blue Boar was one of the busiest coaching inns in London. Stage coaches came and went all day, clattering into the yard and disgorging passengers and their baggage and taking on others going to all points of the compass. It was noisy with shouting and laughter, people saying farewell, others being greeted, horses neighing and chickens squawking.

The air was filled with smells, horse droppings, leather harness, cooking, sweat and perfume, all intermingled. Helen was almost overwhelmed as the cab drew up and the driver jumped down and deposited her and her luggage on the cobbles in front of the inn.

'Carry your bags, missie?'

She looked down to see a little urchin peering up at her with mischievous blue eyes, though his face was filthy and his feet bare. She smiled. 'I think the trunk will be a little too heavy for you, don't you?'

'I'm strong, miss.' He flexed his muscles, making her laugh. 'I can drag it along.'

'I think it would be better if you found me a porter. Would you do that, please?'

He made no move to comply but stood looking up at her and holding out his hand.

'I'm afraid he will not budge until you have put a coin in his palm,' a male voice said.

She swung round and found herself facing a broad blue jacket covered with gold braid and silver lace. Its wearer was so tall she had to tilt her head up to see his face. It was a handsome face, topped by short brown hair which curled over his ears beneath his shako. His clean-shaven chin was as firm as her own, but a great deal larger. But what set her against him was the twinkle of amusement in his brown eyes, as if she should have known the boy would not do as he was asked without being paid for it.

'Where I come from, children do as they are bid without inducement,' she said, noticing, without meaning to, that his wide epaulettes emphasised his broad shoulders, and the cut of his blue pantaloons, tucked into highly polished hessians, enhanced his slim hips and muscular thighs. It was the sort of figure the uniform was designed for.

'How fortunate for you,' he said, smiling openly and throwing the boy a coin which he caught deftly before dashing off towards another traveller; now the soldier had arrived, there was no point in hanging around. 'But I wouldn't class this lad as a child, I'll wager he has been earning a living in like manner for years, ever since he could walk and speak.'

'How dreadful!'

'Dreadful to earn his keep in honest toil, Miss. . .?'

'No,' she said, ignoring his obvious hint that she should tell him her name. 'I meant dreadful it should be necessary.'

'Yes, of course.' He stopped to look at her properly. She was in mourning, which didn't suit her somewhat pale colouring, but her features were good: an oval face, little turned-up nose, a firm mouth, pursed in perplexity, and large green eyes framed by dark lashes. She was obviously a well-nurtured young lady, too young to be travelling alone and he wondered how it had come about.

If she had run away from home, she must have been very resourceful to have crept out with that great trunk. Was she eloping? She was certainly pretty enough and, he imagined, guileless enough to be the target of some unscrupulous young blade and her mourning would preclude a wedding, even if the young man were acceptable. But if so, where was he? She was looking about her in bewilderment as if asking herself the same question. 'Don't worry, he'll turn up,' he said.

'Who?'

'The man. You are expecting to meet a man, are you not? I hesitate to call him a gentleman, since no gentleman worth his salt would allow a lady to struggle alone with a box like that.' He nodded at the trunk standing at her feet.

'It is none of your business.'

'No more it is,' he said cheerfully. 'I bid you good day.'

'Wait!' It was almost a cry of desperation.

He turned back to her, one eyebrow raised and a tiny smile lurking about his lips. 'I can be of service, after all?'

'I need a porter to take my trunk to the coach, but I cannot leave it here while I go and look for one.'

He smiled. 'Tell me, where do you wish your baggage to be taken?'

'I am booked on the coach to Glasgow.'

He had been right. She was off to Gretna Green. No wonder she looked scared to death. 'You can always go back home,' he said gently. 'I'm sure no one will blame you.'

'There is no going back and no question of blame.'

'You will be disappointed, I guarantee it.'

She looked up at him with startled green eyes; could he really see into her heart? 'What do you know about it? Who are you?'

'Captain Duncan Blair, at your service.' He swept her an exaggerated bow. 'I was simply pointing out that it is not too late to change your mind about this undertaking.'

'Oh, yes, it is, Captain, much too late.'

'Then let us find the coach.' He hoisted her trunk onto his shoulders as if it weighed nothing at all and strode into the throng of people. She had perforce to follow.

In no time at all he had located the Glasgow coach, which was emblazoned with the name The Flying Prince and its destination along with a great deal more information which made it look like a travelling bill-board. He supervised the loading of the trunk, handed her in and climbed in beside her, taking off his shako and sitting with it in his lap.

'What are you doing?' she asked in alarm.

'Waiting patiently for the off,' he said. 'You are not the only one setting off for Scotland today. I fancy there will be six of us inside and many more on top. I wish they'd get a move on, I am in the deuce of a hurry.'

They were joined inside by an elderly man in a dark suit, a farmer who, though obviously prosperous enough to afford an inside seat, smelled of cattle and spirits, and a woman of more than middle years, who wore a great deal of face paint and had her hair done up in a style that had been fashionable many years before. The sixth seat remained empty.

Duncan concluded that the unknown lover had lost his nerve, and he was curious to know what the young lady would do. That she was a gentlewoman he did not doubt; her whole demeanour proclaimed it, but she was going to have a rude awakening before many miles had passed, unless her lover was going to board the coach when they changed horses.

He excused himself to lean across her and shout to the guard, who was shepherding the outside passengers up the steps to the roof. 'How much longer are we going to sit here? This coach is due to leave at noon and it is already five minutes past by my watch.'

'Yes, but you see, sir,' the man answered equably. 'We don't go by your watch, we go when that there clock points the hour.' He nodded his head towards the clock above the door of the inn. 'And that lacks two minutes to twelve.'

Duncan subsided into his seat. It was not the least use being impatient; he would arrive when he arrived and he prayed he would not be too late.

Almost immediately the guard called, 'All aboard!' and the coachman appeared. He was dressed in a brown boxcoat with several capes about his shoulders, which flapped open to reveal a striped waistcoat and small clothes which reached down to meet a pair of jockey boots halfway up his calves. Helen watched as he walked slowly all the way round the vehicle, checking the wheels and axles, and then inspecting the horses and their harness before moving to the off-side and taking up the reins in his left hand. As the clock moved to one minute to departure time he took up his whip and climbed aboard. At exactly noon by the clock, the inn staff stood back, and they were off. Duncan smiled at the girl beside him because she was looking decidedly shaky.

'How long does it take?' she asked. Being obliged to him for carrying her trunk and overseeing it loaded safely, she could hardly ignore him and besides, she was no longer in Society and did not need a proper introduction to speak to him. 'The journey to Scotland, I mean.'

So the lovers were travelling separately. If *he* had arranged to carry her off to Gretna Green, he would have made sure he was with her every inch of the way. Already he was beginning to dislike the unknown suitor. 'It's usually twenty-four hours to Manchester, non-stop. That's a good deal less than halfway. After that, it depends on the state of the roads and the weather.'

'Non-stop?' she queried, wondering why she had never asked the question before. 'You mean without going to bed?'

'Yes. We should arrive in Manchester at noon tomorrow, God willing.'

'Surely we must stop to sleep.'

'If you wish, you may stop at any one of a number of inns on the way and continue next day in another coach. It depends on how much haste you are in. Myself, I would rather doze as I go and arrive all the sooner.'

'And I certainly would not!' she said.

'Indeed? You surprise me, I would have wagered you were in haste to reach your destination.'

'You do not know my destination, sir, nor my state of mind,' she said sharply.

'No, I beg pardon,' he said, leaning back and shutting his eyes, effectively ending the conversation.

The farmer was already asleep and snoring and the elderly man was sitting in the corner attempting to read, though how he could do it in the swaying coach Helen could not fathom. The woman sitting opposite her fetched out a packet of food and began gnawing on a chicken leg. They were as motley a collection of individuals as you were ever likely to meet, she decided, and she had to admit to being glad the Captain was there.

She had an instinctive feeling he would protect her — she had recognised the insignia of Prince of Wales's Own Hussars on his shako — but his manner left a great deal to be desired. He spoke in riddles and didn't seem to mind how rude he was. Look at him now. He was dozing.

She did not know how he could sleep in that uncomfortable position, bolt upright with his head lolling because his stiff collar prevented him from dropping his chin on his chest, and with his long legs doubled under him. The passengers sitting opposite prevented him from stretching them out and he could not tuck them under the seat because that space was part of the rear boot.

But like that, he seemed more human, almost boyish, and she supposed he could not be much more than thirty, but there was a slight scar along his hairline and another on the back of his hand which was half covered by his sleeve, and she assumed he had been injured in the service of his country but, judging by the way he had carried her trunk, he was not too badly disabled.

He opened one brown-flecked eye and caught her looking at him and winked at her. Confused and embarrassed, she turned to look out of the window. Mr Benstead had said her status had not altered, but he had been wrong. Yesterday, she had been the pampered daughter of an aristocrat, today she was a nobody whom a common soldier could offend with impunity! She had told her lawyer she must learn to live in the world outside her ken, among people who knew nothing of Society except as a subject for gossip, to accept their ways as her own, but oh, how difficult it was going to be.

CHAPTER TWO

THEY were on a good road and, apart from slowing up for the guard to pay the toll, the horses rarely dropped below a canter. Islington, Holloway, Highgate and Finchley were left behind and then they were approaching Barnet. Helen knew all this because the guard had called out the names as they passed and now he was sounding his horn to warn the next staging post of their imminent arrival.

She was feeling cramped and slightly nauseous and she would be relieved to get out and stretch her legs. Two minutes later they drew into the yard of the Red Lion, where all was bustle as ostlers rushed forward with the new horses while the ones which had carried them thus far were taken from the traces to be rested.

'It takes forty-five seconds, no more,' the Captain said, seeing her hand on the door.

Before she could turn to reply, the guard let out a bellow of rage and dragged the little urchin who had accosted her in London from among the boxes and packages in the rear boot where he had been hiding. It was a miracle he had not been battered to death or thrown out and killed. 'Trying to get a free ride, were you?' he demanded, shaking the child until his teeth rattled. 'In my book that's a crime.'

'Lemme go!' the boy yelled. 'I ain't done nothin'.'

'No fear!' He cuffed him about the ears, rocking his head back on his shoulders.

Helen was out of her seat and down on the ground before anyone realised what she was doing. 'Let him be!' she ordered, pulling at the man's arm to prevent further blows.

He turned in surprise. 'Go back to your seat, please, miss, this here's company business. Riding without a ticket 'as got to be punished.'

The child, feeling the grip which held him slacken, released himself and threw himself at Helen, burying his face in her skirts. 'I meant no 'arm, miss. Only I 'ave to get to me brother and I ain't got the fare.'

'Where does your brother live?' she asked, putting her arm protectively round him, ignoring the fact that he was filthy.

'Don't matter where he lives,' the guard said. 'Now, go back to your seat and leave me to deal with the little slip-gibbet.' He pulled the boy from her grasp. 'I ain't got time to hand you in, so think y'self lucky. Now get you gone.' With a final blow to the head, he pushed the child in the direction in which they had just come.

'You surely do not expect him to walk all the way back to London?' Helen demanded.

'It's all the same to me what he does, but if I see 'im anywhere near one of my coaches again, he'll be for it, I can tell you.'

'But he's all alone. . .'

She became aware that the Captain had left the coach and was standing beside her. 'Please return to your seat, ma'am. There is nothing you can do and you are holding up the coach.' He smiled. 'That's almost as bad a crime as travelling without a ticket.'

'Never mind the coach,' she said crossly. 'We can't

abandon the poor child. He wants to go to his brother.'
She turned from him and called out to the boy, who
had taken half a dozen steps and then stopped when
he heard her spirited defence of him. 'Where does
your brother live?'

'St Albans, miss.'

'Then get in the coach. I shall pay your fare.'

'Oh, no, you don't,' the guard said, grabbing the
child as he went to obey. 'Just 'cos this young lady is a
soft touch, don't mean you can pull the wool over my
eyes; you'd have everyone's pockets picked in the
twinkling of an eye.'

'No, I would not. I ain't a thief.'

'For goodness sake, give him a ticket,' Duncan said,
realising that the young lady was obstinate enough to
stand arguing all day and too soft-hearted by far.
'We've wasted enough time as it is. I'll see he behaves
himself.'

Helen gave him a look of gratitude, which was lost
on him because he had already returned to his seat.
She opened her purse and paid the requisite fare from
London to St Albans, then she took the boy by the
hand and followed, settling him between them.

'Thank you, Captain,' she said, as they set off once
againt several minutes behind schedule.

'Don't thank me. And don't blame me, when he
turns and bites the hand that feeds, because he will,
you know.'

'Of course he won't. Will you?' She smiled down at
the boy, but all he did was grin happily from one to
the other. This was a much better way to travel than
being flung about among the baggage in the boot.

'It's disgraceful!' the woman in the opposite seat

exclaimed, endeavouring not to wrinkle her nose in case she cracked the paint on her face. 'The boy smells and I'll wager he is verminous. We shall all end up infested. I cannot think what the coachman was thinking of to allow it.' She leaned forward and wagged her finger at the Captain. 'As for you, sir, I should have thought you could have prevented your wife...'

'Wife?' Helen repeated, colouring to the roots of her hair. 'You are mistaken, ma'am, I am not the Captain's wife. I am not even acquainted with the gentleman.'

'Indeed?' She paused to look from one to the other, then shrugged. 'Wife or no, he should have stopped you bringing the brat on board.'

The Captain smiled. 'Ma'am, I doubt if anyone could stop the young lady once she has made up her mind to something, I certainly could not. And the bratling is entitled to the ride, his fare has been paid.'

'He could have ridden outside,' the farmer put in.

'It isn't safe,' Helen said. 'And as for smells...' She stopped, realising it would do no good at all to mention the fact that the pungent odour he was emitting masked any smell from the boy. Quarrelling with her fellow travellers would not endear her to them and she felt isolated enough as it was. 'He might have fallen off.'

'And good riddance too,' the farmer said.

'Oh, come now, sir,' Duncan put in. 'The boy is hardly more than a babe, and if the young lady is prepared to endure him, then we must acquiesce with a good grace. He will not be with us for long, after all.'

Helen smiled. 'Thank you, Captain.'

The boy grinned up at her. 'You're a real lady, miss.'

'Huh!' The painted woman's expression said it all.

Helen found herself wanting to answer back, to say, yes, she considered herself to be a lady, but then thought better of it. It smacked of pride and as she had vowed to put her old life behind her, there was nothing to be gained by boasting of it. She had not realised, before now, how much difference it made to how you were treated if people knew you came from the upper echelons of society. But she was learning fast. Instead, she turned to ask the boy his name.

'Ned Barker, miss.'

'And how old are you?'

'Ten.'

Helen was surprised; he was so small she had taken him for much younger.

'And what were you doing alone in London if your family live in St Albans?'

'It's only me brother in St Albans. Pa and Ma went to live in London when I was little. Pa were out of work—a soldier he were, back from the wars—and 'e thought he'd find something in London. It weren't so easy. 'E kep' sayin' one day his ship would come in, but it never did and when Ma die, he give up.'

'Oh, how sad. What happened then? After your mother died, I mean.'

'He took to the bottle, miss . And the dubbin' lay. . .'

'Dubbing lay?' she queried. 'I have never heard of that occupation.'

'It means breaking into houses,' the Captain put in with a smile. 'The boy's father is a thief.'

'Not any more, 'e ain't.' The boy grinned up at her. ''E got snabbled.'

'Arrested,' the Captain interpreted for Helen.

'Oh, dear,' she said, addressing the boy. 'And that left you all alone? Is that why you were working at the Blue Boar?'

'Yes, miss. But it ain't no great shakes as a livin', so I had a mind to go to me brother. 'E's married and settled in St Albans. 'E'll 'ave me.'

'I'm sure he will,' she said. The boy's situation was so like her own, even though it was on a different level, she could feel only compassion for him. That his father was a felon was neither here nor there. Felon or gambler, what difference did it make to the end result?

There was silence in the coach for perhaps a minute, but the boy had evidently not heard the maxim that children should be seen and not heard. He prattled on. 'Them's a good set of wheelers,' he said, nodding in the general direction of the horses.

'Are they?' The only knowledge Helen had of horseflesh was what she had learned from her riding instructor and that was little enough.

'Good strong hindquarters,' the boy went on. 'The leaders ain't bad neither, though one of 'em is pulling to the left.'

'How clever of you to notice,' she said, conscious that the Captain was hard put to stifle his amusement.

The boy switched his attention to the countryside outside the coach, pointing out cows, pigs, sheep, finding something to say about each, asking questions which Helen did her best to answer though she was not very knowledgeable about things agricultural.

'It's a bull,' the farmer said with a grin after the boy had referred to one animal as a 'queer cow'.

Helen felt herself go very red but said nothing.

'I ain't seen one afore,' the boy went on, undaunted. 'Cows in the park in plenty, but not them.'

'Well, they can be dangerous,' Helen said.

'Is that so?' And then, pointing, 'What's that?'

Helen decided she would be wiser not to answer for fear of contradiction. 'A plough, boy,' the farmer put in. 'Don't you know anything?'

'I'll wager he knows the quickest way from Covent Garden to Putney Steps,' the Captain put in. 'The departure times of all the coaches, which hotels throw out the best scraps; the best places to scavenge in the river mud and where to sell the proceeds. I'll wager, too, that he knows when every house in London is likely to have its knocker off.' He smiled at boy. 'When the owners are away, there are rich pickings. Your father taught you that, didn't he?'

The boy grinned. 'You're a sharp cove, but I ain't ever been nabbled.'

'Too slippery,' Duncan said with a laugh.

Helen had only a vague idea what they were talking about but decided it was a subject best not pursued. She opened the small bag she had brought to carry things she would need for the journey and took out a package of food Daisy had prepared before she left, some bread and butter, a slice or two of ham, a few chicken legs, a couple of apples. It was meant to save her having to buy anything until they stopped for the night. 'Are you hungry, Ned?'

'Starvin',' he said, which was nothing less than the truth.

She offered him the package and watched as he wolfed the lot.

The Captain was regarding her with a light in his

eye which might have been mockery, but could equally have been empathy, and she found herself blushing. It was almost as if he knew all about her, knew she was pretending to be someone she was not. 'Oh, dear,' he said, indicating the few crumbs left on the paper on the boy's knees. 'Now you will have to go hungry, Miss. . .?'

Again there was that hint that she should reveal her name. 'It is of no consequence,' she said. 'I ate a good breakfast before I left.'

'And where would that have been?'

'Sir,' she said, stiffening. 'I do not think it is any concern of yours.'

'I beg your pardon, I was simply making conversation.'

'Not very subtle conversation, either,' said a voice from the corner. Helen was startled because the man, who appeared to be engrossed in his reading, had taken no part in the conversation at all. 'But then, what can one expect from a soldier, one of Prinny's Hussars or not. You do not seem to comprehend that not every female will fall into your arms, just because you favour her with a smile.'

'You would have me glower at everyone and never open my mouth?' Duncan queried. He had wondered about the girl, simply because she was so full of contradictions. At times she appeared lost and vulnerable, almost fearful, at others she gave the impression she could take on the world and win.

What had made her like that? Why had she championed the boy, paid his fare, given him all her food, in the face of all opposition, not least his own? Did she like being contrary and having everyone about her up in arms? Or was she simply unaware of the effect she was creating. She was tiny, but no one could ignore her.

'Oh, please, do not fall out over it,' Helen pleaded.

'If you wish for conversation,' the dark man went on, addressing Duncan. 'I will oblige. My name is Tinsley. I am an attorney at law.'

'Blair, Captain Duncan Blair,' Duncan said reaching across to offer his hand. 'Have you been involved in the trial?'

Everyone knew what he meant, even the child, though it was not technically a trial. The House of Lords were debating a Bill which, if passed, would condemn the King's wife as an adulteress and she would forfeit her rights as Queen and be divorced from the King. Every word said and every tiny piece of evidence—some of it was very salacious indeed—was talked about and mulled over by a populace who had no great feelings for either protagonist. It was in the best traditions of a London farce.

'Only in a very minor capacity.'

'The poor woman.' This from the painted lady. 'The King has always hated her.'

'And has never taken the slightest pains to hide it,' Helen put in. 'I have. . .' She had been going to say she had met the Regent at her come-out, but stopped herself; the woman she was supposed to be would never have moved in Royal circles. 'I have heard he is as dissolute a rake as anyone would wish to meet. If I were married to him, I should certainly not wish to live with him, not even to be Queen. Why she did not stay living quietly in Italy, I cannot imagine.'

'Quietly!' Duncan exclaimed. 'She is incapable of

doing anything quietly. She flaunts herself and her...'
He paused, realising there were ladies present, and
corrected himself. '...chamberlain all over Europe and
then expects to come back as soon as the old King dies
and be acclaimed Queen.'

'I can see where your sympathies lie,' the lawyer
said with a smile. 'But then, if I am not mistaken, the
uniform you wear is that of the Prince of Wales's Own
Hussars.'

'It is, sir.'

'How long have you been serving His Majesty?'

'I joined as an ensign in 1808 when I was eighteen.'

'Then you have seen some service?'

'I had the honour to serve under Wellington—
Wellesley as he was then—throughout the Peninsula
Campaign, and again at Waterloo when I was one of
His Lordship's aides.'

'I believe that battle took a heavy toll of His
Lordship's staff.'

'Indeed, it did. I was fortunate to have only minor
wounds which soon healed.'

'You know Old Hooknose?' Ned asked, suddenly
impressed.

'Yes.' Duncan smiled down at him. 'He eats little
boys for breakfast.'

The boy laughed. 'You're gammoning me.'

'You did not consider resigning your commission at
the end of hostilities?' the lawyer asked.

'No.' It was a question he had been asked before
and unable to explain, he gave his usual answer. 'It
seemed to me that there was still work I could do. I
entered Paris with the triumphant army and when
Wellington arrived there as Ambassador, I was

appointed one of his aides. I have lately been in Vienna, working in a minor capacity for the Congress.'

'A notable career, captain.'

'Thank you.'

'I have heard that nothing can touch Vienna for social gaiety,' the painted lady put in. 'You must find yourself mingling frequently with the *haute monde*.'

'There are a great many balls and receptions, plays and operas, which it has been my duty to attend, ma'am, but I have no great love of pretentiousness. I am a simple man.'

'You are unmarried?' she queried, arching her brows and fluttering her lashes in a way which made Helen smile.

'Yes.' He gave no indication of having noticed the coyness.

'I thought so.' The lawyer smiled. 'You have not yet been gentled by a woman's touch. Too blunt by far. If you want something, you demand it. You must learn to tread more softly.'

'Sir, I do not need instruction from you on how to behave. And I have not always found women gentling. In fact, the reverse. They are masters of harshness and many have a rapier wit.'

'You must have been very unfortunate, Captain,' Helen said. 'We are not all unfeeling.'

He was saved from answering by the sound of the guard's horn, warning the next stage of their arrival, and two minutes later they drew up at at an inn where the horses were taken from their traces and substituted with fresh ones. A little over a minute later they were off again, with Ned giving his opinion of the new cattle. 'Ain't a patch on the other lot,' he said. 'Tame as mice.

I could drive 'em m'self.' Which comment set them all laughing as they continued along a good road through open country and then down the hill into St Albans. When they drew up at the Woolpack, Helen was relieved to find they would be allowed to leave the coach for a short while. Even though Ned was small, she had never felt so cramped in her life.

'There will be an hour's stop on account of a repair to one of the traces,' the guard called as they descended. 'Plenty of time for a good meal for those going on. We leave again at four o'clock.'

Helen, trying to find her land legs, stood with her hand on the boy's shoulder, and looked about her. St Albans seemed to be a bustling little town with several inns strung down the length of its long main street.

'Where does your brother live?' she asked him.

'Off Dagnall Lane, miss.'

'Do you know where it is?'

'No.'

'Oh, dear.' She turned to the Captain, who had just got down beside them. 'Do you know where Dagnall Lane is, Captain?'

'No, but I imagine the ostler does.' He called the man over. 'Can you direct this young shaver to Dagnall Lane?'

'It's that way.' The man pointed. 'On the other side of the market place.'

'Come on,' she said to Ned. 'I'll see you safely home.'

'Are you mad?' Duncan said. 'You can't do that.'

'Why not?' she demanded, angry at his rudeness. 'I brought him this far. I feel responsible for his safe arrival.'

'You will get lost, and how do you know the brother will be there? How do you know there is a brother at all?'

'Of course there is. Ned said so, didn't he?'

'Are you always so trusting?'

'I have no reason not to be.' She turned to the boy. 'Come, Ned, we are wasting time and I must be back in time to board the coach.'

'No.' Duncan reached out and held her arm. 'You'll be set upon, robbed, worse. . .'

'Fustian!' She shrugged his hand off and turned to the ostler. 'I shall be back within the hour. Tell the coachman to expect me.' And with that she took Ned's hand and led him in the direction the ostler had pointed.

They had not taken many steps before she became aware that the Captain was walking half a step behind them. She ignored him for several minutes, thinking he was on some errand of his own, but when he turned whenever she did and crossed the road when she did, she was forced to the conclusion he was following her. 'Captain, I do not know what you think you are doing, but I wish you would not dog my heels.'

'Then I shall have to walk beside you,' he said, taking his place beside her and matching his pace to hers.

'Where are you going?'

'To Dagnall Lane, where else?'

'I do not need an escort.'

'You may not think so, but I assure you that you do.'

'You will miss your dinner.'

'And so will you.'

She stopped on the edge of the market place. It was packed with people buying and selling every conceivable commodity: chickens, goats, butter, cheese, vegetables, fruit, cooking pots, garden rakes, bonnets and yards of cloth. They were all pushing and shoving and shouting. A blind fiddler and a one-legged man with a penny whistle added to the din.

She took a deep breath and plunged into the throng, grabbing Ned's hand all the tighter, though whether it was to make sure he followed or to give herself courage she did not know. A moment later she felt the Captain's hand under her elbow and felt reassured, though she would not, for a moment, have admitted it.

He led her through the crowd, ignoring the importuning of the traders and beggars, until they emerged into a quiet street on the other side. 'Now which way?' he asked.

'I don't know. We had better enquire again.'

Having asked a passer-by, they set off again and soon found themselves in a maze of narrow streets, each more dismal than the last. Helen was glad that the Captain was with her. It took several more stops for directions before they stopped at the door of a dingy little house and knocked at the door. 'Let us hope your brother is at home, Ned,' Duncan said. 'I have no wish to track him down all over town if he is not.'

The door opened and a man in his middle twenties stood facing them. He was dressed only in breeches; the top half of him was completely bare except for a mat of hair which covered his chest and disappeared into his navel. Helen gave a gasp of shock.

'I'll deal with this,' Duncan told her. 'Wait for me at

the end of the street. And do not speak to any strangers.' Without waiting for her to reply, he pushed Ned ahead of him into the house and the door was shut.

Helen, shaken to the core, did as she was told, knowing that she had been very foolish to insist on coming. And to think that she had been prepared to come alone! What would she have done, faced with that half-naked man, if the Captain had not been there? And she was lost; they had taken so many turns that she did not think she could find her way back to the inn alone. Her journey had hardly begun and already she had proved her inadequacy.

She was never more thankful to see the Captain striding towards her a few minutes later and they walked in silence back to the Wheatsheaf. Here she was in for another shock, because the coach was on the point of leaving without them and the guard was at that very moment taking her trunk from the boot.

She ran forward to remonstrate. 'Please put it back, I am here now and ready to go.'

'So are we. You don't seem to understand, miss, that coaches have schedules. People expect them to be on time. You made us late leaving Barnet and now you think you can hold us up again. Who do you think you are? Giving orders like a nob. . .' There was more in like vein until the Captain pressed a guinea into his hand and he agreed to return the trunk to the boot, even though it meant re-arranging everything, just when he had it loaded to his satisfaction.

Helen could do nothing but thank the Captain once again, before going to board the coach. He stopped her with a hand on her arm. 'A minute, ma'am.'

She turned to him in surprise. 'We have no time, we must get in or I shall be in trouble again.'

He smiled. 'No, a guinea will buy us another minute or two and I must speak to you privately.'

'Captain, I have thanked you for your escort and your intervention, what else is there to say?'

'I have something for you. If you do not let me give it to you privately, then I shall be obliged to conduct the business in the coach. I am sure you will not want that.' When she hesitated, he added, 'Come, we will sit over there where we can be seen by everyone. You should know by now you have nothing to fear from me.'

Reluctantly she allowed herself to be escorted to a bench outside the window of the inn, where they sat down. 'Captain, I do not like mysteries. . .' she began.

He smiled, carefully removed his shako and tipped it upside down in her lap. She found herself looking down at a lady's purse, a watch and a diamond clip. Instinctively she put her hand to her throat where the brooch had been fastened, but she knew already it was not there and that the one glinting in her lap was hers. And so were the watch and the purse. Almost every penny she possessed was in that purse, which had been attached to the waist of her dress on a drawstring. She had thought it safe, hidden as it was under her mantle. 'They are mine!'

'Yes.'

'Did you take them?'

'Now why should I do that?'

'To teach me a lesson?'

'I had no need to do that, Miss. . . Look here, what is your name?'

After a moment's hesitation, she said, 'Sadler. I am Miss Sadler.' Her father had been a well-known figure and the Captain would have heard of him and the shameful manner of his death, even if he did not know him personally, and she did not relish having her real situation made public. Daisy's surname would do her very well.

'Miss Sadler,' he said slowly, savouring the name on his tongue but not daring to ask her Christian name. 'I guessed the boy would try something of the sort, so before I left him with his brother, who was not exactly overjoyed to see him, I might add, I pretended to help him off with his coat. Ragged though it appeared it had a very strong inside pocket. I relieved him of these items and glad he was to hand them over and not be taken to the magistrate.'

'It seems, Captain, that I am once again in your debt. I can only offer my grateful thanks.'

He smiled. 'You know, it was very foolish of you to keep all your money in one place and one so accessible too. I should hide it away, if I were you.'

'How do you know it's all the money I have?' she demanded, finding herself on the defensive and taking refuge in anger, which was not at all like her and she could not understand it. 'I have ample funds in my trunk. This is simply my travelling money.'

'And speaking of travelling, I cannot understand what you are doing travelling unaccompanied in the first place. Run away, have you?'

'That is not your business, Captain. Now, I think we should rejoin the coach. And please do not concern yourself about me.' She stood up and began to walk towards the coach, her chin jutting.

He followed. 'Do you think I am the kind of man who can sit back and watch a silly chit get herself into a pickle and not be concerned? There are many on the road who would not be so scrupulous; they would rob you blind. Do you not know the risks?'

'Risks or not, I have no alternative, Captain.'

He was about to ask her why because her shoulders had drooped a little and her voice had softened, but the guard was calling impatiently for them to take their seats or be left behind, and he did not say it. On reflection he was glad; she might have assumed he cared what happened to her and he certainly did not want her to think that. Women were the very devil! He climbed up beside her and they were off again, rattling through the main street and out again onto the open road.

The farmer and the painted woman had completed their journeys and now they were travelling with a nondescript-looking man of perhaps thirty who had a hacking cough, and a young mother and her baby. The baby evidently did not like the swaying of the coach and cried incessantly.

Helen sat gazing from the window, hardly aware of anything except the presence of the Captain sitting beside her and the fact that only her skirts and his pale blue pantaloons separated their thighs. Apart from her father, she had never been that close to a man before and his proximity was having a strange effect on her. Her limbs and face burned as if she had been standing too close to a fire and it was difficult to stop her hands plucking at her cloak in a kind of desperate attempt to put distance, if only inches, between them.

There was no room to do so, she knew, and to draw

attention to the fact would only embarrass her, not
him. She had had enough of embarrassment. He had
saved her from her own foolishness and but for him
she would now be penniless, but instead of being well
disposed towards him, she found herself resenting the
obligation he had put her under.

She had had no idea, when she started out, how
difficult it was going to be to maintain her privacy, to
keep up the pretence of being an ordinary young lady
of limited means, used to looking after herself. Everyone, strangers until that day, seemed to expect intro-
ductions and confidences, particularly the Captain.
Could he have some inkling of the truth? She decided
he could not possibly know who she was and she was
being over-sensitive.

Pride comes before a fall, she scolded herself, and
she had no cause to be proud. Having delivered her
lecture to herself, she relaxed a little, telling herself
that at least, sitting next to the Captain and not
opposite him, she was not obliged to meet his eye. She
smiled at the young mother who sat in the opposite
corner and asked the child's name.

Duncan heard her speak and the baby's mother
answer, but he could not have said what they were
talking about. He was immersed in speculation of his
own about the girl at his side. Why should she be so
reluctant to divulge her name? And why did she have
no choice but to travel alone? Had she left home in
disgrace? Whom was she mourning? She was quiet, a
little sad, but she did not act like someone in the throes
of unbearable grief.

Perhaps he had been right all along and she was
meeting her lover and going on to Gretna. But where

was the object of her desire? Was he going to join the coach at some distant stage? Or was he already on it? He looked round. The lawyer had resumed his reading and the unexceptional newcomer hardly fitted the description of a lovelorn suitor. But what was that description? He knew from personal experience there was no accounting for women's tastes. Perhaps it was the man with the cough after all and their attempts at polite conversation were simply a cover.

'Would you prefer the window open?' he heard her ask the man. 'The fresh air. . .'

'No, don't do that,' the mother said. 'The baby will catch a chill.'

'Please do not trouble yourself on my account, ma'am,' the man said, surfacing from the depths of his handkerchief. 'I am perfectly used to my affliction.'

I am not, Duncan thought; the cough was almost as irritating as the child's continuous crying. Why couldn't the mother shut it up?

'Do you think your baby will be more comfortable if you face the way we are going?' Helen asked. 'We could change places.'

'No,' the Captain said, a little too sharply. 'It would be unwise to try and change places in a moving coach. You will make it unstable; we might even go off the road.'

'Oh, I am sorry,' Helen said, chalking up one more reason for disliking the Captain, not because he was wrong but because he was right; the coachman was trying to make up for lost time and was galloping the horses to the next stage. 'Then perhaps I can nurse little Emily for a while.' She held out her arms. 'Come, it will give you a rest.'

The baby was handed over and Helen settled herself against the squabs, gently rocking the child, whose sobs soon faded into hiccoughs and a minute later stopped altogether and she slept, much to everyone's relief.

'Thank you,' the mother whispered, smiling at her slumbering child, while addressing Helen. 'You seem to have the right touch.'

'Yes, I love children.'

'You have children of your own?'

'Goodness, no. I am unmarried.'

'Oh, I am sorry, I thought. . .' She looked in confusion from Helen to the Captain. 'How far are you travelling?'

'To Scotland.'

Duncan had noticed the mistake and was amused by it, though he knew Miss Sadler would not be. She was too top-lofty by far, considering she was probably a governess or a nursery nurse, judging by the competent way she had soothed the child. But she did not behave like a servant at all and in his view was more used to giving orders than receiving them—her manner was a mixture of imperiousness and gentle concern for others.

It was often the case that young women servants learned uppish manners from their employers. But was that true of Miss Sadler? He was more than ever convinced there was something havey-cavey going on and it intrigued him.

The coach rattled through Redbourn and Dunstable, where it stopped for a change of horses and where the man with the cough left them, saying his destination was Cambridge. Then they were off again with only five inside passengers now, but it did not seem to make any difference; Helen felt the Captain was as close as he had been before.

They ran straight through Hockliffe and, six miles further on, stopped at the Swan at Little Brickhill. It was a busy little place where several coaching routes converged and the yard was full of horses and people, and at least two carriages being changed.

The mother stepped down as soon as they stopped and reached up to take her sleeping baby from Helen. 'Thank you, Miss Sadler. My parents live nearby and my father is meeting me. I wish you a safe journey.'

Helen was sorry to see her go and, as it was nearly supper time, wondered if this might be a good place to break her journey. She left the coach, knowing that the Captain was watching her, though he made no move to leave himself, and made her way into the inn. She had never stayed at an inn before, not even with her parents. After returning from India they rarely went far from their London home; it was as if they had had their fill of travelling.

Until her mother's death they always spent some time each year at their country seat in Huntingdonshire, but that could be reached in a day. On the other hand, the prospect of travelling all night in that swaying, jolting coach was more than she could stomach and stiffened her resolve. 'Is it possible to stay here tonight?' she asked the man who was washing down the tables in the tiny parlour. 'I require a private room.'

He looked her up and down. There was no mistaking the tone; she was Quality and travelling alone too. He decided he didn't want to have any dealings with someone so unconventional. 'No private rooms, miss.' He grinned. 'Shared, if you like. . .'

'No, thank you.' Aware of his amusement, she turned and went out.

The guard was looking for her. 'Come along, miss, we can't have you holding up proceedings again, can we? Up you go.' And suiting action to words, he put both hands under her bottom and hoisted her into the coach beside the grinning Captain. She was furious but before she could protest, they were on their way again.

She settled herself in her seat to find herself facing a young fop in a buff greatcoat with enormous brass buttons. It was very long and came down over his calf half-boots, which were almost hidden by the length of his cossacks. He wore a green and white striped waistcoat and a tall crowned hat with a buckle on the band from which swept a long feather. Every time they were jolted, the feather touched the roof and threatened to take his hat off. The other two seats were taken up by a couple of middle years who were both exceedingly plump.

'Late again,' the woman said. 'Stages are supposed to work to time but they never do.'

'It is only five minutes late, my love,' her husband said. 'We shall soon make it up.'

'I'm sorry,' Helen said, realising she was being blamed for the delay. 'I had hoped to stay here overnight, but there are no private rooms.'

'There will be rooms at Northampton,' the lawyer said. 'It is the usual stopping place for passengers on this coach.'

'I hope we won't be late,' the young man said. 'I shall have to hire a carriage to take me on to my home and at that time of night. . .' He stopped and smiled at Helen. 'You are not going to be met at Northampton, are you?'

'No.'

'Pity. I could have begged a ride.'

'Are you not expected?' Duncan asked, unaccountably glad that the lovely Miss Sadler would not be sharing a vehicle with this young popinjay if he were getting off at Northampton.

'No.' He grinned ruefully. 'My father does not know I am returning home. I am at Cambridge, you know.'

'Is that so?' Duncan said. 'Then I'll wager you have been rusticated.'

'Only a prank, sir, only a prank. Went out on the town, got a little foxed, climbed back into the wrong window. Out for the rest of the term.'

'Irresponsible coxcomb,' the woman put in. 'Is that how you squander the opportunities you are given?'

'Ma'am, it was not my idea to go to university,' he told her. 'Papa insisted. I am not a bookish person at all. . .'

'Evidently not,' she said, pursing her lips.

The young man was about to protest again but thought better of it and stared out of the window, but it was already dark and there was nothing to see. Nothing to see inside the carriage either and they all fell silent. Helen leaned back and shut her eyes. She had hardly begun her journey but already she was wishing it were over. Although it was cold outside, the air inside the coach was very stuffy and she was hot and cramped and all she longed for was a comfortable bed.

Captain Duncan Blair, sitting beside her, mile after

mile, was reluctant to let go of his theory that she was going to Gretna to marry and was unaccountably relieved to find that neither the man with the bad cough nor the young student were the object of her affections. What she needed, he decided, was a real man to curb her impulsiveness, a mature man of the world like himself. The thought brought him up short.

He was the last person, the very last person, to say whom she should or should not choose for a husband. What did he know about women? He had avoided having anything to do with them for years, except in a very superficial way, though he supposed that he would soon have to give way to his father's constant demand that he should find a nice young lady with a decent dowry and settle down into marriage and fatherhood. But he was not ready to do that yet.

They passed a house whose upstairs lights shone out across the carriageway and he took advantage of the meagre illumination to look down at the girl at his side. She had closed her eyes and he wondered if she might have gone to sleep, but they were soon in the dark again and he couldn't be sure. He sat very still so as not to disturb her.

Several minutes later he became aware of a weight on his arm and realised she had dropped asleep with her head lolling against him. Slowly he eased his arm out and put it round her shoulders. With a contented sigh, she snuggled her head into his chest. He smiled, savouring the slight scent of her hair beneath his nostrils, content to let her sleep, even though he soon had pins and needles in his arm; it was a small price to pay.

* * *

It was late in the evening when they reached the Angel at Northampton, sixty-six miles from London, where not only the horses, but the coachman and guard were due to be changed. Helen stirred as they drove into the inn yard and came to a stop. She sat up sleepily and pulled her bonnet straight and then gave a gasp of horror when she realised she had fallen asleep and the Captain had his arm around her. She almost fell over her own feet in her anxiety to get down from the coach and escape from him.

The other passengers followed her and she lost sight of him, to her intense relief. He had declared his intention of riding on through the night, and she would be well rid of him. Officer or no, he was no gentleman if he could take advantage of her while she slept.

She started towards the door of the inn and then realised that the coachman and guard were standing between the coach and the inn door, touching their hat brims and bidding their passengers a safe journey. Taking her cue from her fellow travellers, Helen handed the coachman a shilling and a sixpence and the guard a shilling, thinking as she did so, that being coachmen must be a highly remunerative calling if they received a like amount from every traveller every day.

'Thank you, miss,' the guard said. 'The coach leaves again in an hour.'

'Oh, but I think I shall stay here tonight and go on in the morning.'

'But you are booked through.'

'Yes, I know.'

'And now I suppose you are going to ask me for a refund on your ticket.'

'Is that possible?'

Her expression had suddenly lightened with hope and he found himself smiling. Poor little thing, having to go all that way alone and her so innocent. He found himself returning her smile. 'Yes, miss, at my discretion.' He delved into a leather bag he carried over his shoulder and counted seven pounds into her hand. 'There you are, miss, but if you are going to stop overnight again, I suggest you buy your tickets in stages, though it will cost you more in the long run.'

'Thank you.'

'Good luck to you, miss.' And then with a twinkle in his eye, 'Don't let the Captain bully you, miss. You stand up for yourself.'

It was too much. She fled to the door of the inn and then stopped. What would she do if the only rooms available were shared ones, stay or go? But the prospect of continuing in the coach for another minute knowing what had happened and what might happen again if she could not keep her eyes open, was abhorrent. She took a deep breath and stepped inside.

CHAPTER THREE

THE inn was already very crowded and the waiters
were hurrying about with loaded trays, so that it was
some minutes before Helen could attract the attention
of one of them and ask for a room for the night,
stipulating it must be a private room. Having at last
been told that one would be prepared for her, she
ordered onion soup, bread and apple pie to be brought
to her and then looked round for a seat. She realised
at once that finding somewhere to sit should have been
her first step and ordering a bed and food next; there
didn't seem vacant chair in the whole establishment.

'There's a table in the corner, miss,' one of the
waiters said, passing her with a tray loaded with roast
beef and game pie, potatoes and pickles. 'Over there.'
He jerked his head in the direction of a small table and
two chairs almost concealed behind a potted palm. She
thanked him and hurried to sit down before anyone
else could claim it.

She felt quite strange, as if she were still in the
coach; the floor seemed to be moving and her chair
swaying. It was as if she had just stepped on shore after
a long sea voyage and it was several minutes before
her head stopped feeling giddy and her stomach settled
and by that time her food had been put in front of her.
'What would you like to drink, miss?' the waiter asked.

'A glass of ratafia, please.'

'Don't have such refinements as that, miss. There's wine.'

'Wine will do very well,' a familiar voice said. 'The best you have and a carafe of water.'

Helen could not bring herself to look up into his face, though she resented his interference. As if she could not take wine without water! Did he think she was a child? Perhaps he would go away if she pretended she had not noticed he was there. But it was difficult not to notice him, he was so big he towered over her.

'Miss Sadler,' he said. 'I took the liberty of having your trunk taken to your room. You seemed to have forgotten it.'

How could he seem so calm where her heart was thumping with embarrassment? But she could hardly ignore him. 'Thank you, Captain. I was in haste to secure a room for the night. I had not forgotten it.' Liar, she accused herself; the need to escape from him had driven all other thoughts from her head.

'May I share your table?' he asked.

She looked up at him then, to find him regarding her with his head on one side as if unsure of her reaction to the request, though he showed no sign of leaving if it should prove unfavourable. 'Why, Captain, I thought you were determined on travelling on through the night.'

'I still need sustenance, Miss Sadler. The coach does not leave for an hour.'

'Oh.'

'So may I sit down? I fear there are no other seats and if you refuse me, you may find yourself sharing with some less savoury character.'

She was about to retort that she could think of no one less savoury but then remembered the farmer and the student and Ned's half-naked brother, and fell silent. He was preferable to all of those. And if she were truly honest with herself, she had felt safe and comforted in his arms, and that was not a feeling she had enjoyed of late. She managed a tight little smile. 'Please be seated, Captain, or I shall get a crick in the neck looking up at you.'

He flicked up the skirt of his uniform jacket and sat down. A waiter appeared immediately, making Helen resentful that she, an unaccompanied woman, had had to wait so long for service. 'A capon,' he ordered. 'Some turbot, potatoes, a dish of vegetables and a slice of your excellent game pie.' Then to Helen, pointing at her bowl of soup. 'Is that all you are going to eat?'

'Yes, I am not hungry.'

'You have eaten nothing all day.'

'I expect it is the rocking of the coach; it has made me feel a little unsteady and quite taken my appetite.'

The Captain's food arrived, filling her nostrils with its succulent smell. He served himself and smiled at her. His tanned, almost weather-beaten, face creased attractively when he smiled, she noted, and the scar on his forehead almost disappeared. 'Come, let me tempt you to a morsel. There is more here than I can eat.'

'No, thank you,' she said stiffly.

'You are angry with me.' He poured wine for himself and one for her, pushing it towards her.

'Not at all.' She bent to her soup spoon.

'Yes, you are. Tell me why.'

'Captain, I am unaccustomed to being called a liar, or to being treated with such familiarity, even by people I know well, and we have not even been introduced.'

He laughed. 'There is no call to be top-lofty with me, you know. I can give as good as I get in that department, so why not be easy with me. Not half an hour ago. . .'

'Just because I was so foolish as to fall asleep, does not give you the right to take liberties,' she said, glad the light was not good enough for him to see the colour she knew was spreading from her cheeks right down her neck. She took a gulp of wine in an effort to cool herself.

'Good God! Who do you think I am? Bluebeard?'

'No, of course not.'

'I am glad to hear it. I am not so in want of female company I have to wait until a young lady is unconscious before forcing myself upon her. You were the one who fell asleep and if I had not supported you, you would have toppled over face first into the lap of that young dandy. He might have taken far more advantage than I.'

The picture his words created brought a tiny smile to her lips in spite of her determination to retain her hauteur.

So, she had a sense of humour and could laugh at herself; that was good. 'You should smile more often, Miss Sadler.'

'I have had little to smile about lately, Captain.'

'Do you wish to talk about it?'

'No.' She drank a little more wine and was surprised to find her glass was empty. He refilled it.

'Then what shall we talk of? What interests you?

The doings of our fat monarch and his outrageous wife?'

'Not particularly. They are as distant from real life as the man on the moon.'

'You are right, that farce is hardly the stuff of intelligent conversation.'

She smiled then; a genuine smile which lit her piquant face and made her eyes sparkle. 'You do not subscribe to the maxim that young ladies should not converse intelligently, then?'

'Most of those I have met in Society would be hard put to even pretend to having a mind. Empty-headed little flirts.'

'Oh, dear, you do have a poor opinion of the fair sex.'

'I said "most", not all, Miss Sadler. I'll allow there are exceptions.'

'You would like me to prove myself one of the exceptions?'

'Are you?'

'I am not empty-headed, Captain, but I am not so vain as to claim a superior intelligence. I have been fortunate enough to enjoy a good education. . .'

'Good enough to teach?'

'What makes you say that?' She answered his question with another.

'I noticed how you handled that little urchin. There was nothing lily-livered about it.' He smiled suddenly. 'But did you really not know the difference between a cow and a bull?'

She laughed. 'Of course I did, but I did not want to offend the others in the coach if he quizzed me about it.'

'What subjects interest you most, Miss Sadler? Languages, poetry, antiquities. . .?'

'All of those. I read a little Greek and Latin, and I have enough French to converse. . .'

'Gaelic?'

'No. Why do you ask?'

'I collect you saying you were going to Scotland and it is the native tongue of the Scots.'

She did not rise to the bait, but turned the question on him. 'Is it yours, Captain?'

'My father's, Miss Sadler, but being so much from home, I am afraid I have acquired no more than a few phrases.'

'I assume you have spent a considerable time with your regiment?'

'Yes.'

'I imagine it is not all flags flying and bands playing. There must be times when you wish yourself anywhere but where you are. War cannot be a pleasant experience, whether you are victor or vanquished. The sight of all those poor men coming home after Waterloo was heart-rending. I found it difficult to join in the general rejoicing.'

Was that what the mourning was for, a soldier lover who had not returned? But she was too young for that; he did not think she could be more than eighteen now and would have been a mere child at the time. 'Did you know someone who was there?'

'Several young men of my acquaintance served on that battlefield, no one in particular,' she answered evasively. 'Please, tell me something of it.'

She had managed, with consummate skill, to turn the conversation away from herself towards him. So be it; if she did not want to tell him about herself, he would enjoy her company for an hour, bid her farewell and never see her again.

He smiled and talked about the dispositions of the opposing forces and which regiments had distinguished themselves. She ate some of his food, when he pressed her, and drank some more wine and finally relaxed. He was good company and very knowledgeable on a great many subjects, so that she became absorbed by what he was saying and did not notice the other passengers leaving the room to rejoin the coach.

He told her of the triumphant march into Paris and how Napoleon had tried to get onto a British ship and expected the Regent to give him sanctuary. He described Vienna and told her about the arguments and counter-arguments at the Vienna Convention which had been going on for years as the allies carved Europe up between them. He told her about the social life, every bit as hectic as that in Paris, and of the Grand Tour, now re-established for all young men before they settled down.

She answered him now and again and put forward some ideas of her own, but mostly she listened; it was all very easy and very pleasant, and she did not want to break it up and go to bed, though she was feeling very sleepy again and could hardly keep her eyes open.

He did not think she was the sort of girl to swoon at the mention of blood, but he was careful not to frighten her with gory details and was, therefore, very surprised when she suddenly said she felt very hot and would have fallen from her seat if he had not had the presence of mind to catch her.

He sat with her half-lying across his knee and looked

about him. The dining room had emptied and there was no one to be seen but a waiter sweeping the floor. He called to him. 'Fetch mine host's wife, if you please.'

'That's more than I dare do, sir. She's long abed and asleep and she won't want to be disturbed on account of she has to be up betimes.'

'A chambermaid, then.'

'Now, sir, how can I go waking chambermaids?'

Duncan looked down at the girl in his arms. Her face was flushed and her bosom heaved gently, but she showed no sign of regaining her senses. He tried shaking her a little, calling her name, but all that happened was that her head wobbled, her bonnet fell off and she muttered something unintelligible. He cursed himself for a fool. She had eaten hardly any-thing all day and she was very tired; the unaccustomed swaying of the coach had made her giddy and the little wine she had drunk had done the rest. Why had he not noticed?

It was a long time since he had enjoyed a woman's company so much; talking to her and watching her animated face as she spoke to him had filled his mind. He had only been half aware that the coach had gone on without him and completely oblivious to the fact that she was not well. Tomorrow she would hate him. Tonight though, she needed putting to bed.

He knew which room was hers because he had had her trunk taken up to it. He scooped her up in his arms, surprised that she weighed so little, and carried her up to her room, pushing the door open with his foot and depositing her on the bed. Then he lit a candle which stood on a cupboard by the door and stood looking down at her. He could not leave her like that.

He put the candle on a table, sat on the edge of the bed and shook her gently. 'Miss Sadler, wake up, you foolish child, wake up.' When she did not respond, he pulled off her mantle and set about undoing the buttons which fastened her gown up to the chin, but when he had done that, he discovered the layers of underwear. No wonder she had fainted! The sooner she was rid of them and able to breathe freely, the sooner she would recover.

She gave a huge sigh of relief and then giggled as he pulled off the dress and untied the thick petticoat beneath it. 'Oh, Daisy, you are tickling me. . .'

He took off the thick outer layer of underwear and untied her corset and discovered that she was not the dumpy young girl he had thought, but a woman, slight to be sure, but perfectly formed. She certainly did not need the corset.

His own words suddenly echoed in his mind: 'I am not so in want of female company I have to wait until a young lady is unconscious before forcing myself upon her.' He stifled a harsh laugh. It was his fault; he should have been watching out for her instead of allowing himself to be carried away with his own rhetoric. He could not leave her; tomorrow night, if he were not there, someone less honourable might be taking liberties, as she had put it.

The thought of anyone else doing what he was doing made him go hot and cold with anxiety on her behalf. She needed looking after and he cursed the unknown man, whoever he was, who had brought her to this. That it had been a man he was sure. Leaving her in her shift and stockings, he covered her with the quilt, dropped a kiss on her forehead and crept from the room, closing the door softly behind him. Then he went in search of a bed.

Helen woke with a start, wondering where she was. Her head ached abominably and her stomach was churning. She remembered boarding a coach, remembered her fellow passengers and a boy, a dirty little urchin who had stolen her money. It had been retrieved by Captain Blair and she had shown scant gratitude. They had come a long way after that, so where was she now?

Racking her brain, which did nothing to improve her headache, she recalled coming into an inn and sitting over a meal with the Captain. They had talked a lot and she had found him an agreeable companion, but after that her memory was a blank. She sat up and groaned as her head started to spin. She had taken rather more wine than she was used to and the Captain, who could know nothing of those extra undergarments, would undoubtedly think she had been foxed.

How had she got to her room? She must have come upstairs and half undressed before collapsing on the bed. But someone had been with her, she remembered soothing words and gentle hands. The Captain must have fetched the innkeeper's wife or one of the chambermaids to help her. Why was she forever in his debt? Why did she seem determined to prove she could not manage to travel a few miles on her own? He would be gone now and she was glad of that; she refused to admit that she had been grateful for his help.

A month ago, she would hardly have noticed him. She smiled suddenly; no, that was not true, you could not help noticing him, he stood out head and shoulders above everyone else and not only physically; he had a way of commanding attention, a way of concentrating on you as if he were truly interested in what you were saying. It was cultivated, no doubt, along with his skill as a soldier and his extensive general knowledge.

It was probably how he had managed to catch the eye of the Duke of Wellington, so one small, lonely young lady had little defence. But he had been right on one thing; there were sure to be others on the road who would not be so scrupulous and she would do well to be on her guard.

She could hear sounds outside her window; voices and horses neighing and the jingle of harness. She left her bed and padded to the window to draw back the curtains. Dawn was just breaking and there was a coach in the yard which had just driven in. Its passengers were tumbling out, half-asleep, to come into the inn for breakfast. If that was the coach to Manchester, she did not have much time.

Hurriedly she washed in cold water from the ewer, dressed in a pelisse-robe in black bombazine, packed her dusty round dress of the day before and the extra petticoats in her trunk, and went downstairs, carrying her small portmanteau. She met a chambermaid on the way, who bobbed and bade her good morning. Helen smiled, wanting to convey her thanks for whatever had been done for her without actually saying it. 'Would you be kind enough to ask someone to take my trunk to the coach?' she asked, handing her a sixpence.

'Yes, ma'am.' The girl grinned at the unexpectedly large gratuity. 'I'll have Jake do it straight away.'

Helen continued down to the dining room where the smell of breakfast cooking was making her feel decidedly ill, but she needed something to drink, preferably hot, strong coffee, before she could face another day of being jolted about in a coach.

She was surprised to see the Captain sitting over breakfast at a table near the fire. He was dressed in a military-style frockcoat over a kerseymere waistcoat in brown and buff stripes, cut in the Hussar style, and buff nankin pantaloons, so that even in civilian clothes, he still looked every inch the soldier. His dark hair was damp and clung about his neck and ears in tight little curls. He rose, smiling. 'Good morning, Miss Sadler. You are in good time for breakfast.' He half expected her to cut him for taking even more liberties but, to his surprise, she sat down opposite him.

'Good morning, Captain. No breakfast, thank you. Just coffee.'

He called a waiter and the hot drink was soon in front of her. She gulped it greedily and began to feel a little better. 'I am surprised to see you this morning, Captain,' she said, before he could make any reference to the previous evening. 'I collect you saying you were in haste to reach your destination and were going to travel through the night.'

He suddenly realised she did not remember him carrying her to her room and must be thinking she had found her way there by herself. He breathed a sigh of relief. 'I found the company so convivial, I could not

tear myself away,' he said, deciding it would be unwise
to say what was in his mind, that she was so helpless
he could not abandon her. It would have invited a
sharp rebuke and an assertion that she did not need
looking after. 'And this is a passably comfortable inn.'

'Convivial,' she repeated. 'Are you inferring I had
taken too much wine? Because if you are, let me tell
you it was nothing of the sort. I was simply unwell.
The rocking of the coach, you know, and the heat in
the dining room. . .'

'Please forgive me,' he said. 'I am afraid I have been
too long a soldier and do not always choose my words
with care. In truth, I found the heat in the dining-room
somewhat overpowering myself, especially after the
cold outside.'

'I do believe I heard the guard calling up the
passengers for the coach,' she put in quickly, unwilling
to continue the conversation.

He stood up, picked up his cloak-bag and her
portmanteau and waited to escort her. She paid for her
bed and board and followed him. Whatever she
thought of his behaviour, she was obliged to him. She
was feeling far from well and in any case, he was only
treating her like the working woman he believed her
to be and she had to be thankful that he was gentleman
enough to accept her explanation.

As soon as she had purchased her ticket, he handed
her in to her seat, checked that her trunk had been
loaded safely and took his place beside her. They were
joined by an elderly lady in a huge poke bonnet worn
over her day cap, a parson in black robes and a low-
crowned round hat, and a young couple, obviously in
love, with eyes for no one but each other.

Judging by his dress, the young man considered himself something of a dandy; his pantaloons and coat were tightly fitting, his waistcoat colourful and his pale blue cravat extravagantly tied. His wife wore a high-waisted gown of barège with a pleated bodice and a great deal of decoration around the hem, over which she wore a fur-lined pelisse in blue velvet.

Helen could not see the outside passengers but they seemed a noisy group, laughing and calling to each other as they climbed aboard. She could hear the guard calling them to order as he took his own place in the seat above the back boot. A minute later the coachman, having completed his inspection, climbed aboard and they were off.

Helen was glad that her fellow passengers were disinclined to talk; she did not feel like conversation and she was all too aware of the Captain beside her. It was funny how much she remembered of his conversation of the evening before. He had been an agreeable raconteur and she had learned much she had not known about how wars were fought and the magnitude of the task of supplying an army of thousands with horses, weapons, food and clothing.

He had talked of Portugal with affection and of Wellington with admiration and loyalty. Helen had met the great man once, in 1814, in the brief spell of peace when he had come to London to be feted. Had she told the Captain that? What had she told him? She risked a peep at him from beneath the brim of her bonnet.

He was sitting staring into space as if his thoughts were far away, on some battlefield perhaps. Or was he thinking of what was at the end of his journey? He had said he was unmarried, but that did not mean there was not a young lady waiting for him. Where? Where was he going? Did she hope he would leave soon or did she want him to stay until they arrived in Glasgow?

Of one thing she was certain, she did not want him to meet whoever was sent to fetch her because then he would know she had lied, pretending she was something she was not. She surprised herself with how much his good opinion mattered to her.

Duncan had not slept well. Given the option of sharing a room with two or three other men or finding a warm corner of the stables, he had chosen the stables, waking at dawn with his hair and clothes full of straw and an unmistakable odour of horses about him. He had stripped to his waist and stood under the pump in the yard, allowing the cold water to refresh him and then taken a new suit of clothes from his cloak-bag, rolling up the uniform and stuffing it in the bag in its place.

He missed his personal servant, particularly when it came to shaving, but the man had family in London and he had could hardly drag him all the way to Scotland, especially when he had no idea how long he would be at home. If things were very bad, he might have to resign his commission. He had been a soldier for twelve of his thirty years, so perhaps it was time he settled down. But settling down meant marriage, at least in his father's eyes, and since Arabella, he had not trusted himself even to think about it.

He risked a sideways look at the young lady beside him. She was uncommonly beautiful and her figure, now that she had obviously discarded the extra petti-coats, was curvaceous without being plump. He found himself picturing her in lighter colours, pale blues and greens instead of that unrelieved black, and decided that whatever she wore she would be lovely. Neither was she afraid to have an opinion of her own, nor of expressing it articulately.

He had long ago decided she was not eloping; such a forceful person as she was, would not need to resort to clandestine methods to get her own way. Was she affianced to some Scottish gentleman and going to her wedding? The thought made him catch his breath and his heart beat faster, as if it mattered to him whether she were engaged to be married or no, which it did not, he told himself.

She wore no ring and she would surely have told him last night if she had a fiancé. She was probably a nursery nurse or a governess, going to take up a post north of the border. On the other hand, her manner was not subservient, so perhaps she was really a lady, daughter of an aristocrat, royalty perhaps, travelling incognito. But even then she would have had at least one servant somewhere in the background watching over her. Miss Sadler, if that was truly her name, was definitely alone.

Servants often aped the imperious mannerisms of their mistresses, so perhaps that was it; she was a lady's maid. Whom was she mourning? Was she going to Scotland for a funeral? How had she managed to get him to talk about himself without volunteering anything of any import about herself? Almost all he had learned about her, she had divulged to their travelling companions, not to him. Was there a reason for that? Why, however hard he tried, could he not stop thinking about her?

'The countryside is beautiful at this time of the year, don't you think so, Miss Sadler?' he ventured into the silence after they had stopped at Harborough for a change of horses.

It was a moment before she realised he was addressing her, but then she smiled. 'Oh, yes, the changing colours of the trees are quite glorious, but each of the seasons has its own appeal, do you not think? I find that in October, I am in favour of autumn, but in March nothing suits me so well as spring when everything we thought dead is growing anew.'

'A good philosophy, ma'am,' the parson put in. 'One should be content with what God gives us at the time and not be forever wishing it were otherwise.'

'I wish our outside passengers were otherwise,' the old lady put in. 'I do believe they are all drunk. There is one above my head who is banging his heels on the roof. I fear he will put his foot through before long.'

The outside passengers had been growing more noisy the further they travelled and now there was such a drumming on the roof, they began to think the old lady might be right. Duncan got up and put his head out of the door to shout up to them. 'Can you not be a little less boisterous; you are alarming the ladies.'

One of them grabbed the guard's tin horn and blew a blast down towards Duncan, then turned to one of the other young men, whom Duncan could not see. 'Go on, Bertie, I'll act guard if you drive.' And again he gave a toot on the horn, this time directed at the sky. 'Ten guineas says you can't take us to the next post.'

'You're on.'

There was more banging and scraping on the roof and a great deal more shouting of encouragement to the unseen Bertie. Duncan's remonstrances and demands that the coach should be stopped and the young men put off were ignored. A minute later they knew the reins were in inexperienced hands, for the coach began to lurch from side to side.

Duncan returned to his seat. 'I am afraid the coachman has allowed one of those thatchgallows to have the ribbons.'

'What! We shall all be killed!' the old lady said. 'You must stop him at once.'

'Ma'am, I can do nothing unless we come to a halt, or at least slow down enough for me to get down.'

They showed no sign of doing so and in truth began to go even faster, so that the inside passengers were thrown from side to side. Helen, her earlier uneasy stomach forgotten in this new sensation, found herself hanging onto the door strap and praying the young man would realise how reckless he was being and let the coachman have the reins back.

The parson was apparently doing the same thing; his eyes were shut tight and his lips were moving in prayer; the young couple were clinging to each other in terror and the old lady was screaming. Helen reached across and touched her arm. 'Ma'am, pray calm yourself. The coachman, irresponsible as he is, will not allow us to be overturned. We shall slow down directly.'

If anything they went faster and Helen, peering from the off-side door, saw another coach ahead of them, going at a steady pace. Unless they drew up very quickly, she did not see how they could avoid running into the back of it. She shut her eyes and tensed herself for a crash. She opened them when she heard the young lady in the opposite corner cry out and found herself looking right into the other coach as they hurtled along side by side.

'They're racing us,' the young man said. 'We'll never get by.'

Duncan leaned across Helen and shouted to the second coachman. 'Pull up, man. Let us past.'

But the man either did not hear or did not want to hear. They proceeded neck and neck for several hundred yards and then pulled slowly ahead. Helen let out her breath in a long sigh of relief, although they did not slow down. She suspected that the horses were out of control and she could hear their coachman yelling at the man with the reins to relinquish them, but he seemed to be frozen with fear and unable to do anything.

'Watch out!' Duncan yelled as they rounded a bend and he caught sight of a fat, milk-laden cow plodding up the middle of the road towards them. The coachman at last grabbed the ribbons and hauled on them for all he was worth. The horses veered to the left, but the coach, slow to change direction, ploughed into the cow, wobbled terrifyingly and then embedded itself in a pile of stones on the grass verge. The lead horses, unable to pull the coach through the stones, came to a shuddering stop, rearing up and neighing in fright. The outside passengers screamed and the old lady fainted in Helen's arms.

Duncan clambered out, followed by the parson and the young couple, and then Helen, supporting the old lady. There was blood everywhere, which set the young lady into hysterics. Her husband took her off behind the coach to try and calm her. The old lady, fully recovered, left Helen to find out if her baggage was safe.

Only Helen, of the inside passengers, was prepared to help the casualties and it soon became apparent that most of the blood belonged to the poor dead cow. The coachman, who had a broken arm, was cursing the young driver, who had been shot straight over the heads of the horses and had landed in the middle of a thorn bush. His language rivalled that of the coachman, which seemed to indicate he was not all that grievously injured.

Most of the other outside passengers had been thrown from their seats and although they had sustained cuts and bruises, none seemed badly hurt. They had become suddenly sober and shame-faced. It was the guard who gave most cause for concern. He was lying some way off and had been knocked unconscious.

'I'll see to them,' Helen told Duncan. 'You look to the horses.

'Are you sure?'

'Of course I am sure.'

He left her to go and look at the animals and she went behind a tree to pull off her petticoat and tear it into strips. She had hardly returned to the scene when the second coach came round the bend and drew to a stop.

'You cow-handed numbskull!' the second coachman yelled at the first. 'You near had us off the road. Call yourself a coachie, why, you're nothing but a buffle-headed, cork-brained souse-crown!'

'And if you had anything in the attic at all,' the first responded, 'you'd have known there was a green amateur on the ribbons and pulled up instead of trying to race us.'

'More fool you, Martin Gathercole, for allowing a greenhorn to take over.'

There were more acrimonious exchanges, in which the uninjured passengers joined, apportioning blame as they saw fit, while Helen quietly got on with her self-appointed task. Let them argue it out. There was clearly blame on both sides but as long as they did not come to blows and cause more injuries, she was indifferent to the outcome. It was more important that the injured were cared for.

There was little she could do for the guard except make him comfortable with her mantle as a pillow and bathe his face in cold water from the ditch into which they would certainly have tumbled if the pile of road-mending stones had not stopped them. He had a large bump on the back of his head and would need a doctor as soon as one could be fetched. Leaving him, she went to the young driver, who had scrambled out of the bush and was wandering around in a daze, holding his hand to his face. There was blood running through his fingers onto his cravat and down his expensive satin waistcoat.

'Sit down,' she commanded. 'Let me look at you.'

He sat on the bank and allowed her to pull his hand away from his face. 'It's a nasty cut,' she said, dabbing at it with a strip from her petticoat. 'And there's a bruise on your cheek which will certainly spoil your looks for a few days. Whatever did you think you were about? You could have killed us all.'

'It was only a prank,' he said. 'Everyone fancies being a coachie, don't they? It is often done. But the cattle wouldn't answer the whip, mean creatures, wanted to go their own way.'

'Perhaps their way was best.' She smiled suddenly. 'After all, they have probably been cantering up and down this road several times a week for two or three years while you. . .'

'I'm considered a good hand with the ribbons.'

'Driving a phaeton or a curricle with one or two horses at most, I have no doubt, but a four-in-hand is a different matter altogether. I am surprised you allowed yourself to be persuaded.'

'It was a wager, ma'am, couldn't ignore a wager, now could I?'

'Wager! It seems to me that gambling is all young men think of.' Reminded of her father, she added, 'And men old enough to know better too. Could you not have thought of the consequences? We could all have been killed. As it is, the guard has a cracked head and the coachman a broken arm, not to mention the upset to the passengers.'

'I'm sorry, ma'am. I was a little bosky.'

'That is not an excuse either. Now, hold that over the cut, while I look after the coachman.'

Martin Gathercole was still being harangued by his opposite number, holding his injured arm in the good one and obviously in great pain. 'Either help or go,' he yelled back at him. 'I ain't got time to listen to you gabbling on like a fishwife.' And with that he turned and walked round to the front of the coach where the Captain was soothing the horses.

The left leader had taken the brunt of the impact into the stones and was still shuddering. Duncan was speaking gently as if to a child who had fallen and grazed a knee. 'There, my lovely, you've had a fright, haven't you? But all is well. Rest easy. Be calm. There, there.' The horse stood still, blowing a little, but its eyes still reflected its unease. A sudden movement, a loud noise, would set it off again.

Duncan moved to the off-side leader and spoke in the same calm voice. As soon as both leaders were quiet, the heavier wheelers stood still, patiently waiting for whatever orders were given. 'I reckon they'll settle once we are on our way again,' Duncan said. 'It's the coach I'm not too sure about. One of the wheels looks buckled and the nearside door has come off its hinges. It's impossible to tell if it is safe to drive until we get it out of the stones.'

'Then we'd best do that.' Martin turned and yelled at the other coachman. 'Are you going to sit there all day? Or are you going to use those great fat shoulders of yours to do some good?' Feeling a hand on his good arm, he turned to find Helen at his elbow.

'Leave the others to see to it, Mr Gathercole,' she said. 'You need that arm looking after.'

'Go on,' Duncan said to him. 'I'll see to this.'

Reluctantly he followed Helen to sit on the bank a little way from the amateur driver who sat nursing his head. 'I never met such a crank-brained jack-at-warts,' he said, nodding in the young man's direction. 'And a liar to boot. He told me he could drive, said he'd done it any number of times before on the Brighton run.'

'More fool you for believing him,' Helen said crisply. 'You should have had more thought for your passengers. If the Company found out you would lose your job, isn't that so?'

'You'd tell?'

'Not me, but the other driver might. He was angry enough.' She glanced over to where all the uninjured passengers and the coachman and guard from the second coach were putting their shoulders to the wheels of the stranded vehicle while Duncan, standing at the front of the horses, urged them to pull.

'Not he.' He gave a laugh but it changed to a grunt of pain as Helen bound his arm to his chest. 'All wind, that's what he is. Done for the benefit of his passengers. He's a good mate.'

And it did seem to be true, for the man was huge and strong and was not sparing himself in his efforts to free the coach. Slowly, inch by inch, it was dragged from the stones and stood once more on the hard surface of the road. The passengers gathered round it, wondering if they dare trust themselves to it again. The young couple stood with their arms about each other, the old lady was threatening to sue the Company, though what injury she had sustained they could not see. The parson was looking at the bent wheel and muttering.

'I reckon it will go, driven slowly,' Martin said. 'We'll have to stop at the next inn and have it repaired.'

'That's all very well,' the parson said. 'But who's going to drive it, a one-armed coachman or a be-fuddled guard who doesn't seem to know which way is up?'

'I'll drive,' Duncan said.

'Give me strength, more amateurs!' exclaimed the old lady. 'I'm not getting back in that thing, not for the world.'

'Then you'd best ride on with us, ma'am, we've got

two spare seats,' the second coachman said. 'We'll take one of the others too.'

'Then it had better be that young scapegrace, Bertie Billingsworth,' Martin said. 'For I have seen and heard enough of him for one day.'

The old lady's luggage was transferred and the two passengers climbed aboard; the coachman manoeuvred the vehicle round the first one and they were gone, disappearing round the bend in the road.

'Now, let's help the guard inside,' Duncan said. 'And you, young shaver.' He pointed to a young lad who had been knocked out when he was thrown from the roof and was still looking very dazed. 'You too, Mr Gathercole, if the Reverend does not mind sitting outside for a few miles.' No one seemed in the least surprised that he was directing operations and none objected.

'Not at all.' The parson clambered up on the roof beside some of the other outside passengers who had resumed their places, sobered by what had happened.

'Not on your life!' the coachman said. 'I've never ridden inside my own coach afore and I'm not starting now. I'd die of shame.'

'Yes, you are. You are in no fit state to ride on the box. And we are wasting time.' Duncan turned to the young husband. 'If you would not mind giving up your place, Mr. . .?'

'Smith. Tom Smith,' the young man said. 'Of course. . .'

'No!' shrieked his wife. 'No! You must not leave me! You really must not.' She burst into noisy sobs.

'Dearest, it is only for a few miles.' He tried to soothe her, but she would not be pacified.

'I wish I had never come with you. If I had known it was going to be like this, nothing would have induced me to undertake the journey. I want my mama.'

'And how are we to produce your mama, ma'am?' Duncan queried, all but losing patience with her. 'You have your husband, is that not enough? He will be sitting directly above your head.'

'He's not my. . .' She stopped suddenly and looked round at the company all agog. 'Oh.'

'Let him stay with her,' Helen put in quickly before the young lady could make any more revelations. 'I'll ride on top.'

Duncan turned to her. 'Don't be foolish. Ladies do not ride outside.'

'This one does. Come now, you were the one complaining we were wasting time. I shall be quite comfortable.'

'Then you sit on the box beside me. At least I can make sure you do not fall off.'

And so it was arranged, not without much grumbling from the coachman, but as he was in a great deal of pain, he allowed himself to be helped into the coach beside the young couple. The door was tied with a piece of rope, Duncan retrieved Helen's mantle and helped her to climb aboard, guiding her left foot onto the wheel-hub, her right onto the roller-bolt, then left onto a step and the right on the foot-board. She hitched along the seat and he picked up the reins and sprang lightly up beside her.

'Everyone ready?' he called, wrapping the mantle round Helen's shoulders and the coachman's rug about her knees.

'Aye,' came a chorus from behind him.

'Then here we go.' To Helen, he said. 'Hold onto me, if you feel unsafe.'

Slowly they drew away from the scene, over two hours behind schedule.

CHAPTER FOUR

'I AM surprised he did not put up a greater fight,' Helen said, as they proceeded at a walk.

'Who?'

'Mr Gathercole. After all, we had all but been overturned by an amateur and he was scathing in his remarks about them, and yet he allowed you to take over. . .'

Duncan chuckled. 'There are amateurs and amateurs, Miss Sadler. I am well known to the coaching world as a safe pair of hands.'

'You mean you have done what that young ninny did?'

'Run a coach and four off the road? No, Miss Sadler, I have never done that, but I have shared the box with with some of the best coachmen on the road and they have asked me if I were wearing my driving gloves.'

'A hint that they are open to a bribe, I suppose.'

He laughed. 'Yes, but I do believe no one inside the coach has ever been the wiser.'

'Why do you do it?' She watched his brown hands on the reins; he seemed only to need the slightest pressure of one finger, a turn of the wrist or a little flick of the whip and the horses moved unerringly down the road, somehow managing to avoid the worst of the potholes, though they could not help but go through one or two and then Helen had to hang on tight.

'Why? Oh, for the challenge, the exhilaration of guiding a team of excitable horses down a narrow country lane in a poor light, managing a top-heavy vehicle in a gale, ploughing through snowdrifts, fording swollen streams, turning the whole equipage on a sixpence, bringing everyone safely to the next stage. There is more to driving a four-in-hand than sitting on the box with the ribbons in your hand, Miss Sadler.'

'I am sure there is, so please enlighten me.'

He looked sideways at her, wondering if she were teasing, but she looked perfectly serious. 'First of all, you must know what each horse is doing the whole time. You must be aware if a leader is pulling to one side or if he is too eager, and be able to check him without upsetting the others. And if a wheeler is not pulling his weight, to give a touch of the whip which only he responds to.

'You must decide whether to hold the horses back going downhill or let them have their head, whether to stop and have the shoes put on the back wheels or whether the wheelers can hold the coach without them. You must judge to a whisker how much rein to give on a bend in order to get the wheelers to follow the leaders in a smooth arc without turning too soon. Wheelers sometimes have a habit of taking the commands of the rein to the leader in front and turn too soon if they are not held in check. You have to point your leaders and shoot your wheelers.'

She smiled. 'Whatever does that mean?'

'Well, if the bend is a right-hand one, the leaders have to be pointed into the turn, neither too soon nor too late, the nearside wheeler has to be held back slightly and the off-side wheeler urged on, so as to keep the pole between the leaders. For a left-hand bend it is the opposite. Watch me on this next bend, it needs only the slightest touch. Put your hands over mine, if you wish.'

She watched his hands, tanned, sure, capable hands, but resisted the temptation to do as he suggested, afraid of the intimacy.

'Go on. Feel how it is done. I shall not mind.'

She reached out and put a gloved hand over each of his, but she sensed nothing of his driving, only a quivering sensation passing along her arms and right down into the pit of her stomach. Hastily she returned her hands to her lap.

'You must be able to tell the speed you are doing, even in the dark,' he went on, apparently unaware of her reaction. 'Seven or eight miles an hour is safe, though there are times when this is exceeded, going downhill, for instance, or on a good stretch of road when it is possible to make up for time lost elsewhere.'

'How did you learn to do it?'

'From one of the best coachmen on the road.' He laughed suddenly. 'He used to say, "Horses are like women. Never let them know they are being driven; don't pull and haul and stick your elbows out. Don't get flurried, let every horse be at work and handle their mouths gently, then you might even drive four young ladies without ever rustling their feathers or their tempers."'

She smiled at the image he was creating; was he as good at handling young ladies as he was horses? 'I can understand that, but surely it is wrong for inexperienced pranksters to attempt it. And the coachmen should never allow it.'

'No more they should, but some are indulgent and see it as a way of adding to their income.'

'To put lives at risk for money seems to me to be nothing short of criminal.'

'You intend to report the matter?'

'No, but I fancy the old lady will. She was threatening to sue. Mr Gathercole will lose his job if she does, won't he?'

'Perhaps, but perhaps the Company will do no more than issue a reprimand and fine him.'

'Which he will pay from whatever the young scapegrace gave him and his gratuities. It seems to me they do very well from those, considering they have wages as well.'

'Do you begrudge paying a little extra for your comfort, Miss Sadler?'

'No, but I shall not tip this one.'

He laughed. 'No, I did not think you would. I heard you ringing a peal over him, and that poor sapskull who drove us into the stones. Just like a schoolma'am. Indeed, that is what I think you must be.'

'Then you would be wrong.'

'Oh?' He turned briefly to look down at her. 'What are you then?'

'Nothing. Nobody. I wish you would not give it another thought.'

'You are certainly not a nobody,' he said softly. 'But I think you must like to keep people guessing. Perhaps you are a princess. Yes, a princess, travelling alone and incognito for a dare.'

She laughed suddenly. 'How clever of you to guess.'

He fell silent at what was obviously a put-down, and concentrated on driving. They turned onto a broader, straighter road and he risked a trot. He hated secrets. Ever since Arabella had deceived him, he had found it difficult to trust any woman. And this one was more infuriating than most, managing to parry every enquiry, every light-hearted conjecture, so that he was eaten with curiosity.

But wasn't that what she wanted, for his interest to be aroused, for him to be charmed by her? No one could be so ingenuous and yet so compellingly feline. A kitten, a kitten with claws, that's what she was. Spirited and headstrong, she would be a handful for any man, but a handful a man could rejoice in.

He turned to look at her, sitting beside him, drinking in the air as if it were wine. Wine. She had been funny when tipsy, funny and lovely, and in her shift utterly desirable. It had taken all his resolve to leave her, even for a few hours' sleep. And now she was sitting beside him, not in a stuffy coach but on the narrow wooden seat of the box, in full view of the outside passengers, but private just the same, in a world of their own.

Helen sat upright, enjoying the feel of the cool air on her face, the steady rhythm of the horses' hooves hitting the road, the creak of the carriage. She was so high up, she could see over the hedgerows for miles, could see across the fields where the grazing cows looked up without interest as they passed and the workers in the fields waved them on.

This was good hunting country and away on the horizon, she saw a band of huntsmen galloping after a fox; she glimpsed its red back and tail disappearing into a copse and found herself wishing it would escape. And there a kestrel swooped and then rose with a small creature in its beak. A boat glided down a strip of grey water, its sails filled.

Her nausea was forgotten; she felt alive for the first time for weeks, alive and enchanted by all she saw. Was that what he meant when he talked about the exhilaration of driving a coach and four?

It was strange how everyone had taken it for granted the Captain would take charge of everything, would sort out the muddle, find a way of getting them going again, would tell the coachman what to do. Being an officer, he had been used to commanding soldiers, but today he had shown he could order civilians too. He had a presence about him which invited trust. She knew she could trust him.

She smiled to herself. It was incredible that, two days before, she had never ridden in a public coach, let alone sat on the box of one. Less than a month before she would not have dreamed of speaking to a man to whom she had not been properly introduced and she would certainly not have dined with him alone. Her reputation would have been in shreds and there could have been only one possible outcome; the man would have been in honour obliged to marry her.

She wondered if the Captain would have succumbed to that kind of pressure and decided he would not. Not that she would ever have allowed herself to be compromised in that way. So what was different now?

Everything, she told herself. She was no longer a member of the *haute monde*, no longer a potential catch for any young blade who fancied his chances, no longer financially independent. She was poor, so poor she had to count every penny she spent, so poor she could not afford a maid. Was it any wonder he took her for a working-class girl, a teacher, a governess, someone to tease with jests about being a princess?

But would his manner be any different if he knew the truth? She would hate it if he began to behave like some of the fops she had known in London, dressed exquisitely, cravat just so, waistcoat dangling with fobs, hair cut and curled in the latest fashion, boots polished until you could see your face in them, pretentious coxcombs looking for heiresses to marry.

It was one of the reasons she had not enjoyed her come-out year, though she would never have upset her parents by saying so, particularly her mother, who had set great store by the proper behaviour. What would she think if she could see her daughter now, thigh to thigh with a man on the box of a stagecoach? The thought made her smile.

He turned towards her briefly and noticed the slight twitch of her lips. 'A penny for your thoughts, princess.'

She was tempted to tell him what she had been thinking, knowing it would make him smile too, but then remembered she was not supposed to be one of the idle rich. 'I fear they are not worth a penny, Captain.'

'Let me judge their worth. Come, tell me what was making you smile.'

'I was remembering the look on that young driver's face when he found himself sitting in a thorn bush,' she invented. 'He was using the most shocking language and most of it to do with his clothes being spoiled. And that when everyone else was in fear of their lives.'

'I do not recall you laughing at the time. I distinctly heard you roasting him.'

'He deserved it.'

'So he did, but I am glad I was not the object of your displeasure. I should be quaking in my shoes.'

'I cannot imagine anything frightening you,' she said. 'Certainly not a helpless woman.'

'Women are never helpless,' he said, as they approached the outskirts of a village and he slowed the horses to a walk. 'They have weapons more terrifying than anything man could invent.'

Before she could reply he drew the coach into the yard of an inn with a creaking sign which proclaimed it to be the Jolly Brewers. 'I think we had best stop here. The wheel must be repaired and our injured people looked after.'

Helen was the curious one now. His comment about women had sounded bitter, so what had made him like that? Had he been badly let down? If so, where and when? He had been very young when he joined his regiment, could it have been someone he met during the war? Portuguese? Spanish? French even, one of the enemy? Or more recently, someone in Paris or Vienna, both places reputedly full of intrigue and romance?

But she could not question him, not only because he would give her a decided put-down for her impertinence, just as she had done to him, but because there was so much activity around them as the outside passengers climbed down from the roof and the young couple emerged from the interior.

A bent old man with wispy ginger hair and a stubbly beard emerged from the inn and hurried towards them.

'I've been expecting you,' he said. 'The coach ahead warned me. I have sent for a doctor. Bring the injured men in. I have a room for them.'

Helen watched as the guard was carried from the coach. He looked very pale and she was afraid the movement of the coach, for all the Captain's care, had not helped his injuries. She turned to help the coachman but he shrugged her off. 'I ain't in need of help, miss, it's my arm that's broke, not my legs. As for travelling inside, give me the box any day.'

'Yes, I am sure,' she said soothingly. 'The Captain did his best not to jolt you too much.'

'Oh, I ain't complaining about the Captain's driving, miss. I know he is a nonpareil of the highest, one of us, you might say. It was lucky he was with us. There ain't many I'd trust with my cattle.'

She looked up to see if the Captain had heard this remark but he was busy talking to the ostler about the horses, which were being unharnessed. 'They will settle given rest and a good long drink,' he was saying. 'The coach needs a wheel repaired; it was lucky it carried us this far.' He helped the ostler lead the horses to the stables and Helen followed the other passengers into the inn.

They discovered the old lady and young Bertie Billingsworth ensconced by the parlour fire, having already had a good meal. They were not talking and Helen sensed that the old lady had spent most of the time castigating the young man and he, resentful, was sulking. As soon as the old lady set eyes on the coachman, she began all over again to grumble and threaten to sue. 'Shaken to bits, I was,' she said. 'I could have had a seizure, I could have died. . .'

Helen bit back the retort she had on her tongue and said, 'Indeed, ma'am, we could all have died. Fortunately no one did, though the guard is injured and must be looked after.'

'That means more delay. I can see it will be Christmas before we arrive.'

'Oh, no!' Young Mrs Smith, who had come into the parlour hanging onto her husband's arm, sat down suddenly on the nearest chair. 'We cannot stay here. Tom, tell them we must proceed at once.'

'But, my love, how can I? The coach has to be repaired and we have no driver or guard.'

She grabbed his hand. 'But we must go on. We must hurry. Find another conveyance. Do something. Surely you do not want us to be overtaken?'

'Of course not, but. . .'

Duncan came into the room at that point. 'I am told the wheel can be given a temporary repair, which will be good enough to take us on to Leicester, where they will be able to fit a new wheel and mend the door. It should be done by late afternoon.' He turned to the landlord. 'If you can provide the ladies with a room in which to rest and refresh themselves. . .'

'I haven't any free rooms,' the man said. 'They must make do with this.'

The room they were in was intended for people coming in to eat while their horses were changed, or while waiting for a connection, and had nothing but a wooden settle against the wall, several hard chairs set about small tables and an armchair by the fire, now occupied by the elderly lady. It was not conducive to comfort and it was certainly not suitable for a lady to change her clothes, which Helen wished to do.

She was very conscious of her ripped petticoat, dangling about her knees under the bombazine of her dress.

'I need to change my clothes,' she told the innkeeper. 'And the young lady is very upset. I think she should lie down for an hour or two.'

'I'm sorry, ma'am, but the bedrooms are all in use and you can't have the best parlour on account of the doctor is in there examining your guard.'

Duncan drew the man to one side, whispered a few words and handed him something which chinked. When he turned back to the ladies, the innkeeper was smiling. 'You can use our bedroom, ladies. My wife will go and prepare it. Please be seated and have some refreshment while you wait.'

Ten minutes later the innkeeper's wife arrived to conduct them upstairs. The old lady declined to accompany them. 'Soft, that's what young chits are nowadays,' she said. 'Always wanting to rest and change their clothes. Why, in my young day, we thought nothing of travelling the full twenty-four hours in the same garments and been fresh as a daisy at the end of it.'

The young lady giggled suddenly, even though a minute before she had been weeping. 'Fresh!' she whispered to Helen. 'I'll wager her fellow passengers kept their distance.'

'If she is right, they would all have been as bad as one another,' Helen murmured, as they left the old lady to her grumbling and climbed the stairs behind the innkeeper's wife to a bedroom at the back of the house.

There had been frantic efforts to tidy it, the quilt

had been hastily thrown across the bed and there was still dust on the dressing table where a white garment poked from one of the drawers, but the water in the ewer was fresh and there was soap and clean towels laid on the washstand. Helen's trunk and the young lady's portmanteau stood in the middle of the worn carpet.

'Thank heaven,' Helen said, undoing the hooks and eyes that went down the front of her pelisse robe from neck to hem and revealing the torn petticoat. 'I felt everyone could see my legs.'

The young lady sat on the edge of the bed, watching her, doing nothing to help herself. 'You are very capable, but then I suppose you must be used to looking after yourself.'

'One can become accustomed to anything if one tries hard enough,' Helen said evasively, delving into her trunk for a fresh petticoat.

'I don't think I could. I hate this. I hate the dust, the dirt, not having anyone to help me, not having anything except that old portmanteau. I didn't know what to pack in it. I've never packed in my life before. I've never even undressed myself. . .' She stopped suddenly and her eyes filled with tears. 'Oh, it is so dreadful. And if Tom leaves me. . .'

Helen looked at her in surprise. 'Why should he do that?'

'I made him angry. He said I made him look small in front of the Captain and the others. He admires the Captain, you see. I believe he would like to have travelled on the box with him and I would not let him.'

'He would not leave you for anything so trifling. He seems devoted to you.'

'I wish I could be sure. I am not at all certain I should have undertaken this journey at all. What will everyone say? I had thought I could carry it off, but I can't, I know everyone is staring and talking about us.'

'I collect you saying Mr Smith is not your husband?'

'Did I?' She answered vaguely. 'That just proves I cannot carry it off.'

'An elopement?'

'Yes. You see, everyone has guessed.'

'It doesn't matter what people think they know. It's what you feel about Mr Smith that matters.'

She laughed shakily. 'His name isn't Smith, it's Thurborn. Tom Thurborn. He is from Canada. And my name is Dorothy Carstairs.'

Helen had wondered about the young man's accent. 'Mr Thurborn is a long way from home.'

'That's just what Papa said. He forbade me to see him or speak to him. He said he didn't know anything about his family or background. He said he would not have me affianced to some ne'er-do-well with no money and no prospects who would carry me off to the other side of the world, where I was bound to be miserable.'

Helen could quite see Mr Carstairs's point of view. 'How did you meet Tom?'

'At a ball at the American Embassy in London at the beginning of the season. Papa is a diplomat, you see, and it is my come-out year. Oh, it was such a glittering occasion, with the whole of London Society there. My card was full almost from the first. As soon as I saw Tom, I fell in love with him. He is so handsome, don't you think?'

'Indeed, yes,' Helen said, though the young man was

a parrot compared to the Captain's eagle. 'Do go on. I shall respect your confidence.'

'Oh, you don't know the relief of being able to talk to someone who understands. You do understand, don't you?'

'I think so.'

'We danced twice and went into supper together, which made Papa cross because he had almost promised Lord Danminster I should go into supper with him. I think he had already spoken to Papa about offering. I meant to refuse him, even if Tom had not come along. He is thirty if he is a day and fat, too.'

'How old are you, Miss Carstairs?'

'Oh, do call me Dorothy. We are hardly strangers, after all we've been through today. I am seventeen. When I told Papa I could not love a man so old, he said I had been reading too many novels and love had nothing to do with it. Do you not think love between husband and wife is very important, Miss Carstairs.'

'Please call me Helen. Yes, but then I would be considered a little eccentric for saying so.'

'I knew you would understand! Tom and I fell in love from the very first. We both said afterwards we became aware of it at the same moment, halfway through supper. I found myself feeling hot and breathless and he took me onto the terrace because it was cooler. We were not alone, there were any number of other people out there and Tom behaved perfectly properly.

'We talked a great deal, I cannot remember what about, but afterwards he crossed one of the names off my card and waltzed with me. I did not think anyone had noticed, but Papa was furious, he said I had no idea what I was about and Mama agreed with him, though she was nothing like as angry. They forbade me to see Tom again, but I managed to meet him at a friend's house.

'He was angry with Papa for denying us our happiness. He asked him for an interview. I don't know what they said to each other, but Tom left without speaking to me and I was locked in my room for a week afterwards. I was only let out when I promised to be good and obedient.'

'I imagine you were nothing of the sort,' Helen said dryly.

'I had to do something, didn't I? I sent Tom a letter, asking him to meet me in the garden after everyone had gone to bed. Papa saw us from the window and came down in his dressing-gown with a sporting gun. You can't know how frightened I was and thankful he did not use it. Tom bolted over the garden wall. The very next day Papa sent me to our country house in Norfolk. I thought I would never see Tom again and wept all the way.'

'Tom followed you?'

'Yes. He watched the house until he saw my maid, Jenny, coming out and gave her a letter for me.' She sighed. 'It was a beautiful letter, saying how much he loved me, how he could not live without me and if Papa and Mama could not see that, then he would carry me away to be married in secret.'

'So, you decided to elope to Gretna Green?'

'Yes. Tom hired a chaise and waited for me in the lane behind the house. It was still dark when we set off. We had to leave the chaise in Northampton to be picked up by its owner and caught the stage. I thought it would be a wonderful romantic adventure, but everything keeps going wrong. I never imagined coach travel would be like this, crammed into a jolting wooden box with all manner of other people, vulgar people too some of them, and being jostled against them, with hardly room to breathe. People asking questions when it is perfectly obvious you do not wish to talk. And when the coach ran off the road. . .' She shuddered. 'I thought I was going to die for my wickedness, I truly did.'

'We were all very alarmed,' Helen said.

'Tom called me a faint-hearted pudding,' she said. 'He has never been angry with me before. I begin to wonder if he truly loves me at all.'

'We all say things we do not mean when we are under stress,' Helen said. 'I am sure he did not mean to hurt you.'

'I miss Mama and Jenny. I want to go home.' She looked round the ill-furnished room with distaste. 'I half wish Papa would catch up with us.'

'Do you think he will come after you?'

'Yes, but he will be very angry. I do not know which is worse, his anger or Tom's. And if Tom decides he has had enough of me, I will be quite ruined. And I shall have to stay here forever and ever.' And again her eyes filled with tears.

Helen bit off the comment that Dorothy should have thought of that before setting out, and instead offered to help her off with her dress so that she could wash.

'I wish I could remain as calm as you do,' the girl said, as she stepped out of her dress and stood in her petticoat and chemise. 'Nothing seems to upset you.

Look how you tended the wounded. I could not have done that, the blood made me feel sick.'

'Most of it belonged to the cow. And truly, I did nothing exceptional. Shall I find you another gown?' She opened Dorothy's portmanteau and pulled out a flimsy lace nightgown, a pair of satin shoes, two petticoats and a round gown of pink gauze with a satin slip in deep rose. It had a very full skirt, caught up with little garlands of silk roses, but it had been rolled up and stuffed into her bag without thought and was so creased as to be unwearable, even if it had been suitable for travelling. 'Is this all you've got?'

'Yes. I told you I had never packed before.'

'Then I will brush this one.' She picked up the worn gown from the floor. 'Have a wash, you will feel better.'

Given something specific to do, Dorothy complied. 'Have you been a lady's maid?' she asked, as she towelled herself.

'Me?' Helen asked, startled. 'Good heavens, no. What gave you that idea?'

'You seem to know exactly what to do.'

'Do I?' she repeated. 'It is only common sense, you know. Think what you would do if you were at home and then do it. Now you would sit and brush your hair, would you not?'

'Jenny would.'

'Yes, of course.' Dorothy was homesick, it did not need a soothsayer to tell that, and thinking of home and what her life used to be like made Helen homesick too. She envied Dorothy having parents who cared for her, who would be worried by her disappearance, who would, she was sure, forgive her and welcome her back into the family fold. For Helen there was no going back, only an uncertain future. She smiled, unwilling to let Dorothy see her misery. 'But if you want me to do it, then you must wait until I have washed and dressed myself.'

'I'm sorry I am so helpless.'

'It is not your fault. But if you are to survive, you must learn to be a little more self-reliant. Is Tom able to provide you with a maid?'

'No, not yet. Later, when we are settled.'

Helen wondered what Tom had told her about his prospects, if anything at all. 'Why don't you both wait for your papa to catch up with you? I am sure he will understand and forgive you. If you want to marry Tom after that, I doubt he will put obstacles in your path, knowing how determined on it you are.'

'Do you think so? Do you really think so?' She sounded so eager to accept the idea that Helen prayed she was right.

'Yes.' She helped Dorothy back into her dress and did the buttons up at the back, glad that she herself had had the foresight to make sure her dresses were easy to get into and out of. 'Now you rest on the bed. I am going downstairs.'

'You will not leave me?'

'No, but do you mind if I tell Captain Blair what you have told me? I am sure he can be relied upon to be discreet and he may have some advice to offer.'

'No, but do make him promise not to repeat it.'

Why she had suggested the Captain, Helen did not know, except that she had come to rely on him. She wanted confirmation that she had been right to suggest the young couple should wait for Mr Carstairs and beg his forgiveness.

She found him in the parlour alone. He was sitting on the settle under the window and staring out onto the cobbled yard, deep in thought. 'Captain?'

He started up at the sound of her voice, as if he had been in another place, another time, listening to voices she could not hear, seeing people she would never know. 'Oh, Miss Sadler, I beg your pardon, I was in a brown study.'

'Fretting at the delay, Captain?'

'Yes, among other things. Did you wish to speak to me?'

'Yes. I have just come from Miss. . .' She stopped. 'The young lady who has been travelling with us.'

He smiled. 'She has pitched herself into a bumble-bath, hasn't she?'

'Yes. She and the young man, Tom Thurborn she tells me his name is, are eloping.'

'That much was obvious from the first.'

'Oh, do you think so? I did not notice anything amiss until the accident when she admitted he was not her husband. She is in a very excited state and I am quite concerned for her. She is beginning to regret her foolhardiness. I came to ask your advice.'

'My advice, Miss Sadler? What can it possibly have to do with me? Or you, either. They got themselves into this mess and must get themselves out of it.'

'But she is very confused and quite helpless without her maid. I have advised her to wait until her father comes and to beg his forgiveness.'

'Is that what you would do, Miss Sadler? In her shoes, I mean.'

'I do not know. If she really does love the young man. . .'

'*If*. That is the question. It seems to me, she does not know her own mind.'

'I am sure she must do. No young lady would contemplate such an enormous step and risk everything she values, if she were not truly in love. . .'

'Love what is love, but "an abject intercourse between tyrants and slaves"?'

'Oliver Goldsmith,' she said, green eyes twinkling. 'I am familiar with the quotation, but is a bitter comment on life. Surely you are not so cynical?'

'It is what I have come to expect.'

'Then you have been very unfortunate.'

'And you have not? Love has treated you kindly?'

'It has not been unkind. But we are not speaking of me, but of Tom and Dorothy. It must be truly dreadful when parents refuse to consent to a match when two people are in love. No wonder they eloped.'

'Would you elope, Miss Sadler?' His dark eyes seemed to be burning into hers, trying to make her reveal her innermost secrets, and she knew she would need all her strength to resist. But it had become a kind of deadly serious game between them; him probing, her parrying, asking, refuting, finding out things about each other and scoring points for how difficult or how easy it had been, losing them when the fantasies were exploded.

What made it worse was that there were no rules about telling the truth. Who would be the winner, the one who discovered the most or the one who revealed nothing, the liar or the truth teller?

'Does it take so long to decide?' His voice came to her through her reverie.

'To decide?'

'Whether you, being in love, would ever consider eloping?'

'That is irrelevant.'

He laughed. 'Oh? But do you know, that's what I thought you were doing when I first saw you at the Blue Boar, when you said you wanted the Glasgow coach. I wondered where your lover was.'

'You forget, sir, that there would be no question of my having to elope. I am of no consequence at all, an ordinary young woman, who has to earn her living and who is certainly old enough to make up her own mind on the subject of marriage.'

'How old are you? Nineteen, twenty?'

'Sir, you are very wanting in conduct to ask me that. And we are talking about Tom and Dorothy, not me.'

'I crave pardon,' he said, but there was a twinkle in his eye. 'I can ask a working girl her age, but not a princess. I should have remembered.'

'I am not a princess and it is unkind of you to mock me.'

'Oh but you are. No one but a princess could be so top-lofty.'

'I am not accustomed to. . .' She stopped suddenly. That was exactly what he meant; she was giving herself away all the time. She wished she were a princess then she might pass the whole thing of as a prank—the reason for her journey, her poverty, her obligation to him. She tried again. 'I am not used to dealing with men like you, helpful one minute, hateful the next. It is almost as if you were two men, not one.'

She had done it again; she had turned the conversation right round so that they were talking about him and not her. Two men indeed! But was she right? 'You have brought it on yourself by being so secretive.'

'Why should I satisfy your curiosity? That is all it is, idle curiosity. If you had been a woman, I would have set you down as a gabble-grinder with nothing in your head but gossip.'

'But I am not a woman,' he said, refusing to be offended, though that was what she had intended. 'I am a mere man, with a man's instincts to look after those who are weak and vulnerable.'

'I am neither weak nor vulnerable.'

'I stand corrected.' He laughed aloud, throwing back his dark head so that the long line of his throat showed against the pale lemon of his cravat. He had a mole beneath his chin, she noticed, and felt a sudden urge to reach out and touch it. Then, seriously, 'But you think Miss Carstairs is?'

'Yes.'

'What do you want me to do about it?'

'Talk to Mr Thurborn, find out his intentions. . .'

'I fancy the young lady's papa has already done that and found the answers unsatisfactory.'

'Yes, but you could point out how this escapade is affecting Dorothy, see if a solution can be found.'

'Where is the young man?'

'I saw him in the yard five minutes ago.'

'Very well.' He sighed heavily and stood up. 'Wait here for me. We will talk some more.'

Why had he said that? he asked himself as he strolled out to the yard in search of Tom Thurborn. What did it matter to him whether she was a princess or a servant and why was he so determined to find out? Was it simply curiosity? He had told her to wait for him, though there was nowhere she could go. Would he wait for her if she asked him to? He knew the answer without thinking. He would wait forever, he could never leave her. Princess or pauper, it did not matter.

He shook himself as he crossed the yard to where the young man stood kicking at stones with dusty hessians, watching the ostlers. He was being ridiculous. She was nothing to him, simply a young woman on a coach, amusing herself baiting him. And he was fool enough to fall for it.

Tom looked up at his approach. 'Hallo, Captain. This is a deuced inconvenient business, ain't it?'

'Yes. I fancy more for you than for me. I am told you are expecting to be pursued.'

'How do you know that?'

'Miss Carstairs confided in Miss Sadler, who told me.'

'It is none of your affair, sir.'

'I couldn't agree more,' he said, smiling. 'Unfortunately, Miss Sadler has made it her affair and that means I cannot avoid becoming involved.'

'I cannot think why Dorrie should even mention it.'

'Are you blind? Have you not been aware of Miss Carstairs' distress?'

'Of course, I have. It is the accident, the delay, you know what women are.'

'No, I don't think I do. Do you?'

'Oh, you know what I mean. Dorrie will be as right as ninepence when we are on our way again.'

'You are determined to go through with it, then?'

'Good God, Captain, you surely do not think I would abandon her?'

'She apparently thinks you would.'

'Why? I have never given her the slightest reason to doubt me. I would not. She is everything to me.'

'And yet you took her from her parents and put her through an ordeal which would have strained the stoutest heart. . .'

'Miss Sadler manages very well.'

Duncan smiled. 'Yes, not all young ladies are as practical and self-reliant as Miss Sadler. You cannot measure Miss Carstairs against that young woman. The cases are very different.'

'No, but what else could I do? Her father would have none of me, though I am not the penniless cur he believes me to be. I come from good stock, farmers who left England half a century ago and made good in Canada. Out there, we are in the top one hundred, not quite what it is in England, but well enough. In any case, I have an inheritance in this country, a small estate in Berkshire, I have no intention of uprooting my darling, if she does not wish it.'

'At this moment I believe she wishes she was safe back home.'

'No, I do not believe that.'

'Could she go home if she wanted to? Would there be any reason why she should not go back unmarried?'

'What?' He looked puzzled. 'Oh, you mean. . . No, Captain, I would not harm a hair of her head and I'd kill anyone who tried. She is still the innocent.'

'Then take her back. Speak to her father again, perhaps he will relent.'

'I doubt that.'

'Then enrol the help of the mother. Women understand these affairs of the heart better than men. Let Mrs Carstairs be your advocate.'

'If that is what Dorrie wants, but I must hear it from her own lips.'

'I'll send Miss Carstairs out to you.'

Duncan returned to the inn, leaving Tom to dwell on what he had said, though whether he would take it to heart, he was unsure. Miss Sadler was sitting where he had left her, a slight, downcast figure in unrelieved black, but not dull, by no means dull. She was like a beacon in the wilderness, lighting a path to...

He stopped. Where? Where was she going and why? She was frowning a little as if trying to solve a puzzle, and her lips were pursed. Very kissable lips. For one brief moment he allowed himself to imagine what it would be like to kiss her. Behind him he heard the door open and Miss Carstairs came into the room.

Helen looked up and saw them both, the man, dark and brooding with a half-smile on his lips, the girl, all flounces and eagerness.

'I could not stay on that bed a moment longer,' Dorothy said, sitting down beside Helen. 'I should not have poured the whole story out to you like that, complaining about everything. It is not your fault. It was only the upset of nearly being overturned in the coach and seeing all that blood which made me behave foolishly and caused my doubts about what we were doing. I have no doubts at all. I want to marry Tom as soon as I can. If you can put up with the inconvenience for the one you love, then so can I.'

Duncan drew in his breath audibly making them both turn to look at him. So there was someone. Miss

Sadler had confided in the chit that she was going to meet a lover. He should have known. Oh, what a fool he had been!

'Excuse me, ladies,' he said. 'I have arrangements to make for my onward journey.' And with that he turned on his heel and strode from the room, intending to hire a riding horse, or walk on to the next village and see if there was another coach going on, anywhere, away from the girl in black with the huge luminous eyes who had made him want to protect her, who frustrated him beyond endurance.

'I must find Tom,' Dorothy said into the heavily laden atmosphere. Helen and the Captain had quarrelled, judging by the thunderous looks he had given them when he stormed out. She hoped it had not been over her and Tom. 'Have you seen him?'

'The Captain was talking to him outside.'

'Will you help me look for him? Oh, I do hope he has not disappeared.'

'Of course he hasn't disappeared,' Helen said, more sharply than she intended. The Captain had been upset about something or why had he left so abruptly, as if he were washing his hands of the whole affair? She knew he had not wanted to be dragged into it, but he had gone off to speak to Mr Thurborn quite happily. What could they have said to each other to have brought about such a change?

And what was that Dorothy had said? 'If you can put up with the inconvenience for the one you love'? Where had she got that idea? But that would not have caused the Captain to take himself off. After all, he had thought she was eloping and that only strengthened his surmise. Why did she wish Dorothy had never said it? Why did it matter so much?

She stood up and followed Dorothy out to the yard where they searched high and low. There was no sign of either man. 'I saw the young one walking down the lane that way,' one of the ostlers said, when Dorothy spoke to him.

'Was he alone?' Helen asked.

'Yes. Gone for a stroll until the coach is ready, I'll be bound.'

But Dorothy did not believe that. She began to wail that Tom had left her and Helen was obliged to put aside her own concerns to comfort her. 'Come back inside, he may be there.' She put her arm about the girl's shoulders and drew her indoors, wondering what she would do if the young man did not turn up. She could not leave her and neither could she afford the expense of extra nights' lodgings waiting for Mr Carstairs to turn up. He might not come or he might miss them.

And now the Captain had gone too, bored with their game and exasperated by the eloping couple and who could blame him? But without him to guide her, she knew she would be lost, whatever she had told him to the contrary. Two days she had known him, only two days, and yet she already knew that life without him would be bleak indeed.

CHAPTER FIVE

Tom was nowhere to be found inside the inn either and Dorothy became inconsolable, crying loudly enough to have everyone in the building running to see what was wrong. 'Whatever shall I do? Whatever shall I do?'

'Stop weeping all over Miss Sadler, for a start,' Duncan said, pushing his way past the innkeeper, the innkeeper's wife, the old lady and assorted passengers, to her side.

Helen, her arms round Dorothy, looked up to see his tall figure standing over them and breathed a huge sigh of relief and pleasure. He stood looking down at them with a quirky smile; so, she was pleased to see him back, her expressive eyes gave her away. 'Now, tell me, what the matter is this time,' he demanded, doing his best to sound severe.

Dorothy was incoherent and it was left to Helen to explain what had happened. 'I do not know what you said to him,' she said. 'But you seem to have driven him away instead of making him face up to his responsibilities.'

'I did no such thing.' He had got no further than the stable door in his quest for a riding horse, deciding he could not leave her, however much she infuriated him, however many loves she had waiting for her at the end of her journey. At the rate she attracted problems,

113

other people's as well as her own, she would never reach journey's end.

He was torn between his need to get home as soon as possible and wanting to stay and do what he could for her. It was an inclination so strong that to deny it was to deny his inbred sense of chivalry. But there was more to it than that; she held him like a magnet and he could not tear himself away. Yet, if he did not do so, where would it lead? To more heartache, more humiliation? He was gambling with his hard-won peace of mind.

And now, for his pains, he was saddled with not one but two helpless females and his own homecoming was destined to be delayed still further. 'If the foolish muckworm hasn't the ginger to face up to what he has done, it is none of my doing.'

'You are not to speak of Tom like that,' Dorothy cried. 'I love him. He is a good kind man. . .'

'Then where is this good kind man?'

'I do not know.' She dabbed at her eyes with a lace handkerchief. 'But it is all my f-fault. I am not usually such a w-watering pot but I could not h-help it and he was so angry with me. . .'

'You do not seriously think he has abandoned you because you cried?'

'Y-yes. N-no. Oh, I don't know.'

'Merciful heaven, save me from weeping women. It is bad enough having to watch over one helpless female. . .'

'Captain, are you by any chance referring to me?' Helen put in, wishing she had not so readily shown her pleasure at seeing him again. His reference to facing up to what you had done reminded her of her father;

the Captain would undoubtedly condemn him out of hand. 'I am not helpless and I do not need watching over. If you have assumed the mantle of my protector, then it was entirely unnecessary. And you are being cruel to Miss Carstairs who is too upset to defend herself.'

'She doesn't need to defend herself when she can get other people to do it for her.'

'And why should I not speak up for her?'

'Because you have enough to do looking after yourself. I never met such a one for getting into scrapes.' The only way he could control the feelings which threatened to run away with him was to keep his sympathy well in check; any sign of weakness and he would be lost.

'And you, sir, are so hard and unfeeling you cannot recognise true distress when it is right under your nose. I fancy you have been too long a soldier. We are not one of your men, to be bullied into submission. I do not know why you came back, if you have nothing helpful to offer. You could have been halfway to wherever you are going by now.'

Oh, why had she said that? Now he would leave and this time he would not come back. Why did she say one thing when she meant another? She wanted him to stay. So why was she behaving so waspishly? It was no longer a game, it was a clash of minds and hearts, a fierce battle and her only defence was in attack and that made matters worse.

'So I could. Is that what you wish?'

She could not truthfully say yes and her pride would not allow her to say no. 'You must please yourself.'

They were so absorbed in their exchange, they had

almost forgotten the cause of it, when Dorothy cried out. 'There he is!' and dashed from the room, along the corridor and out into the yard, where Tom had returned and was speaking to one of the ostlers.

The watchers from the window saw her fling herself into his arms, saw him comforting her, talking gently to her, taking both her hands in his and kissing them one by one.

'Oh, what it is to be in love,' Duncan said wryly. 'I think I would sooner have indigestion.'

'Now, Captain, you know you do not mean that,' Helen said, thankful that she could relinquish responsibility for Dorothy to Tom.

'I am not in the habit of saying things I do not mean.'

'Then you are cynical beyond belief.'

'Perhaps I have reason to be.' His dark eyes reflected a remembered pain, but she would not allow herself to feel sympathy.

'If you have suffered at someone else's hands, it is hardly civil of you to belittle other people's feelings,' she said, wishing she understood her own. 'I, for one, am pleased for Miss Carstairs and wish her happy and if you cannot do the same, then you should not have come back. You should have left us to manage.'

'I am not so easy to shake off, Miss Sadler,' he said. 'Nor such a scapegrace as to leave any young lady to her fate, however much she might deserve it.' If he had said it with a smile instead of something approaching a scowl, she might have felt better.

A few minutes later the young couple returned indoors hand in hand to where Duncan and Helen waited. 'It's all right,' Dorothy said. 'He hadn't left me. He just wanted to go away and think about what to do.'

'A trifle late in the day, don't you think?' Duncan murmured. 'The thinking should have been done long ago.'

Tom ignored the jibe. 'We have decided to go on to Derby.'

'I have an aunt there,' Dorothy explained. 'We will go to her and send word to Papa that we are there, then he will come and fetch me. Aunt Sophia will help us to persuade him to let us marry.'

'Recruit the distaff side to your cause, how very clever,' Duncan said, laughing.

Tom coloured but made no comment.

'Oh, I am so happy,' Dorothy said. 'I really shan't mind riding in the coach knowing it is not for long. Papa is sure to bring the carriage.'

'That is a splendid idea,' Helen said. 'Derby is not so very far away.'

'In miles, perhaps not,' Duncan said. 'In time, it is another matter. The coach is not yet repaired and we shall be kicking our heels here for several hours more. We will be lucky to reach Leicester tonight, let alone Derby.'

'Then I, for one, shall go for a walk,' Helen said. 'I need a little exercise.'

'Alone, princess?' queried Duncan, raising one well-shaped brow, making the scar on his forehead stand out.

'Dorothy and Mr Thurborn will come too, won't you?' she appealed to the other girl.

'Of course, but surely the Captain. . .?'

'That goes without saying,' Duncan said, with a

lopsided grin. 'I don't think I dare let Miss Sadler out of my sight.'

'I should think not, either,' Dorothy said, taking Tom's arm. 'Come, Helen. Captain Blair.'

Duncan chuckled and held out his arm to Helen. 'Come, princess, let us play chaperone to young love.'

There was nothing she could do but lay her fingers on his arm and accompany him from the inn and even that small physical contact was giving her shivers.

'I believe there is a very pleasant park nearby,' Tom said, as they walked. 'I glimpsed it while I was out earlier.'

'Wistow Hall,' Duncan said. 'During the Civil War, its owner, Sir Richard Halford, was host to Charles I before the Battle of Naseby. I believe it belongs to Sir Henry Halford now.'

'Isn't he one of the Royal physicians?' Helen asked, and could have bitten off her tongue. She had made up her mind not to mention anything which could connect her with London Society, even if any well-read young lady could have known about it.

'Yes. He treated the late King and I believe the present one. Wellington and Pitt too.'

'Do you think he is at home?' The last thing she wanted was to meet anyone who might have known her father.

'It is doubtful.' Detecting the slight concern in her voice he turned to look down at her, but all he could see was the brim of her black bonnet, a wisp of curl and a pert little nose. 'Are you afraid of meeting him?'

'No, why should I be?' She laughed a little unsteadily. 'But I should hate to be accused of trespass.'

'Then we will avoid the gentleman's residence.' He

pointed to a lane to the left, running through a spinney. 'This looks a pleasant little byway. Shall we take it and see where it leads?'

It led, they discovered, to a tiny village with a quaint little church and a handsome manor house. Having admired both, they resumed their walk, turning south along the bank of a river.

'How peaceful it all is,' Helen said. 'It is difficult to imagine it was the scene of a great battle.'

'The battle was a little to the south,' Duncan said. 'But I can imagine the countryside would have been filled with troops, horses and pikemen, supply wagons and hospital carts being marshalled to their positions, trampling down the crops, taking over farmhouses and buildings.'

'It must have been dreadful for those who lived in their path, whichever side they favoured,' Helen said.

'War is always terrible,' he went on. 'But civil war especially so, neighbour fighting neighbour, brother against brother, son opposing father. I am glad I did not live in those times.'

'Would you have opposed your father?'

'One opposes my father at one's peril,' he said, somewhat caustically.

'Oh.' He was evidently speaking from experience and she wondered just what he had done to displease his father. Had he formed an unsuitable attachment or refused to obey him in some other way? Had he been banished? Was that why he had been so long a soldier? She would have liked to ask him, but knew he would not welcome her questions any more than she wished for his.

'I fought for King and country, Miss Sadler, not in a

Civil War,' he said. 'Being a second son, it was expected of me.'

'How hard it is always to do what is expected of one,' she said softly.

'Yes.' He did not elaborate, leaving her feeling unsatisfied.

'Oh, look!' Dorothy cried, pointing. 'The hunt is out.'

They stood and watched as a band of noisy horseman hallooed after a pack of hounds in full pursuit of a fox, thoughtlessly flattening a carefully ploughed field and tearing down hedges as they jumped them. Helen, watching them, realised that the damage they were doing was minute compared to what an army would cause, but it was bad enough. 'Tomorrow, some poor labourer will have to plough the field again and mend the hedges,' she said.

'He will not mind that,' Duncan said. 'It is work, after all, and he will be paid.'

'I suppose so, but I abhor wanton destruction, either of crops or animals.'

'Very commendable, but have you ever hunted, Miss Sadler?'

She paused, casting her mind back to happier times, to visits to their country home near Peterborough, before everything had gone so badly wrong. She had hunted with Papa then. She was considered a good horsewoman and had enjoyed the exhilaration but had always been relieved when the fox escaped, but she could not tell him that. A schoolma'am, which is what he thought her to be, would certainly not have hunted. Unwilling to face the cross-examination if she told the truth, she took refuge, once again, in lying. 'No.'

'Then you can know nothing of the excitement of the chase.'

'No, but I have eyes to see.'

'What you see, is not what you feel. To feel something, you must experience it.'

'Is that so?' Had he ever experienced the confusion she was feeling now? She doubted it; he seemed so self-possessed, so iron-hard, and yet she detected a softness he tried hard to disguise.

'Do you ride, Miss Sadler?' he asked, changing the subject abruptly. 'I imagine you must have taken a gentle hack in the park.'

'That pastime is for ladies,' she said, evasively. He was still playing their game of cat and mouse, still probing, and she knew he would counter any reply with more questions. To stave them off, she must divert him. 'I prefer walking, there is time to see so much more. I used often to walk in Hyde Park.'

'I wonder you found the time,' he murmured. 'Being a working girl.'

'I thought Miss Sadler must be a lady's maid,' Dorothy put in. 'But she tells me I was mistaken.'

'Of course you were mistaken,' Duncan retorted. 'Can you not tell she is a princess in disguise?'

'No!' She looked from him to Helen, both of whom were unsmiling, and then laughed. 'You are gammoning me.'

'Of course he is,' Helen said. 'He has a very strange sense of humour.'

'Then if you must earn a living, how do you do it?' It was Dorothy's turn to ask questions and these were not so easy to parry. She could hardly snub her.

'I was a companion to an elderly lady, a widow to a

wealthy nabob who had made his fortune in India.'
Worse and worse! Not content with being evasive, she
was being inventive; until now she would never have
believed it possible.

'India?' queried Duncan, his interest aroused. 'Who
was she? I have been in India, I might be acquainted
with the lady.'

Helen felt the colour flooding her face; being a liar
needed more wits and guile than she possessed. 'I do
not think so, she was not much in Society,' she said
lamely.

'What happened? Did you lose your position?'

'No, she died.' Oh, where was it all going to end?
She was falling deeper and deeper into the mire.

If that was the reason for the mourning, Duncan
thought it a little excessive unless the old lady were
related. 'My condolences, Miss Sadler.'

'It must be dreadful being a companion,' Dorothy
said before Helen could find a suitable reply. 'I should
hate it, being at the beck and call of an old lady's every
whim. "Fetch my wrap." "Read to me." "Make me a
drink." No time to yourself at all. . .'

'But Miss Sadler has just said she did have time to
walk in the park,' Duncan said pointedly.

'Carrying the old lady's parasol, I'll wager,' Tom put
in. 'Going at a snail's pace.'

'She was very good to me,' Helen said, deciding she
may as well be hung for a sheep as a lamb. 'She
allowed me two half-days off a week when I could
please myself what I did.'

'Goodness me, two half-days!' Dorothy exclaimed.
'How fortunate you were. I know someone who is
companion to a friend of my mother's, who has no free

time at all. She is a poor little thing with no spirit at all.'

'I should think that spirit is the last trait you would need for that occupation,' Duncan said, smiling at Helen. Of all things, she was undoubtedly spirited. 'Would you not agree, Miss Sadler?'

'Not necessarily. If people behave like mice, then they cannot complain if they are treated like mice.'

'But if your bed and board are dependent on doing as you are told. . .'

'Captain, have you never heard of compromise?'

'Naturally I have. One must tread the tightrope, is that not so, Miss Sadler?'

The barb went home and she lapsed into silence. How much had he guessed? Did he know she was lying through her teeth and did not even know why? She supposed it must be her pride driving her. Unhappy and disappointed in her father, penniless, having to pretend to be inferior to Dorothy Carstairs, travelling alone to heaven knew where, she had been forced to call on her pride to sustain her. It was all she had left. Pride. And according to her old nanny, that came before a fall.

How much further could she fall? Were there greater depths? She straightened her back and strode on, so that the others were obliged to quicken their pace, until they came within sight of the inn.

'You have ample time to have a meal before you go,' the innkeeper said, coming from the back regions as they entered the parlour. 'The coach is not yet ready and my wife is the best cook in the county. You will fare better here than in Leicester. It will be late by the time you arrive and all that's left will be scraps.'

Duncan had a fair idea that the old man had told the wheelwright not to hurry over the repair and at any other time he would have roasted him for it and insisted on haste, but this afternoon had been more enjoyable than he had expected it to be and a good meal in the quiet surroundings of this out of the way inn would round it off nicely. He was becoming philosophical about the constant delays; it was fate and it was never a sensible policy to kick against fate. He smiled. 'What do you recommend?'

'The partridge pie is very fine and so is the stew. Finest scotch beef went into that, Captain. There's oysters too and a roast capon. Syllabub and apple pie to sweeten the taste buds and wine to wash it all down.'

'All of it,' Tom said heartily. 'I am hungry as a hunter.'

Having succeeded in persuading them to stay, the innkeeper set about proving his claim that the cooking was the best in the county, which he did to everyone's satisfaction. It grew dark while they ate and their host lit the lamps, but they hardly noticed, being absorbed in cheerful conversation. Not until they had all declared they could not eat another thing, did he tell them the coach was ready in the yard with the horses, now nicely rested, back in the traces.

Duncan insisted on paying the bill, then left them to oversee the stowing of their luggage and speak to the coachman who, with his broken arm still strapped to his chest, was busy inspecting every inch of the equipage.

'How is the guard?' Duncan asked him.

'Staying here. The doctor said it would be unwise to

move him tonight. I'll call for him on the return journey.'

'And you?'

'Middling fair.'

'But not yet able to drive, I'll wager. I'll take us on to Leicester, if you like.'

'I was hoping you might offer, Captain, but I'm not travelling inside again, not nohow. And you'd best wear my spare coat; it'll be cold on the box.' He dragged a heavy buff benjamin out from under the box and handed it to Duncan. 'You may as well look like a coachman.'

Ten minutes later, everyone was back in their seats and Tom, who had purloined the horn from the long basket attached to the side of the guard's seat, blew a tantivy into the night and Duncan, muffled from neck to heels in the big coat, set the horses in motion.

Helen half wished she were still on the box, but then decided it could not be so pleasant in the dark with nothing to see of the countryside and unknown obstacles lurking in the shadows. The glimmer of the lamps on each side of the coach illuminated little more than the backs of the wheelers. Driving an unknown team must be ten times more hazardous at night and she did not envy the Captain.

But then he seemed able to deal with any and every situation that occurred with unerring self-confidence, from petty thieves and amateur whipsters to eloping couples and driving a coach and four, not to mention giving orders to ostlers and innkeepers and making one and all jump to obey. He had been a thoughtful and agreeable travelling companion, when he was not grumbling at her for some misdemeanour or other. He had made an unbearable journey bearable, almost a pleasure.

If he were to leave her, as he almost had at the last inn, she would feel bereft, as if her last ally had deserted her, which was absurd. They were strangers on a journey, thrown together by circumstance, never to meet again. And it was just as well, she told herself, she had lied to prevent him discovering who she really was. It had started as self-preservation, an unwillingness to divulge the reason for her journey, to admit that she was ashamed of her father and afraid of the future, but the future had to be faced.

The journey would eventually come to an end. If Captain Blair was still with her when she reached Glasgow, he would see, perhaps speak to, whoever had been sent by her guardian to meet her and that would mean her deception would be uncovered. She had to make sure they parted before then.

Telling herself it was of no consequence made not the slightest difference; it was as if she had known him all her life, right from the beginning in India, a time she could not remember at all. But that was foolish. He had said his home was in Scotland, not India, though he had admitted he had been there. Why had she been so foolish as to tell that Banbury tale of the nabob's widow?

'There's a nasty bend ahead with a high bank which won't take feather-edging, so don't point the leaders too soon,' Martin Gathercole advised Duncan. 'And you've a couple of steep hills too, so watch what you're at. Don't let them drop to a walk going up or you will lose the horse's draught and when you get to the brow, don't stop to put the chain on; without the guard to do it, it would be asking for trouble. I've known many a coach and four gallop off down a hill without its driver.'

'I can imagine it,' Duncan said, smiling. 'But I shall take your advice and stay on the box.'

'I can get down and put the shoe on if we have to,' Martin went on. 'But I reckon they'll hold well enough and the tackle is good, I checked it particularly before we left. We should make the outskirts of Leicester in about fifty minutes, though we might have to put the drag on going down the last hill.'

Duncan grinned to himself in the darkness, taking the advice in the spirit in which it was given, though he did not need instruction. He had not been boasting to Miss Sadler about his prowess and his eyes were younger than the coachman's; he could see the dark shadow of the trees on the bend. He negotiated it to perfection, eliciting a 'Good turn, Captain,' from the coachman.

Helen, her name was, he had heard Miss Carstairs call her that. Helen, wife of Menelaus. Wasn't she reputed to be the most beautiful woman in the world? She had run away with Paris and caused the ten-year siege of Troy which ended in the destruction of the city. But this Helen would not behave so shamefully, he was sure of that. He chuckled to himself in the darkness, which made his companion turn and look at him in surprise. 'Captain?'

'Nothing. I was pleased with the compliment.'

'And very forward it was of me to utter it.'

'Not at all.'

Helen. How did he know that she would not behave

shamefully? He was a fair judge of character when it
came to his own sex; he could tell when a trooper
could be trusted, by looking in his eyes. He could tell
a trickster at the card table simply by his hands. There
had been men in his own command he would not have
given an inch to, and others among the enemy he
would have trusted with his life. But nothing in his
experience had led him to believe himself a fair judge
of the ladies, whatever their station.

Dorothy Carstairs, for instance. She was a spoiled
empty-headed chit, selfishly taking it for granted that
everyone would fall in with her wishes, taking and
never giving, assuming Miss Sadler would wait upon
her. His aversion to the young lady was not based on
anything except her behaviour when confronted with a
situation she had never met before.

Was that how you should judge everyone, by taking
them out of their normal environment and putting
them to the test? In that case, Miss Helen Sadler had
passed with flying colours, because he was convinced
she was not what she said she was. Every incident on
the journey, her behaviour towards the different
people they had met on the way, scraps of information
she had let drop into the conversation, had revealed
just a little more of her character, of Helen Sadler, the
woman, a woman of spirit and compassion, culture and
education, but as to how those traits were acquired,
her family and upbringing, not a thing.

He was convinced it was deliberate, but why the
deception? What was she hiding? Shame, dishonesty,
scandal? Such a situation was not new to him. He had
suffered at Arabella's hands. Years ago it had been,
when he was green and trusted everyone, before he

learned that beautiful young ladies could not be relied on.

He had been home once or twice since then, to visit his father and brother, Andrew, but he had never stayed very long and had never strayed onto the neighbouring estate where he might come across James, his one-time friend, now Lord Macgowan, or his lady wife. Such an encounter would be painful and embarrassing to them both. But now his father had been taken ill and, according to Andrew, was asking for him. He had been given leave to come home, but oh, how slow the journey was proving to be!

He had ridden horseback from Vienna to Calais and that had been bad enough, then the packet from France had been delayed by adverse winds and a terrible storm, which had everyone but the hardiest of sailors sick in their bunks. His horse, which had carried him faithfully for years, had broken free in its terror and been so badly injured he had been obliged to shoot it. He had taken the mail from Dover to London but missed the ongoing mail on which he intended to continue and been obliged to take the slower stage. Ever since then it had been one thing after another.

If he had gone on with the coach instead of staying the night at Northampton, he would have been at least twelve hours ahead, but that would have meant forgoing that delightful meal with Miss Sadler and carrying her up to her bed. He did not regret that for one moment. For the first time for years he had forgotten his avowed antipathy to the female of the species and enjoyed her company; she had been intelligent, funny, naïve. He smiled to himself in the darkness. Fancy wearing all those clothes! Did she imagine they were travelling to the Arctic?

But she had also been clever enough to parry every attempt to find out where she was going and why, and was not in the least over-awed by him. But why should she be? She did not know who he was other than his name and he had no intention of revealing his antecedents and spoiling the rapport they had built up, soldier and lady's companion, nobodies enjoying each other's company for a day or two, even if it was all a sham.

But supposing she did know who he was, supposing it was all a game to her? Many a man had been ensnared by a woman's apparent helplessness; they were not helpless at all, but artful, as he knew to his cost. What had set him thinking along these lines? Deceit and dishonesty, that was it, and whether Miss Sadler was capable of either.

For the first time since Arabella's betrayal, he was unsure of his judgement. All the evidence told him he was being a fool, that the more he became entangled the more difficult it would be to extricate himself. On the other hand, his curiosity had been aroused; he would not be satisfied until he knew all there was to know about Miss Helen Sadler. But it was more than that, it was the girl herself.

She was as unlike Arabella as it was possible to be. Arabella was fair-haired and blue-eyed, with a rounded figure which he had to admit might become even rounder as she grew older. It was a fashionable figure and she had been a fashionable young lady, dressed in the latest mode, her conversation tempered by the instruction she received from her mama. It was not her fault she could not stand up to the pressure of her parents, he told himself in those early days of his disappointment, but she should have told him, not waited until he came home and found out for himself.

Miss Helen Sadler, on the other hand, was tiny and dark with huge green eyes which looked straight at you, a girl with a mind of her own and who was not afraid of expressing it. What she lacked in stature she made up for in fire; he could not imagine her allowing herself to be coerced into a marriage she did not care for.

'There's no call to go at a snail's pace, you know.' A voice at his elbow broke in on his reverie. 'You'll have the cattle asleep as they walk.'

'Sorry,' he said, flicking the reins alongside the leaders and setting them going at a trot. 'I was thinking.'

'The only thinking you should be doing, Captain, begging your pardon, is what you are about. Once over the next crossroads, you can spring 'em to the top of the next hill. Then you'll be able to see the lights of the town ahead of you.'

Duncan smiled and shouted over his shoulder to his passengers. 'Leicester coming up.'

His answer was a toot on the guard's horn from Tom.

Ten minutes later they drew up at the staging post and everyone tumbled out. Duncan, standing by the coach in true coachman fashion, tipped his hat to each of the passengers and wished them a safe onward journey, not in the least disturbed when he was given a coachman's gratuities, even from the old lady, who was by now so tired that she did not recognise him. Tom, in the spirit of the jest, handed over half a crown, saying, 'Thank you, my good man, a very pleasant ride. I congratulate you.'

'And you?' Duncan asked Helen, speaking softly, his brown eyes looking down into her uptilted face, making her insides quiver. 'Was it a pleasant ride for you?' For a brief moment they held each other's gaze.

'Yes, thank you,' she said then, averting her eyes, delved into her reticule. 'I suppose I had better tip you too, or I shall be labelled a pinchcommons.'

'Oh, indeed you must.' The moment of intimacy was gone like a dandelion seed on the wind.

She gave him a handful of loose change, which he took and sorted out in his palm. 'This will do nicely,' he said selecting a farthing and returning the rest to her. Then he turned and tipped all but the farthing into the coachman's good hand. 'Give this to your guard when you see him next.'

'I will, Captain.' He touched his low-crowned beaver. 'I wish you both a pleasant journey.'

Duncan pealed off the huge coat and handed it back to its owner before offering Helen his arm. She put her hand on it and they walked into the inn behind Tom and Dorothy. The old lady had completed her journey, the parson was making a local connection and the outside passengers were either retiring to their beds or joining another coach which was getting ready to leave.

'Tom and I are going to stay here for the night,' Dorothy said, as they joined them. 'If we go on to Derby now, we shall arrive in the early hours and we cannot wake my aunt up then; it would give her a seizure. Besides, we shall both be tired and not in a fit state to explain ourselves. I want to be fresh when I come face to face with her.'

'That's very wise of you,' Helen said.

'You and the Captain must be in haste to continue your journey,' Tom said. 'So please don't let us delay you. We will manage very well.'

'I could not possibly leave you now,' Helen said. 'I am determined on keeping you company until we reach Derby.'

'You think Miss Carstairs is in need of a chaperone?' Duncan queried, sighing heavily.

'Yes, don't you? It will help her when it comes to telling the story to her aunt if she is able to say she was not alone with Mr Thurborn.'

'So you intend to stay yet another night? Three days on a journey intended to take twenty-four hours. At the rate we are going we shall have to buy the coaching schedules for the whole of Britain.'

'We, Captain Blair? There is no call for you to stay.'

'Goodness, you surely have not quarrelled,' Dorothy said, looking from one to the other.

'No, of course not, but what has that to do with it? What the Captain does is his own affair. We are not travelling together.'

'You're not? But I thought...' She stopped in embarrassment.

Duncan laughed. 'Oh, my dear Miss Carstairs, please do not be discomfited. It is perfectly simple. Miss Sadler is determined to look after you, whether you will or no, and I am determined to look after her, even though she maintains she is perfectly able to manage alone. We will, all four, stay here for the rest of the night and journey on together tomorrow morning. I will endeavour to procure rooms.' And with that he sketched a small bow and left them to seek out the innkeeper.

Dorothy smiled conspiratorially at Helen. 'Your secret is safe with us, is it not, Tom?'

'What?' He was busy watching how Captain Blair handled the innkeeper, intending to learn by his example. 'Oh, yes, of course, perfectly safe.'

'My secret?' echoed Helen. How did they know? Had she some time in the past, met Miss Carstairs and forgotten it? But Miss Carstairs had said she thought Helen was a lady's maid; why had she said that if she knew the truth? Was she testing her, trying to find out just how far she would go to deceive?

'Yes. We will not say a word.'

Before Helen could try to explain, Duncan rejoined them. 'There is a room available for the ladies on the first landing,' Duncan said. 'I am afraid you will have to share, I hope you do not mind.'

'Not at all,' Dorothy said.

'I have asked for your baggage to be sent up.'

'Thank you, Captain,' Helen said coolly. 'If you do not mind, I think I will retire. It has been a very long day.'

If she had hoped to be allowed to go to bed and straight to sleep, she was mistaken. Dorothy needed help undressing and she was determined to talk, notwithstanding that Helen was being very quiet.

'Oh, I am so sorry if I put you out of countenance with the Captain,' Dorothy said over her shoulder as Helen stood to undo the buttons on her gown. 'I would not for the world have put you to the blush, but I did not think it was meant to be such a secret.'

'What was?' She was weary beyond imagining, not

only from the journey, but from watching every word, playing her little game with Captain Blair and looking after Dorothy, who seemed to have recovered completely from her distress and was now bright and cheerful and anxious to exchange confidences.

'Your elopement. I did not think it mattered mentioning it, considering we are all on the same errand.'

'My elopement?' So the secret Dorothy thought she had uncovered had nothing to do with her identity, after all. But to imagine she was running away to marry was ludicrous. 'My elopement! It is Tom and you who are eloping, not me. . .'

'But you and the Captain. . .'

'Good Heavens! I am quite sure Captain Blair did not tell you that.'

'No, but it is obvious.'

'Not to me it isn't. I do not know the gentleman.'

'Oh, come, Helen, be blowed to that for a Banbury tale. You and he already behave like an old married pair, arguing all the time. . .'

'That is because we do not agree and I am not so pudding-hearted as to let him have it all his own way.'

'That's exactly what I mean.' She stepped out of her gown and rummaged in her luggage for her nightgown. 'I'll say this for you, you are carrying it off with a great deal more aplomb than Tom and me.'

'Once and for all,' Helen said sharply, leaving the girl to tug a brush through her own hair, pulling at the tangles and hurting herself. 'I am not eloping with Captain Blair. He does not even like me. In truth, he does not like women at all; he as good as told me so.'

'Fustian! Anyone with half an eye can see he is in love.'

'Not with me.' She got into bed beside Dorothy. 'Now, if you do not mind, I want to go to sleep.'

But she could not sleep. She was wide awake long after Dorothy's heavy breathing told her that her bedmate was out to the world. Whatever had given Dorothy the idea that Captain Blair was in love with her? He had been chivalrous, to be sure, but that meant nothing more that he had been well brought up to care for the weaker sex and he obviously looked on her as weak and helpless and needing protection.

The trouble was, she did need him. Without him she would have been robbed by everyone with whom she came into contact: coachmen, ostlers, innkeepers, urchins with honest blue eyes. You couldn't call that love, could you? Not only had they met just two days before, but she also knew very little more about him than she had at the beginning and that only what he chose to reveal.

But it was equally true she had not been very open either. She had led him to believe she was a lady's companion, which was not, she decided, the sort of person a captain in the Prince of Wales's Own Hussars would consider as a wife, especially as he had said he was a second son. That usually meant he had come from a titled family. But would such a man be travelling on a public coach without a servant? Had he invented it? But wasn't that exactly what she was doing, pretending to be someone she was not? She really ought to put an end to the pretence, tell him the truth, apologise. But if they were both playing the same game, why apologise, why be the first to admit defeat? Oh, why couldn't he have ridden on into the night, out of her life?

CHAPTER SIX

'MISS SADLER, Miss Sadler, do wake up.'

Helen opened her eyes to see Dorothy sitting on the bed half-dressed. 'Oh, dear, have I overslept?'

'A coach has come in the yard and I heard someone shout it was the Independent for Manchester. That's the one we want, isn't it?'

'I believe so.' Helen scrambled out of bed and hurried to wash and dress. 'We must make haste if we are to have breakfast before we leave.'

They went downstairs to find Tom and the Captain already at the table with food enough for four in front of them, though Tom had evidently only just arrived and was grumbling about his accommodation. 'I had to share a room with half a dozen others all of whom snored in a different key,' he was saying. 'I hardly shut my eyes all night. If it had not been for Miss Sadler, Dorothy and I could have booked a room to ourselves. . .'

'Mr Thurborn!' Helen exclaimed, realising he had not noticed them arrive. 'I do hope I have misunderstood your meaning.'

He looked up and had the grace to look ashamed. 'We would not have shared a bed, I promise you.'

'As the opportunity did not arise, there is no point in wasting conjecture on it,' Duncan said.

'I'll wager you managed a room to yourself,' Tom

went on, addressing Duncan. 'You seem to be able to command the best without putting yourself out at all.'

'On the contrary, I chose the stables. Horses do not snore and they are infinitely preferable to sharing with assorted other livestock.'

Helen shuddered, wondering about the bed she and Dorothy had shared, but the sheets had been newly laundered and the blankets clean. She suspected the Captain had made sure of that when ordering the room to be made ready. 'And were you able to sleep?'

'As a soldier I have learned to sleep anywhere whenever I can. Do not give it another thought. Please have some breakfast, we must leave soon.'

The girls had hardly begun to eat when a guard came in and announced that the Independent was about to leave. 'All aboard as is coming aboard,' he called. Reluctantly they prepared to abandon their breakfast and follow the other passengers outside.

'Sit down,' Duncan said. 'Finish your breakfast.' Then, to Helen's amazement, he looked about him to make sure no one was watching, gathered up the cutlery on an adjoining table which was littered with the remains of a half eaten breakfast, and put it into the empty teapot.

The innkeeper, following in the wake of his departing guests, began to clear the tables and suddenly missing the cutlery, set up a hue and cry. 'I've been robbed! Someone has gone off with the silver.' Then to one of the waiters, 'Stop the coach! Stop everyone! No one leaves until I have my belongings back. It's bad enough people walking off without paying, but to take the knives and forks... How is a body to make an honest living? You, sir.' He pointed to a burly countryman in a huge topcoat. 'What have you got in your pockets?'

'A kerchief and a purse,' the man said, turning to go, but his way was blocked by the waiter, who required him to turn out his pockets.

'Eat up,' Duncan told the girls, who were so interested in what was happening they were forgetting to eat. 'The coachman will not let him hold us for long.' Suiting action to words, he calmly resumed his own breakfast, while the furore went on all around them, with the innkeeper accusing and the passengers angrily maintaining their innocence. 'Time to put an end to it,' Duncan said at last, picking up the teapot and shaking it, making a great play of finding something inside it. 'Landlord, is this what you are looking for?' he asked, producing the missing cutlery.

The innkeeper dashed over to him and grabbed the knives and forks, while everyone in the room was convulsed with laughter. 'Someone hid them,' he said, glaring at Duncan. 'Some people never grow up, do they?'

'And some are too quick to accuse,' Duncan said, though how he kept his face straight Helen had no idea. 'Now, if you would be so good as to stand aside, we have a coach waiting for us. Come, Miss Sadler, Miss Carstairs, it is time to go.'

Helen's eyes were so filled with tears of laughter she could hardly see where she was going and they began the next stage of their journey in high good spirits. As there were only the four of them travelling inside, they were far less cramped.

Miss Sadler, so beautiful in repose, was equally attractive when animated, Duncan mused, as they took their seats. She ought to laugh more often. He would make it his business to make her laugh. She should not be grieving for an old lady who doubtless treated her with disdain.

'Mr Gathercole told me some extraordinary tales about his life as a coachman,' he said, deciding to amuse her with a few anecdotes and see if he could make her green eyes sparkle again.

'If the incidents we have met with are any measure, I imagine his life is never dull,' Helen said. 'But he brings his troubles on himself if he allows widgeons to take over the ribbons.'

'Oh, I am inclined to forgive him,' Dorothy put in. 'It brought us together, did it not? Instead of sitting here stiff and silent, we are the best of friends. I would be happy were it not for the thought of confronting Aunt Sophia. I wish. . . No, I could not ask it of you.'

'We are both in haste to reach Scotland,' Duncan said quickly, before Helen could offer to accompany the young lady to her aunt's. 'There has already been too much delay.'

'Yes, of course. I understand how impatient you must be.'

'Captain, you were speaking of Mr Gathercole,' Helen put in quickly to prevent Dorothy explaining how she thought Captain Blair was eloping with her; the young lady evidently preferred to believe her own theory than the truth she had been told. 'Do tell us some of his tales.'

'He told me that a coach was left unattended outside an inn while the coachman and guard went in to lubricate their throats, but the horses apparently knew the importance of keeping to schedule better than their crew. They set off without them at a smart trot. The only outside passenger was a fishwife, who waved her arms at everyone they passed, pointing to the empty box but to no avail, no one could stop them. Thankfully she had the sense not to scream and upset the horses. The inside passengers assumed the coachman was in his usual place on the box and were completely unconcerned.'

'How far did they go?' Helen asked.

'Seven miles. Apparently they negotiated all the hazards on their route, including oncoming traffic, a bridge and a tollgate before coming to a halt outside the next stage dead on time.'

'I do believe you are gammoning us,' Dorothy said. 'The horses must have known there was no one on the box.'

'If they did, they thought nothing of it,' he said. 'When horses cover the same ground day after day, they learn the way blindfold. Some are quite blind, you know, especially those on night runs, where sight is of little significance. There was a one-eyed coachman who boasted that he and his four horses had only one eye between them.'

Helen smiled. 'Ah, but it was the coachman who had the eye.'

'Yes, but horses can be as unpredictable as people, you know. There is another story of a horse dealer who was offered a horse for ten pounds, a price which made him immediately suspicious because it looked as though the animal was worth five and thirty pounds at least. He was promised it was sound in wind and limb and would never kick and so, in spite of his misgivings, he decided to buy it. It was only when the beast was put into harness he discovered he would not budge and nothing would make him do so. Even setting light to straw beneath him did no more than make him jump and throw himself to the ground.'

'I assume your friend turned his whip on the vendor,' Tom said.

'No, for he had been given no warranty. He took the horse down to the canal and persuaded a bargeman to hitch him up with his two horses, but the animal was as recalcitrant as ever. He bucked and reared and threw himself down on his haunches, but the other two simply plodded forward as they had always done, taking no notice of him at all. He tried his tantrums again, but all that happened was that he rolled right off the towpath and into the river. After his wetting he decided to surrender and became a model of a good coach horse.'

'I do believe you are every bit as bad as the coachmen with their Canterbury tales,' Helen said. 'I have heard they like to embroider their stories when they have a gullible audience.'

'Why not, if it helps to enliven a dull journey? It is for the listener to decide whether to believe them or not.'

'Do tell us more, Captain,' Dorothy begged.

'Mr Gathercole is the master, not I,' Duncan said. 'But he did tell me a tale last night about a gentleman who boarded a night coach and wiled away the hours talking to a fur-coated gentleman beside him, only to discover, when dawn came, that his travelling companion was a performing bear.'

'Now I know you are teasing us,' Helen said, though she was laughing. 'He must surely have wondered why his fellow passenger never offered a comment of his own.'

'Some people like the sound of their own voices,' he said, pleased that he had succeeded in making her smile again.

'I heard of a coach being attacked by a lioness,' Tom put in, not to be outdone.

'Fustian!' Dorothy said. 'There are no lions in England.'

'Yes, there are! It had escaped from a circus. And there's another tale of two ladies who joined a coach where the only other inside passenger was another lady, but she had unfortunately died on the road an hour or so before. Rather than walk, they shared the coach with the stiffening corpse all the way from Chelmsford to Norwich.'

'Ugh!' Dorothy said. 'I do not wish to hear another word on the subject.'

'Neither do I,' Helen said, as they stopped for a change of horses. 'I have had enough adventures these past two days to last me a lifetime.'

'Then I hope the remainder of your journey is uneventful,' Dorothy said.

'From here to Manchester is plain sailing,' Duncan said. 'After that, who knows? We could have tempests and floods, roads washed away, bridges down.'

'Captain Blair,' Helen said. 'Are you determined on frightening me?'

'I doubt that is possible. Such a staunch and valiant traveller I never met before. I am simply saying we must not be complacent; delay could be serious.'

'I recollect you are in haste,' she said. 'You may rest assured I am entirely in agreement with that.'

'I should think so too,' Dorothy said, almost wist-fully. 'I almost wish we were coming too. I am not at all sure of my aunt's reception.'

'I am persuaded she will be perfectly content when you tell her everything,' Helen said. 'How could she be otherwise when she realises how much you love each other?' She heard Duncan give what sounded like a grunt of derision but chose to ignore it. 'And your papa too, when he realises how determined you are. That is the secret, being determined.'

'And you are an authority on the subject?' Duncan interposed. 'You can tell how a father is going to behave over his daughter's disobedience without even meeting him? You know how he will react to determi-nation which he will view as nothing but wilfulness?'

'Oh, you think he will be dreadfully angry, don't you?' Dorothy countered; tears welling in her eyes again. 'Why did you tell Tom to face up to Papa if you believe that?'

He controlled his exasperation with an effort; after all, she was little more than a spoiled child. In some ways she reminded him of Arabella and that was perhaps why he had so little patience with her. He softened his tone. 'Not at all, I was simply pointing out to Miss Sadler she can have no knowledge of how your father will react and she should not pretend she has.'

'And you, sir, are so cynical, it is a wonder you have survived at all,' Helen said. 'You must allow people to have hope. . .'

'Even misplaced hope?'

His quirky smile belied the harshness of his words. His apparent arrogance was at odds with the hurt she could see in his eyes. Helen felt as if she wanted to hit him for his stupidity and hold him to her breast to heal his wounds at one and the same time. Not for the first time she wondered whether there was a woman in his past who had caused the contradictions in his character. Perhaps she was still there, still plaguing him. It was extraordinary how annoyed that thought made her. 'Why not?' she countered. 'Wasn't hope the only thing left in Pandora's box after all the evils of the world had flown out to plague us?'

He smiled and his eyes softened. '*Touché*, Miss Sadler. You must forgive an old grouch who has seen too much of the evil and too little of the good.'

Two minutes later they heard the guard's horn and in another minute drew up at an inn in Derby where the horses were due to be changed and where Tom and Dorothy got down, a little despondent at parting from their new friends and anxious about the future.

'Have no fear,' Helen said, smiling. 'Whatever faces you, it cannot be any worse than what is ahead of me if half the Captain's Banbury tales are true.'

Dorothy laughed, putting a hand up to where Helen's rested on the door. 'In that case, perhaps I am glad I am going no further, but I shall miss you dreadfully. Do write when you are settled, won't you?'

'Yes, of course.'

She moved aside to allow two new inside passengers to board and then stood beside Tom, waving until they were out of sight. Helen turned in her seat and leaned back against the squabs, sorry to part from the young couple. They had acted as a buffer between her and the Captain and now she was bound to be thrown more in his company than ever. And if he started quizzing her again, she would give herself away.

There were ony two other inside passengers, an army sergeant with a curly moustache and a thin little man who looked as though he had not eaten in several days, both of whom were dirty, unshaven and malodorous. They ought to be travelling outside, she mused, but then if they were, she and Captain Blair would be alone in the coach and the thought of that sent her heart racing and the colour flaring in her cheeks.

'I never met such poor beasts,' the sergeant said, nodding towards the horses. Stretching across the little man, he put his head out and shouted up at the coachman, 'Spring 'em, driver. Let's see what they can do.'

Helen felt, rather than saw, the Captain stiffen, but fortunately the driver paid not the least attention and continued at the regulation canter wherever it was possible to do so, but the terrain, though beautiful with gorse-covered moorland and craggy outcrops of rock, did not lend itself to a steady pace. They found themselves dashing down the hills in order to give themselves a good start up the next, with the sergeant shouting encouragement and the little man sitting in the corner with his chin on his chest in brooding silence. He did not seem to be aware of his surroundings but he must have been carefully watching for an opportunity because at one spot when they were reduced to a crawl by the steepness of the gradient, he opened the door and would have flung himself out if the sergeant had not grabbed his coat tail and hauled him back inside, beating him about the head with his fists. 'Oh, no you don't, you little runt,' he said.

'Really, sir, there is no call to attack the poor man like that,' Helen protested, shrugging off the Captain's restraining hand on her arm. 'What has he done to deserve such violent treatment?'

'No one escapes Sergeant Hollocks and lives to tell the tale.' He gave him one or two more blows for good measure and then turned to Duncan. 'Be so good as to hold on to him, sir, while I tie him up. Seems he can't be trusted to behave himself. Promised me he wouldn't cut and run and I was fool enough to take his word.'

The Captain leaned forward and grasped the man's shoulders while the sergeant fetched a rope from his belt and tied the man's hands together and secured them to the door handle. 'That should fix him.'

'What has he done?' Helen asked, feeling sorry for the poor man whose lip and nose were pouring with blood. 'You can't sit there and let him bleed.'

'Beg pardon, ma'am, you ain't about to swoon, are you?' the sergeant asked. 'Look the other way, you'll soon come about.'

'Of course I am not going to faint. I am concerned about your companion.'

'Companion! I would rather have a snake for company.'

'Here, wipe his face,' Duncan said, pulling his cravat from his neck and handing it to the sergeant.

The man complied, none to gently, after which he offered the neckcloth back to its owner. Duncan shook his head, whereupon the blood-soaked muslin was pocketed.

'What do you suppose he has done?' Helen whispered to Duncan, disinclined to risk speaking to the sergeant again.

'He's a deserter,' the sergeant said, before Duncan could venture an answer. 'A runaway, a lily-livered coward, what's disgraced the King's uniform. I'm taking him back to the regiment.'

'Where is that?'

'We're barracked near Manchester.'

'Is that where he deserted?'

'No, sir, he left the field of battle, "deserting in the face of the enemy" it's called.'

'I know what it's called,' Duncan said. 'Which battle?'

'Beg pardon, sir, am I to assume you are a military gentleman?'

'Yes. Captain Blair of the Prince of Wales's Own Hussars. I am presently on leave.'

'Then you, sir, will know the battle. He ran from the field at Waterloo.'

'But goodness, that was over five years ago,' Helen said. 'Surely. . .'

'The army never gives up on deserters, ma'am.'

'What will happen to him?'

'He will be tried and hanged.'

'Hanged! Oh, no, that's too barbaric.'

'You think he should be shot? That's only for officers, not for the likes of this thatchgallows.'

'No, I did not mean that. I do not see why he should die at all. I expect he was afraid and who can blame him for that?'

'Deserting in the middle of a battle is the worst crime a soldier can commit, ma'am. Isn't that so, Captain?'

'Yes.'

'But surely you do not hound a man for five years. . .'

'Please do not argue, my dear,' Duncan said. 'You really do not understand.'

'I understand cruelty and injustice.' She turned to the little man who had been looking from one to the other, saying nothing on his own behalf. 'Tell me what happened.'

'My dear, I really do not think you want to know about it,' Duncan said.

'Of course I do, or I would not have asked,' she said, wondering why he had twice called her 'my dear'. She had never given him any indication she would allow such familiarity. She looked across at the sergeant who was grinning as if he were enjoying a secret joke.

'Go on.' He nudged his captive. 'You may tell the Captain's wife your sorry tale, I shan't stop you.'

Helen opened her mouth to deny she was related in any way to the Captain, but stopped when he gripped her arm so tightly she winced. She looked round at him and saw him shake his head imperceptibly. So, he had deliberately given that impression and perhaps he was right. She was a lone female among three soldiers and the Captain was definitely the lesser of two evils, the third being trussed up like a chicken for the oven.

'You do not have to, if you do not wish to talk about it,' she said to the trooper. 'If it is too painful. . .'

'I don't mind tellin' you, ma'am, no one else will listen. I've been a soldier all my life, since I was little more than a nipper and I've been in many a battle, but Waterloo, that was different. I never met the like. Hour after hour of artillery barrage and then the charges. Give old Boney his due, he knew how to direct a battle, ain't that so, Captain?'

'Yes, it was very bad. Wellington had it right when he said it was a close-run thing. We were never so near defeat.'

'As far as I could tell, we were done for,' the soldier went on. 'Everyone round me fell. God knows how I survived. I found myself alone with a whole troop of Boney's cavalry advancing on me. It was fight and be killed or captured or run for me life.'

'And so the little coward ran,' the sergeant put in.

'It weren't like that. I left the sector intending to join others still fighting but I lost me way. I wandered about the battlefield for hours, but all I could see were dead and dying. I found a road. It was full of people, mostly wounded but there were hundreds of others fleeing on foot or on horseback, whole regiments of them, all going in one direction, so I went too. No one took any notice of me. We ended up in Brussels. I hadn't meant to desert, not then. I walked about the city looking for mates or officers, anyone who could tell me what to do, but there weren't no one. The wounded were being evacuated by barges, so I tied a bandage round me 'ead and joined them and no one stopped me. We went to Antwerp and got on a hospital ship. When we got to London, I slipped off without being stopped and walked all the way home.'

'My goodness, I do not think that was cowardly at all,' Helen said. 'But how were you caught now, so long afterwards?'

'I told my wife I'd been discharged but I couldn't find work and she was forever nagging me, telling me she'd be better off if I was still in the army and I begun to wish that m'self.'

'So you decided to give yourself up?'

'What, and be hanged! I ain't that dicked in the nob. It was just my bad luck the sergeant came from the same town. He was on leave and recognised me. So, here I am.'

'I cannot think you will be punished after such a long time,' Helen said. 'And your story cannot be exceptional. . .'

'What has that to do with the matter?' the sergeant said. 'He knew what he was letting himself in for as soon as he got on that barge in Brussels.'

'Captain. . .' She turned to Duncan for support but all he said was, 'Let it be, my dear. We are nearing the next stage. Would you like me to fetch you anything, a drink or something to eat?'

'No, thank you.'

They drew up at an inn, the exhausted horses were taken from the traces to be rested and new animals brought forward. Duncan and the sergeant took the opportunity to get down and stretch their legs, leaving Helen facing the prisoner.

'Ma'am, it is terrible uncomfortable sitting like this. I've got cramps and me nose itches. I beg of you to untie me.'

'I cannot do that. What will the sergeant say?'

'He won't dare say anything, you being the Captain's wife. Come on, ma'am, I promise not to run for it and you may tie me up again afterwards.' He grinned suddenly. ''Less, of course, you was to scratch me nose for me.'

The idea of doing that made her shudder. She looked out of the window. The Captain and the sergeant were deep in conversation with the guard, each with a pint pot in their hands. Quickly she moved over to sit beside him and untied his bonds. 'There, hurry up and do what you have to so I can tie you up again. They will be back soon.'

'Sorry, ma'am,' he said, pushing open the door and jumping down. She watched in horror as he disappeared behind a coach house and then reappeared on the road, dashing across it into a copse of trees on the other side. She opened her mouth to shout, then decided to give him a fighting chance and shut it again. But the sergeant, and probably the Captain too, would be furious that she had done nothing to alert them. She got down and walked over to them. 'I have changed my mind about that drink,' she said. 'I should like a glass of water.'

'Very well, but we must be quick.' The Captain took her arm to conduct her into the inn, leaving the guard and the sergeant to continue their conversation and finish their ale. 'I assume you found the man's company distasteful. We should not have left you with him.'

'He is bound up, what harm can he do? I simply did not feel like listening to him any more.'

'No, but you did ask for it.'

'So I did.'

He called to the innkeeper who fetched a glass of water, which she drank quickly. 'I suppose we had better return to the coach.'

'Yes. At least they are only going as far as Manchester. . .' He stopped when he heard the sergeant shout. 'Something has happened.' Leaving her to make her own way, he raced back to the coach.

Helen walked more slowly, knowing the cause. When she arrived, she found the sergeant, his face red with fury, insisting that Captain Blair go with him to help fetch the prisoner back. 'You too,' he shouted at the guard and then pointing up at the coachman. 'Wait here, he can't be far away.'

'I've got a schedule to keep, I can't dally around waiting on your pleasure, sir,' the coachman said. 'And I need my guard. You may come or not, as you please.' To Helen he said. 'Madam, be so good as to take your seat.'

Helen found herself wishing she had not been so foolish. Now she would have to go on without the Captain and the thought of all that had happened and might yet happen filled her with alarm. She did not want to be carried away without him. She put a hand on his arm. 'Please. . .'

'I cannot refuse to help,' he said. 'Go on. Wait in Manchester for me. . .'

'Wait?' she echoed in surprise.

'Yes, wait. You will not have to complete your journey alone.'

'Come on, Captain, we are wasting time, and there is no need for your wife to worry,' the sergeant said, before Helen could find a reply. 'The coach is going nowhere without us.'

'If you do not board this instant, it most certainly is,' the coachman said.

'No, for I have the power to hold you until I have caught the man and we can all resume our journey. I am on the King's business and the King's business takes precedence over everything, ain't that so, Captain?'

Duncan was not at all sure the sergeant was correct, but the thought of the lovely Miss Sadler continuing without him and possibly finding herself in more scrapes decided him. He looked up at the coachman, whip and reins in hand. 'I am afraid the sergeant is right, coachman. He can demand assistance and we must accede or find ourselves in trouble with the law.'

Helen heaved a huge sigh of relief as the coachman put down his whip and looped the reins over the back of his seat. 'Hold 'em,' he said to the ostler who stood at the leaders' heads. 'I might as well do my bit to hasten our departure.' With that he clambered down and followed the Captain, the guard and the sergeant into the copse, to the accompaniment of cheers from the outside passengers.

'They've come out onto the field further down,' one of them shouted after a few minutes. 'No sign of the quarry though.'

'There he is!' One of the others grabbed his arm and pointed.

'Oh yes, I see. Tally ho!' he cried. 'Tally ho!'

'What's happening?' the ostler called up to the outside passengers on behalf of all the people on ground level who could not see above the hedges.

'The hounds are in full pursuit. The cunning fox is dodging them, doubling back into the wood.'

'Now the gentleman is heading him off. He's surrounded.'

'Oh, he's nabbed.' The other man's voice dropped in disappointment. 'I thought he'd give 'em a better run for their money.'

Two minutes later pursuers and pursued returned to the coach, the coachman climbed on the box and took up the reins again, the guard took his place on the back seat and pulled his horn from its basket beside him, Duncan helped Helen into her seat and the sergeant, having tied the deserter more securely than before, got in behind him.

'How did he get hisself undone?' the sergeant demanded as they drew away. 'I reckon he must have been 'elped.' He glared at Helen. 'Anyone aiding and abetting a deserter is breaking the law and could go to prison for a very long time.'

'Sergeant,' Duncan said. 'You forget yourself. Mrs Blair is not to be accused in that impertinent fashion. The man is back in custody, that is all that need concern you.'

'Beggin' your pardon, Captain, but there weren't no way he could ha' got away by hisself.'

'Then look elsewhere for your conspirator. My wife was with me in the inn at the time, as you yourself know.'

Helen shot him a look of gratitude but his face looked thunderous and she knew he had no illusions about her complicity and was decidedly angry. If she were really his wife, she would be due for a scolding as soon as they were alone. In truth, she did not think the fact that she was not his wife would make the slightest difference to him.

'It weren't the lady's fault, if you didn't tie them knots tight enough,' the soldier said. 'I slipped out o' them m'self and much good did it do me.'

The sergeant gave him a murderous look, but said nothing. The Captain was duty bound to defend his wife, but he knew the truth and so did everyone else. She had shown an uncommon interest in the prisoner, felt sorry for him, that was obvious, so it stood to reason she would help him if she could. If she hadn't

been married to the Captain, he'd have roped her in
as well.

He sighed and gazed out of the window, wishing
they could move a little faster. Why, he had made
more miles an hour on the back of a gun carriage in
the mountains of Spain. You couldn't call these little
bumps mountains, nor even hills, and a coachload of
people wasn't any heavier than a gun on its limber.
And now it was beginning to rain. What a way to finish
his leave! But there might be a reward for bringing a
deserter, a few shillings to wet his whistle. He could
look forward to that.

Helen, seeing the rain and hearing it beating on the
side of the coach, was reminded of the Captain's
stories. Perhaps he had not been teasing, in which case
she was very glad he was sitting beside her even if he
was silent as the grave. His hands were folded and his
head was sunk on his chest, a position made easier by
the absence of his cravat, but she did not think he was
asleep. She had come to think of him as a man who
never slept.

Her supposition was born out when he turned his
head slightly and she saw his brown eyes regarding her
with a faint hint of mockery. She did not know which
was worse, his mockery or his anger, or why his good
opinion mattered so much to her. But it did and she
was dismal over it.

Another two changes of horses, when the sergeant
sat and glared at his prisoner, defying him to move so
much as a whisker and they arrived at the Bridgewater
Arms in Manchester, just as it was getting dusk. Helen,
descending ahead of the Captain, found the coachman
and guard at their usual place, touching their hat brims

to the passengers and apologising for their late arrival. 'We leave you here,' the coachman was saying. 'But no doubt you will make up for lost time on the next stage.'

Helen handed over her usual gratuity with a smile, unwilling to let anyone know that she found the constant tipping onerous. Buying one's ticket was only the beginning of the expenses of travelling; bed and board took a vast amount, and drinks at the shorter stops and the endless tipping were taking their toll of her purse.

The Captain had offered to pay for her on several occasions but the only time she had allowed it was when they had dined with Tom and Dorothy. She was determined not to be under any more obligation to him than she could possibly help, but the further they went the more she depended on him to smooth her path, to alleviate the discomfort of travel, to amuse and enlighten and pull her out of the bumblebaths she was constantly falling into.

She had realised that coach travel might be cramped and cold, that sometimes her fellow travellers would not be congenial, but never had she imagined it would be so packed with incident. She had had one adventure after another and, if it had not been for the Captain's presence, she did not know how she would have managed.

The sergeant disappeared into the darkness with his prisoner while the outside passengers, wet and shivering, were escorted to the bar parlour, where they were assured there was a good fire, leaving Helen and Duncan to make their way into the dining-room. 'I'll see about your room,' he said curtly and disappeared.

So, there were to be no more cosy dinners, no more rapport. She smiled wryly, being his so-called wife was far less agreeable than being a stranger. She was suddenly struck by the thought that he might want to prolong their fictitious relationship; she had given no indication she did not like it. Was he even now arranging a room for a married couple?

She hurried to the door, intending to search out the landlord and make her own arrangements and bumped straight into the Captain at the door. She found herself held firmly in his arms, her head on his broad chest, with her bonnet hanging from its ribbons down her back. She could feel his heartbeat right against her ear, fast and erratic, as if he were gripped by fear or agitation of some kind, though he gave no outward appearance of being anything but calm. 'Princess,' he murmured, making no move to release her. 'Where were you off to in such haste?'

'To see to my trunk.' Her voice was muffled against his kerseymere frockcoat. 'I forgot it again. I didn't want the coach to carry it off.'

She moved her head slightly and found herself looking up at his throat. She saw him swallow hard before he chuckled. 'No, that would have been one more disaster to contend with and I am becoming tired of them. Your baggage is safely in your room.'

'Thank you.' She tilted her head up to see into his face and wished she had not. His soft voice belied his looks; she could tell by the twitching of the muscles in his cheeks and the fierce expression in his brown eyes that he was still angry. Then why were his arms still around her, his thighs pressed against her skirt, making her shiver with something she refused to recognise as desire? 'Are you going to let me go?'

'Let you go?' He sounded puzzled. 'Go where?'

'To my room.'

He released her at once. 'Of course. I have ordered a tray to be taken up. I shall find convivial company in the tap room. There is a game of cards I have a mind to join.'

'Oh, you are going to gamble.'

'Is there any reason why I should not?'

'What you do is no concern of mine,' she said crisply. 'If you choose to lose your money at the gaming tables, that is your affair.'

'Indeed it is.'

'Please excuse me.' And with that she rushed away from him up the stairs. At the top she stopped. Which was her room?

'Number seventeen,' he called after her.

Without answering, she made her way along the corridor until she found the room with her trunk standing in the middle of the floor. She went in and shut the door behind her with a bang, then sat on the edge of the bed, her hands in her lap, staring at the closed door.

It meant nothing to her that he was going to spend the night gambling. It was not her money he was playing with, not her inheritance slipping through his fingers. Would it have made any difference if it were? Would he still take the risk, just as her father had done, just as countless other irresponsible men did to their families every night of the week? Oh, how disappointed she was in him!

It just went to show how foolish it was to make

judgements about people you had met only three days before. You could not possibly know what a man was really like in so short a time, and you should never make up your mind that this was a man with whom you would be content to spend the rest of your life. She brought herself up short. What, in God's name, was she thinking about? The rest of her life? They were strangers brought together by unusual circumstances, no more than that. The journey would come to an end and they would say good-bye without any regrets.

No regrets? Oh, there would be regrets in plenty. She had lied to him; their whole conversation had been one enormous hum, a contest of strength with no thought for the outcome. Just when they were getting on so much better, just when they had established a rapport, shaky though it was, she had to go and spoil it all by untying that man and making him angry. He would dislike her all the more if he ever found out the truth. She could not bear that.

She had not fallen in love with him, that was too outrageous an idea even to contemplate, but she was hurt by his changes in mood, the sudden desire to seek other company, the curt way he had said he was immune to a woman's wiles. As if she had set out to trap him! Oh, he was above everything conceited and she had best put him from her mind, eat her supper and go to bed.

In spite of that conclusion, she could not eat the food on the tray though it looked and smelled delicious. Neither did she do anything to prepare for bed. He might knock on the door before retiring himself, just to say goodnight, and she would sleep all the better if they were not at odds with each other.

She fetched a book from her trunk and settled down to read. But she could not concentrate on the printed page; her whole being was tense, listening to the sounds coming from the room below her where the men were playing cards. There were long silences, followed by gusts of laughter and then murmured conversation and the chink of coins.

The book dropped from her lap, as she sat straining her ears for signs the game was finishing, for cries of goodnight, footsteps coming up the stairs, the gentle knock at the door. She would not let him in, of course, but just to hear him say goodnight was all she wanted. She was so very, very tired.

She heard the clock strike one and then two. Had he even arranged for a room for himself? Was he going to roll into the straw of the stable as dawn lightened the sky? Would he lose? What would that mean to him? Ruin, just as Papa had been ruined? Oh, why did she let it trouble her so much? She stirred herself and stood up to undo her dress. It was nothing to do with her what he did with his life or his money and she was being foolish worrying about him. She finished her toilette and climbed into bed, too weary to think about it any more.

Duncan had intended to play cards, had even had his hand on the door of the taproom, when he thought better of it. He would not have his mind on the game and he would be bound to lose. He was not enough of a gambler to risk that. He went out into the town for a walk. The rain had eased a little but the wind was cold and it was wet underfoot. He was glad of his greatcoat and the good leather hessians he wore. But the air cleared his head. Not that it helped him to come to any conclusions about Miss Helen Sadler.

It had been the height of folly to allow himself to become involved with her, but what else could he have done? He could not have turned his back on her. Their lives seemed to have become intertwined, at least for the duration of the journey, but after that? He did not even know her final destination; all she had said was that it was Scotland and then she had been speaking to their travelling companions, not to him. Almost everything he had discovered about her, he had learned through a third party, as if talking directly to him demeaned her in some way. Was she afraid of him? He did not think that for a minute.

She was a consummate liar, of that he was certain. Her manner was at odds with her supposed station in life and her clothes, though black, were exquisitely cut in the most expensive materials, not what you would expect a lady's companion to wear mourning her employer. She was so spirited and headstrong he wondered why she had not come to a bad end long before. But her apparent innocence was her greatest strength, making people protective of her, as he was. But she wasn't the one needing protection, he was.

She had managed, in the space of three days, to aid a pickpocket, assist in an elopement, set free a deserter and upset the whole schedule of a notable coaching company and, in the process, charm everyone with whom she came into contact, himself included. He had said he was immune but that was far from the truth; he had become ensnared and he would have no peace while she continued to wreak havoc all around, particularly with his heart.

Slowly he made his way back to the inn and up the stairs to his room. Outside her door he paused, then smiled and crept away. Tomorrow was another day.

CHAPTER SEVEN

HELEN dreamed she was sitting at a card table opposite Captain Blair. His features were clear enough though the other two players were hazy; she thought one of them was her father. There was a pile of money and jewels heaped up in the middle of the table. She looked down at her hand. King, knave, ten of hearts. Who had the queen? Dare she risk all on it being the Captain? Could she stand up and walk away? Which was the greatest gamble? She felt a sense of panic, of not being able to breathe, of someone shaking her.

'Miss, the Captain said I was to wake you at five. The coach is due to leave at six.'

Helen opened her eyes, to find herself looking into the face of a chambermaid, only inches from her own. 'The Captain said he thought you would like breakfast in your room, so I've brought it up.' She indicated a tray on the table beside the bed, lit by a lamp she had just placed beside it. 'There's bread and butter and ham and eggs. And a pot of coffee.'

'Thank you.' Helen struggled to sit up. Supper in her room and now breakfast; she felt like a naughty schoolgirl being punished for some misdemeanour, too mischievous to be allowed to eat in the dining-room. Not since she was fourteen had such a punishment been dealt out to her and she could not remember now what she had done to deserve it.

'He said to help you dress and make sure you

weren't late,' the girl went on. 'Very particular, the Captain is.'

'Too particular,' Helen said, throwing back the covers. 'You need not stay, I can manage.' She found her reticule and handed the girl a coin. 'Please ask someone to come in fifteen minutes to take my trunk and bag down.'

'Yes, miss.' The girl bobbed and left, grinning.

As soon as the maid had gone, Helen scrambled from the bed, washed in the hot water which had been brought along with the breakfast and then searched in her trunk for a warm dress. The further north they went, the colder it was likely to become, and she did not want the Captain to misinterpret her shivering.

She pulled out a merino round gown with a fan-shaped silk insert in the bodice front. It had leg o' mutton sleeves and white fur trimming around the hem. With her mantle and ankle boots, she would be warm enough. Having packed her trunk again and fastened the lid, she picked up the tray and carried it down to the dining room.

Captain Blair was sitting at one of the tables, calmly enjoying his breakfast and reading a newspaper, with no sign of the raucous night he had passed in the taproom. He looked wide awake and his clothing was as pristine as it was possible to make it under the circumstances. Although he wore the same coat, he had changed his shirt and put on a brand new cravat. She carried the tray over to where he sat and set it on the table. 'Captain, if I wish to have my meals in solitary splendour then I will request it myself.'

'Good morning, Miss Sadler,' he said, looking up at

her angry little face. 'You must have slept well, you
are as sharp as ever, I see.'

'I slept tolerably, sir.'

'I am glad to hear it,' he said, deliberately returning
his attention to his newspaper.

She sat down opposite him and made a pretence of
enjoying the food, though by now the ham and eggs
and the coffee had gone cold. 'There is something of
import in the paper?'

He put it down. 'Not unless you count the collapse
of that idiotic trial.'

'The Queen has been found guilty?'

'No, that farce has degenerated into slapstick.
Liverpool moved that the Bill do pass this day six months,
which is a parliamentary term for abandoning it.'

'Does that mean she is still Queen and the King has
to acknowledge her?'

'In theory, yes, but in practice. . .' He shrugged. 'It
is impossible to make a man love someone he holds in
aversion and I doubt he will live with her again. But it
does make the succession a problem. While Caroline
is Queen, the King will never have another legitimate
offspring. It might not have been so bad had Princess
Charlotte or her child survived. . .'

'All that fuss, all those months of accusation, stirring
up the most disgusting evidence,' she said. 'All that
hate and invective, and nothing has changed. I feel for
them both, I truly do. I could never enter into an
arranged marriage.'

'Sometimes, there is no choice, *noblesse oblige* and
all that.' He smiled suddenly. 'But you are a princess.
Is that your problem, a marriage you do not relish?'

'No, certainly not,' she said, deciding not to persist

in telling him she was not a princess. He didn't really believe it anyway; it was all a game to him. 'I shall marry whom I please. There is no one to gainsay me.'

'And the poor man who has the misfortune to fall in love with you?' he ventured. 'What of him?'

'There is no such person.'

'No?' he queried softly. 'I'll wager otherwise.'

'Then you would lose your money.'

'Oh, I do not think so.'

'My goodness, how confident you are. But isn't that what gambling is all about, betting on something you can have no knowledge of?'

'There is skill as well as luck involved, Miss Sadler. It comes down to using the information you have to make rational judgements.'

'I collect you were going to play cards last night,' she said. 'Did you win?'

'I almost always win,' he answered evasively, wondering why he did not tell her he had been nowhere near the card table.

'And that attitude is the height of folly. Sooner or later, everyone loses, even you.'

'And you are an authority on the subject of risk, I presume.'

'No, but I abhor gambling. It is the worst of vices.'

'The worst?' He raised one eyebrow at her, a tiny smile playing about his lips. 'I should think pretence and deceit are equally abhorrent. At least, they are to me.'

'Oh.' She looked down at her plate to hide her confusion and shame. He knew she had lied! But he didn't know why. Should she tell him? Should she confess and hope that he would understand and forgive? He did not seem to be in a forgiving mood, judging by his coolness since the episode with the deserter. She allowed the opportunity to pass.

'Do you never gamble, Miss Sadler?' he went on.

'No.'

'Then, pray, what are you doing now? Life is a gamble, Miss Sadler, and yours more than most, and I'll gamble on that too.' He leaned forward the better to look into her eyes and was surprised to see tears glistening on her lashes. He had touched a raw spot and wished he had not teased her. He reached out to her hand but thought better of it and picked up the coffee pot instead.

'You are still angry with me,' she said.

'I would not be so uncivil.'

'Oh, yes, you would. If I am cause for annoyance, why did you stay? You could have gone on.'

'And left you to fall into more scrapes. First it was the young shaver who stole from you and then you must help Dorothy and Tom and yesterday was worst of all. We could both have been in the most serious trouble. You did untie that man, didn't you?'

'I felt sorry for him. And he promised me he would let me tie him up again after he had scratched his nose.'

He suppressed a smile. 'And you believed him!'

'He seemed so honest.'

'Honest? I doubt a single word of what he said was true and even if it were, I hold no brief for him. You can have no idea what it is like to be in the middle of a battle and have to depend for your life on the man either side of you doing his duty and staying firm.

Breaking ranks can have disastrous consequences. Courage does not come into it.'

'But have you never been afraid?'

'Often, and any soldier who tells you differently is a liar, but I have never turned my back on my companions.'

'No, I cannot imagine you would, but all men are not so steely.'

'That is not the point, Miss Sadler. The point is that the man was under arrest, being taken back to a court martial, which is not a matter to be treated lightly. What you did was criminal and I would have been the one to be blamed if he had got away.'

'But you were not the one who set him free,' she cried.

'I said you were my wife. I would be held responsible for your actions.'

'But you did not have to let them think that, did you? You could have denied it. We are strangers sharing a coach, that is all.'

'Yes, that is all,' he repeated. 'Strangers on a coach, ships that pass in the night. But when one of those ships looks set to founder, then the other must come to her aid, it is the unwritten law of the sea. Now, eat up, you have twenty minutes before the coach leaves, I would advise you to waste no more time.'

'You do not mean to hide the cutlery again, then?' she queried with a smile, trying to lighten the atmosphere.

'Not today. Those tricks are for schoolgirls. There is none here.'

She put down her cutlery and stood up. 'Excuse me,

I have to pay my bill and I believe I heard the coach arrive.'

He rose, inclined his head in a sketchy bow and watched her leave, then he returned to his breakfast and his newspaper, chuckling at the salacious evidence brought by the Queen's accusers. He did not doubt for a minute she was an adulteress, but she knew how to use publicity to her advantage. She was wildly popular wherever she went and even people who had never seen her in their lives, swore her innocence. The poor King had not stood a chance.

Miss Sadler was right, arranged marriages were full of pitfalls. On the other hand, an arranged marriage eliminated the greater hazard of falling in love. He had escaped both, not quite unscathed, but as near as made no matter and he meant to keep that way.

'Anyone for Carlisle?' a voice boomed from the doorway. He looked up to see a guard, muffled in a greatcoat with at least six capes and with a wide brimmed hat pulled firmly down on his brow, indicating the weather outside was no better. 'The Rob Roy is about to depart.'

Duncan rose hurriedly. Where was Miss Sadler? They could not go without her. He strode outside to find she was already in her seat, along with a florid gentleman in a yellow waistcoat, checked trousers and a huge neckcloth; a thin faced man with a wart on the end of his nose; a woman in widow's weeds and a young boy of about twelve who was obviously the woman's son. They were back to the discomfort of six inside passengers. He took his place beside Helen, the grooms stood back from the horses and they were off once more.

The girl beside him was silent, brooding about what he had said no doubt, but then she had asked for it, always sparring with him, causing mayhem. But now the fire had gone from her eyes and she looked tiny and vulnerable. He had not noticed her lack of stature before because of her apparent self-confidence, but now he wanted to take her in his arms, tell her everything would be all right, he would always protect her; she need not look so worried.

'Hartley,' the man in the yellow waistcoat said, leaning forward and offering Duncan his hand. 'I am in cotton, import the stuff from the Americas. Visiting the mills hereabouts.'

'Captain Duncan Blair, Prince of Wales's Own Hussars,' Duncan said, shaking the man's hand. 'I am going home on leave.'

'Where are you bound, Captain?' the widow asked.

'Scotland, ma'am.'

'Oh, then we shall be travelling together until Lancaster.' She leaned forward and smiled at Helen in friendly fashion. 'My name is Mrs Goodman.'

'And mine is Helen Sadler.' What else could she say? Lies were becoming second nature to her now.

'Oh, then you are not. . .' She stopped, looking from Helen to Duncan. 'I am sorry, I thought. . .'

'Unfortunately not,' Duncan said with a smile.

'Oh, I beg your pardon.' This to Helen. 'I would not for the world. . .'

'Oh, please, think no more of it,' Helen said. 'Unhappily I am obliged to travel alone and I am glad to have congenial company.'

Mrs Goodman poked her son in the ribs. 'Say how do you do to Miss Sadlert, Robert.'

He obeyed with a mumble.

'I am very pleased to meet you, Robert,' Helen said.

'You have also recently suffered a bereavement?' Mrs Goodman went on, indicating Helen's black clothes.

'Yes. My father. He died two months ago.'

'Your father?' Duncan queried. 'But I thought. . .'

She turned to him and smiled. 'What was that you said about using the information you have to make rational judgements, Captain?'

'*Touché*, Miss Sadler. But I wish you had told me.'

'Would it have made any difference?'

'Of course it would. May I offer my condolences now?'

'Thank you.'

'And are you also going to Scotland?' Mrs Goodman asked her.

'Yes, I am going to Killearn.'

Killearn! How many more surprises was she going to spring on him? Killearn was his home town. He found himself mentally listing everyone he knew, wondering who might need a companion or a governess, but he could think of no one. It was probably another of her fabrications; perhaps she did know who he was, after all and was baiting him. One day, perhaps, she would surprise him with the truth.

'I have just buried my husband,' Mrs Goodman volunteered. 'I had the boy home for the funeral. I am taking him back to school now.'

'Oh, I am dreadfully sorry.'

'He weren't my father,' the boy said, almost defiantly.

'Father or stepfather, what's the difference?' his

mother snapped. 'He brought you up, provided for us.' She smiled at Helen. 'I've buried three husbands now. Robert's father was the first, when I was very young indeed, no more than a child bride.'

'Oh, how dreadful for you,' Helen said, then added hastily, 'losing your husbands like that.'

'Careless, you mean,' Duncan whispered in her ear.

'Yes, indeed.' Mrs Goodman had thankfully not heard the comment. 'But they left me well provided for.'

Helen heard Duncan mutter, 'And now she'll be looking for a fourth,' and smothered a smile with some difficulty.

'My husband, the last one, died of wounds received last year at Peterloo. You have heard of that, Miss Sadler?'

'Indeed, yes. My condolences, ma'am. Such a dreadful thing to have happened. It was intended as a peaceful demonstration, wasn't it, a meeting to air the grievances of the handloom weavers? I believe they have been very distressed by all the new machinery coming into use.'

Duncan groaned inwardly. This could be contentious, especially with a cotton importer in the coach with them, but Helen never seemed to sense danger. She jumped straight in with both feet and was surprised when she found herself in deep water. And the meeting had ostensibly been about Parliamentary reform, a platform for Orator Hunt.

'That's no reason to start a riot,' Mr Hartley said. 'Workers have to move with the times, it is the only way. Shouting the odds and demanding rights they do not have, is no way to go on.'

'My husband was not one of the rioters, you under-stand,' Mrs Goodman put in quickly. 'He was simply doing his duty as a militiaman.'

'Oh, I see, one of the law enforcers,' Duncan said with a note of irony in his voice which was not lost on Helen. The militia had been even more enthusiastic at putting down the insurgents than the army itself and there were those who firmly believed the whole epi-sode had been created by *agents provocateurs*. Mr Goodman, perhaps, or people like Mr Hartley, with an axe to grind?

'Yes,' Mrs Goodman agreed. 'The militia were ordered to charge the mob. There were thousands of them, carrying banners and sticks and suchlike and chanting insults against the troops who were sent to calm them.'

'You were there?' Helen queried. 'You saw the massacre?'

'I was not on the spot, but it could be heard from miles away. If I had been there, I might have prevented Francis being hurt. He was run through with his own sword, taken from him by one of the mob.'

'Oh, I am so sorry,' Helen murmured, realising her mistake. 'I did not mean to distress you.'

'A year he lived afterwards, a year and two months, lying there in his bed, staring at the ceiling, unable to move except the fingers of one hand, unable to speak properly. I nursed him night and day, but he never knew I was there. To me he died that day in August last year, not two weeks ago. It was only the burial of him that was delayed. And no one brought to book over it. They won't be now, of course, he took too long in the dying.'

Helen could hardly say she was sorry again, but what else was there to say? This coachride, besides being a journey into the unknown, was a journey of discovery; so many different people, so many harrowing stories, so much to learn. She was beginning to realise how easy her life had been up to now. She should be thankful for what she had had, the happy childhood, the loving parents, not spend her time blaming her father for deserting her, or being afraid of the future.

'You think I am callous, don't you?' Mrs Goodman went on. 'That I should be weeping behind my veil?'

'I imagine you did all your weeping twelve months ago,' Helen said.

'I did that. It was fortunate Robert was at school most of the time and knew little of it. He is a good boy and very clever, like his father. He was an engineer, you know.'

She went on in like manner for mile after mile, with an occasional comment from Helen and Mr Hartley, while the thin man with the wart on his nose sat in the corner with a small case on his lap and uttered not a word, and Duncan smiled wryly.

Killearn. But where in Killearn? Did it matter? He could hardly go calling on his friends and acquaintances simply for the pleasure of seeing one of their employees, and his father and brother would think he had run mad. Arabella! If memory served him, James and Arabella had a child just the age to begin a little tuition at home. If she were going there. . .

He stopped his thoughts running back to his hurt. He had been no more than a naïve youth and Arabella had been a childish dream. But when you are very young you do not have the wisdom to see such things in proper perspective; every emotion, high or low, every joy, every hurt is doubly felt, remembered with embarrassment.

But he had put it behind him, made himself get on with a life that was full and interesting, except that he never *quite* trusted himself to fall in love again. He had almost forgotten that early hurt until he met Miss Helen Sadler. But why should meeting her bring it all back? She did not look like Arabella, did not sound like her, certainly did not behave like her.

He glanced out of the window as they slowed over a particularly bad patch of road, so full of ruts they were bounced and bumped about like potatoes in a sack and all conversation ceased while they held on to their seats. Thankfully the rain had ceased, but the potholes were full of water and it was difficult for the coachman to see which holes, being the deepest, were best avoided.

It was no surprise to Duncan when a sudden lurch sent them all sprawling in a heap on top of Mr Hartley and the thin little man in the corner seat. Duncan, who had managed to save himself from joining them, grabbed Helen round the waist and hung onto her until the rocking of the coach stopped and they came to rest.

'God's teeth!' This from Mr Hartley as he scrambled off the little man. 'Are you hurt?'

'No, I do not think so, though my hat is broken.'

Duncan opened the door on the offside and helped Helen to alight. To Robert he said, 'Come on, young shaver, out you come and let me help your mother.'

Robert emerged, followed by Mrs Goodman, complaining that she thought her last hour had come, then Mr Hartley and finally the little man and his battered hat. The coachman, the guard and the solitary outside passenger had all descended unhurt and were standing on the nearside verge looking at the back wheel, which was smashed beyond repair.

'Oh, not again!' Helen exclaimed, as she joined them. 'How many more disasters are we to suffer?'

'It's not a disaster,' Duncan said. 'No one is hurt, not even the horses. It is simply a setback.'

'And one I would rather do without,' the coachman said. 'We'll never make Carlisle tonight now.'

'Can it be repaired?' Mrs Goodman asked.

'I've got tools for minor repairs,' the guard said. 'But this ain't minor, not nohow. This is major. A new wheel, no less.' He bent down and examined the underside of the carriage. 'And an axle-tree.'

'And where are we to find those?'

'In Preston. There will be a coachbuilder and wheelwright there.'

'But that is miles away,' Mr Hartley said. 'I have important business to transact, I cannot waste my time, sitting in a broken-down coach counting the hairs in my beard. Something must be done and done at once.'

'Of course something must be done,' the coachman said somewhat irritably. 'And the first thing is to get the vehicle off the road. If we leave it where it is, someone is bound to run into it and then it won't be an axle-tree we'll be needing, but a whole new carriage. And I could do with help, not hindrance.'

The guard and all the passengers, except Helen and Mrs Goodman, heaved at the coach while the coachman, standing at their heads, urged the horses to pull, until it was half-hauled, half-manhandled to the verge and allowed to drop lopsidedly onto its broken axle. 'They might have a spare coach at the next staging post,' the coachman said, unharnessing one of the leaders. 'I'll ride on and see what I can find.' Then to the guard, 'Charlie, you look after our passengers and keep your eye on their belongings. And walk the horses. I'll be back as soon as I can.'

There was nothing for it but to wait and try to keep warm until help arrived. The little man elected to settle down in the lea of the coach with his battered hat on his head and his chin in the turned-up collar of his coat, while the guard released the horses from the traces and began to walk them up and down the road. Robert ran back the way they had come and climbed onto a knoll which gave him a good view of any approaching traffic which might take some of them on.

His mother paced up and down, avoiding the water-filled potholes, accompanied by the outside passenger and Mr Hartley, who found in her a willing listener. Helen, pulling her cloak closely round her, walked up the road a little way, to see what was beyond the group of trees which surrounded them. Duncan, unwilling to let her out of his sight, accompanied her, matching his stride to hers.

The bitterly cold wind whirled her bonnet off and would have taken it away if it had not been securely tied under her chin. It hung down her back on its ribbons and she left it there. Her raven-black hair escaped from its pins and tendrils of it drifted across her face. Her eyes were bright and her cheeks glowing. He had never seen anyone so beautiful, so full of life.

He walked beside her, watching her, watching the way she tipped her head back and lifted her face to the sky, the way she put up a gloved hand to push the hair back, the sudden smile and just as sudden frown, dainty feet picking her way over the rough ground. Everything she did was a delight. And yet, in the back of his mind were doubts, doubts about her, doubts about his own feelings. She had lied, of that he was sure, but what he did not know was why. What was her secret? And did it matter?

'I am truly sorry,' she said, breaking in on his thoughts.

'Sorry, Miss Sadler?'

'Yes. You seem to have appointed yourself my escort and though I did not ask for it, I have been grateful for your kindness. I am sorry I was such a crosspatch this morning, ringing a peal over you because of a game of cards. It was very impertinent of me.'

'It is of no consequence. Think no more of it.'

'But for me you would have been safe home by now.'

'Perhaps,' he said, as they left the trees behind and emerged on a slight hill. The road, empty of traffic except for a farm cart in the distance, wound through moorland dotted with sheep and disappeared below the hill towards a distant hamlet; there was no sign of the returning coachman. 'But just think of the adventures we have had. I would not have missed them for worlds.'

'It is unkind of you to tease me.'

'I am sorry,' he said contritely. 'But you make it so easy.'

She ignored his comment and marched on. He really was insufferable. Why she had bothered to apologise she did not know. The wind was biting through her clothes and she could not stop herself shivering. 'How long do you think the coachman will be?'

'Not long, I hope.' They turned to go back. 'Let's go this way, it is more sheltered.' He took her arm and guided her off the road between the trees where a narrow path wound its way parallel to the highway. It was not quite so windy there, though they could hear it soughing in the tops of the branches. They walked side by side without speaking, their feet scuffling the fallen leaves.

She could not understand him; the two sides to his nature were so at odds. He was a perfect escort, except for the fact that he was obviously acting against his will. He wanted to be riding on and rid of her, and yet he stayed glued to her side. He had spoken of duty, was that how he saw it? But why? Strangers on a coach, they had agreed on that. He had no duty towards her and she had no obligation to be grateful. It would be the same with the Earl of Strathrowan when she arrived in Killearn. When she arrived. *If* she arrived.

Busy with her thoughts, she failed to see the tree root sticking up in her path and stumbled over it. She put out her hands to save herself but she was not allowed to fall; the Captain caught her in his arms almost before she knew it had happened. He stood there, his arms about her, feeling her body shaking, like a tiny bird trapped in a net. 'Helen.' His voice was hoarse.

Hearing him say her name, she tipped her face up to his. The brittle look had gone from his eyes and the hard line of his jaw had softened; it was as if she saw him through a haze. For the first time she glimpsed the man beneath the shell. He bent his head and put his lips to hers, softly at first, then more urgently.

Somewhere in the depths of her being something stirred, something new and exciting which filled her whole body with a tingling sensation which spread from her arms down to her stomach and thighs. It was both exhilarating and weakening, so that she could hardly support herself. She pressed herself closer, allowing the kiss to deepen, opening her mouth to his, tasting the essence of the man, clinging to him with her hands about his neck. The wind took their hair and intertwined it about their faces, her cloak blew across his thighs, making them a single being, alone among the leafless trees.

How long she would have allowed it to go on, she would never know because a voice, loud and insistent, brought her suddenly to her senses. 'Captain! Miss Sadler! Where are you?'

She sprang away, scarlet with embarrassment. He did not move. She turned and ran, darting out of his sight among the trees, towards the sound of Robert's voice.

Duncan stood and watched her go, cursing himself. Just as he thought he was making headway, he had spoiled it all with that impulsive kiss. He would have to behave more circumspectly than that if he wanted to win her in the end. He pulled himself up short, wondering exactly what he meant by that. Did he mean to enjoy her charms as one would a mistress or make her his wife? He could not believe he had had either thought in his head.

Lady's maid or governess, she was hardly the sort of wife of whom his family would approve and she was far too young to make a satisfactory mistress. Had she known what she was doing to him? Was she the little innocent or a woman who knew exactly what she was about? 'Damnation!' he muttered, following more slowly.

Helen stopped her headlong flight. She could not dash into the company like a frightened rabbit; they would know instantly that something had occurred. How could she have been so wanton as to allow it to happen? She had trusted him and where had that trust led her? Down into the depths.

How could she have been so wrong about a man? She had thought he was dependable and kind, when all the time he was a philanderer and gambler. He had taken her for a simpleton the moment he she had asked for his help at the Blue Boar in London and ever since then had been playing with her as a cat plays with a mouse, waiting for his chance to catch her unawares. And, oh, how he had succeeded!

'Miss Sadler.' Robert appeared through the trees. 'Mama sent me to find you. The coachman has returned. Did you not hear him?'

'No.' She managed a smile, settling her bonnet back on her head and pushing her hair up under it. 'I expect the wind drowned the sound of the horse's hooves.'

'Where is Captain Blair?'

'Captain Blair?' She swallowed hard. 'I have not seen him for some time.'

'I'll go and look for him, if you like.'

'Yes, do. The sooner we are away, the sooner I shall

be pleased.' And if Captain Blair had managed to get himself lost and they left without him, she would be even more pleased. How was she going to endure the rest of the journey, sitting beside him, pretending nothing had happened, she did not know. Robert darted off, calling the Captain's name and she made her way slowly back to the coach, trying desperately to compose herself and behave naturally.

Beside the broken-down coach stood another, which hardly looked in better shape except that it had four wheels. It was very small and its paintwork was scuffed and old leather curtains hung in the windows instead of glass. There was no rail on the roof for the outside passengers. Two old horses stood in the traces. The guard was busy transferring their luggage, some of which had to be strapped onto the roof. Helen stood and stared at it.

'It's all I could find,' the coachman said apologetically. 'But it will carry us to the next village.'

The little man rose from behind the broken coach and climbed inside without speaking, settling himself in the corner as if he had changed coaches at a normal stopping place. Mr Hartley, who had struck up a rapid rapport with Mrs Goodman, took her arm. 'Come, my dear, let me help you up.'

'Where is Robert?' she asked, looking about her.

'He has gone to look for Captain Blair,' Helen said, surprised that her voice sounded perfectly normal. 'They will be here directly.'

Almost before she had finished speaking, Duncan and Robert appeared and Mrs Goodman climbed in, followed by Helen. It was cramped and there was no room for anyone else. Momentarily she wondered if

the Captain might be left behind, which would have
served him right, but quickly realised that was unlikely.
She sat there, staring straight ahead, wishing they could
be on their way and this dreadful journey over and
done with.

The whole thing was a nightmare, it must be. Soon
she would wake to find herself in London, safe in her
own bed with Daisy hovering over her with hot water,
and the sun shining in the window and her father
downstairs sitting over his breakfast without a care in
the world. And later she would go shopping and buy a
new gown, something light and frivolous, not this
dreary black. Black was for mourning.

She pinched herself hard and knew it was no dream;
she really was sitting in a battered old coach surrounded by strange people, not least a man who
thought it was perfectly permissible to grab hold of her
and kiss her without so much as a by-your-leave.

'Ah, there you are, Captain,' the coachman said.
'Will you ride one of the spare horses?'

'It will be a pleasure.' Duncan said, looking at Helen,
who was busy rolling up the leather blind to let some
light into the coach. A little smile played about his lips.
The ghost of Arabella had been well and truly laid to
rest, Miss Helen Sadler had seen to that. She noticed
the smile and turned her head away. He was laughing
at her, laughing at her naïvety, at the easy way he had
conquered her. It increased her fury, not only with
him, but with herself for her weakness.

'If you would ride the leader, Captain, Charlie can
ride one of the wheelers and lead the other.' The
coachman's voice seemed loud in her ears, interrupting
her jumbled thinking.

'Yes, of course,' Duncan said, taking the bridle of one of the horses, while the guard mounted another and took up the reins of the third.

'You sit on the box beside me, young shaver,' the coachman said to Robert, much to the boy's delight, and then to the solitary outside passenger. 'If you sit close behind and hang onto the back of the box, you'll be right as ninepence.'

It was soon arranged to everyone's satisfaction and they set off at a shambling gait which suited the two old horses, who were more used to pulling farm carts than coaches. At least, Helen thought, she did not have to sit beside Captain Blair.

It was getting dusk as they drew into a yard where chickens flew up squawking at their approach and where a solitary coach lamp hung at the door. An old man hurried out towards them, a huge grin on his face. It was evident as soon as the passengers alighted that here was not a coaching inn. 'What have you brought us to, coachman?' Mrs Goodman demanded. 'This is nothing but a hedge tavern. Can we not go on to something a little more agreeable?'

'Sorry, ma'am, but this is where the coach and horses belong and they have to be returned.'

'So what are we to do?' Mrs Goodman looked from Mr Hartley to the Captain. 'We surely cannot all stay here. It looks a dreadful place.'

'It's better than the roadside, ma'am,' Duncan said. 'And I am sure we shall be made welcome.' They would be welcome, there was no doubt. How often did a coachload of people arrive on this particular doorstep with no alternative but to accept its hospitality? He strode over to the door, ducking his head under its low lintel. There was only one parlour, low-ceilinged and dingy, the smell of stale tobacco smoke clinging to the air.

He went through a door at the other end and found himself in a kitchen, where a fat woman was stationed over a stove stirring something in a pan and a scrawny girl stood at a table cutting up a cabbage. They looked up when his large frame filled the doorway.

'We need food,' he said, laying two sovereigns on the table beside the cabbage. 'The best you can manage. And a bedroom for two ladies.'

'The food you can have,' the fat woman said. 'But we don't have no beds. This ain't an inn.'

'That is evident,' he said. 'But you must have one room with a bed in it.' He put down two more coins which chinked beside the first.

'Only my own, if that's what you had in mind.'

'That will do but clean sheets and blankets, mind you.'

It took the couple and their daughter all of two hours to produce a meal which turned out to be surprisingly good. All the passengers, even the man who travelled outside which was unheard of, dined together around one large table with the tavernkeeper and his wife, a situation which pleased Helen. There was no intimacy with Captain Blair and she could allow the conversation to drift around her without feeling she had to take part.

From now on she would hold her tongue, and no matter how many more untoward incidents occurred, she would stay out of them. Perhaps Captain Blair would then realise he had made a very grave mistake;

she was not the sort of woman to fall into his arms at the drop of a hat. But she had, oh, she had, and God forgive her, she had enjoyed it, had wanted it to continue, had felt her insides turn to quivering jelly. There must be something very dissolute in her make-up for that to happen and she must be very wary of it.

Perhaps, when they reached Preston, which was the next town of any size, he would decide he had had enough of her company and ride on. The thought of that filled her with dread. What was the matter with her? Did she want him to stay or to go?

If only there was someone she could confide in, but there was only Mrs Goodman, and somehow Helen did not think she would receive very good advice from that quarter. The lady in question was doing her obvious best to captivate Mr Hartley who seemed not to mind at all, laughing at her jokes and agreeing with everything she said, calling her 'my dear' and beaming at Robert, who had seen it all before and simply scowled back at him. Helen was reminded of the Captain's comment that the good lady would be look-ing for husband number four and found herself smiling in spite of her anger with him. Unless she missed her guess, number four was already hooked.

Helen and a reluctant Mrs Goodman were the first to break up the party and were shown up to the room under the rafters where the landlord and his fat wife usually slept. Helen was doubtful about the sheets, but their hostess assured her they were freshly laundered, and accepting her word, she undressed and crawled into bed beside Mrs Goodman, hoping fervently that that good lady would draw breath long enough to fall asleep. She need not have worried; without the gentle-

men to entertain, she was not in the least interested in
conversation and was soon snoring. Helen turned her
back on her and stopped her ears and in a little while,
exhausted from all that had happened, she fell asleep
herself.

A wheelwright arrived next morning in a flat-bottomed
cart containing spare wheels, a couple of axle-trees, a
hub or two and the tools of his trade. He was taken
out to the abandoned coach by the coachman and the
guard, riding two of their original horses and leading
the other two, long before the passengers woke for
their breakfasts. All except Duncan.

While the other three men passengers and Robert
had curled up under blankets on the hard floor of the
parlour, if such a dismal room could be given that
grandiose name, and the landlord and his wife tried to
share a settle in the kitchen, he had chosen to sleep in
the hayloft above the horses, who being more than
usually crowded themselves, snorted and snuffled the
whole night long. As soon as dawn crept between the
cracks in the wooden slats of the building, he rose and
went for a walk to clear his head.

He prayed his father had recovered from his illness,
or if not, that it was not as serious as everyone had at
first thought. Duncan loved his father, just as he loved
his brother and his nephew and niece, but he could no
more have left Helen to go to them than take wings
and fly. Mind you, he told himself wryly, he wished he
could fly, wished he could take Helen Sadler by the
hand and whisk her into the sky.

He looked up at the lowering clouds; there was bad
weather on the way or he missed his guess and the

sooner they left the better. He heard the drum of hooves and the clatter of wheels and returned to the yard to find their old coach, with a spanking new yellow-painted wheel, being loaded with their luggage and the little old tavernkeeper dashing about trying to be helpful but in reality getting in the way of the coachman and guard who were, once again, their professional selves. He joined the other passengers and climbed aboard.

Helen, sitting once again thigh to thigh with Duncan, was acutely aware of his presence beside her. It seemed as though he had been sitting there, her uninvited escort, since the beginning of time instead of just four days. Why didn't he go on? He could long ago have changed to the mail or acquired a horse to ride; either would have been quicker and he had said more than once he was in a hurry.

She felt as if she were doomed to be riding in a coach, mile after mile, stage after stage, flitting from one incident to another, to eternity. It was difficult to think about how it had come about, to remember the lovely old house where she had lived in such comfort, difficult to recall the face of her beloved mother or the father who had decided to end it all.

Nor had she ever seen the place where she was going: could not picture the man she was going to meet, her guardian. It was as if she had no past and no future, flotsam buffeted by life's storms. No wonder she had clung to the lifeline thrown out by Captain Blair. They were strangers at the outset and they were still strangers. She knew nothing whatever about him, except that when he had kissed her she had been able to offer no defence at all and even thinking about it made her burn with shame.

She had an itch in the middle of her back and would dearly have loved to put her hand behind her and given it a good scratch but she could not move without disturbing the man beside her. She tried not to fidget, knowing as the itch moved from one place to another, that she had probably picked up a flea or two and, in spite of herself, smiled. There was a first time for everything, for kisses and for flea bites.

Duncan saw the smile and wondered what had prompted it; only a moment before she had looked on the verge of tears. He knew he had caused her distress and hated himself for it, but he also knew that a public apology would make matters worse. Until he could speak to her alone, he would do better to pretend there was nothing wrong and that was made easier by Robert, who was determined to quiz him, asking if he had ever met Napoleon or the Duke of Wellington and was the King as fat as everyone said he was? Had His Majesty really led a charge at Waterloo?

Duncan humoured him, answering his questions, telling him that if His Majesty imagined he was leading a charge, then who was he to say differently, but he wondered how he had managed to mount the horse because he hadn't been able to do that for years. And not even a King could be in two places at once.

'But you were there, sir?'

'Indeed I was, along with a few thousand others.'

And so it went on until, at last, they arrived in Lancaster where Mrs Goodman and her son were whisked away in Mr Hartley's carriage, which had been sent to meet him. Helen said goodbye and watched them go, with a tired heart. Travelling was like that, bone-shakingly tiring, a time for making new acquaintances whom you never saw again after the journey ended, a time for conversation and for reflection, but not a good time for making decisions; it was too transitory, too unreal. Everything seemed unreal, even the tall shape of Captain Blair with his firm jaw and laughing brown eyes, as he escorted her into the inn as if nothing at all had happened.

CHAPTER EIGHT

THERE was time only for a hasty meal and none at all for conversation and Helen was glad of that; the last thing she wanted was to talk to Captain Blair. He, sensing her mood, made sure she was comfortably seated and some food ordered and then excused himself. She had no idea where he had gone and told herself she did not want to know. An hour later she returned to the coach, to find the wart-nosed man already in his seat, hugging his case on his lap as if he had never moved. His hat with the broken crown was still on his head.

Captain Blair was talking to the coachman at the head of the horses. He seemed to have an easy rapport with everyone, Helen noted, high or low, it seemed to make no difference.

Seeing her, he came over and handed her in without speaking and sat down beside her. She hitched herself as far away from him as she could and stared out of the window so that she did not have to look at him, because looking at him would remind her of that kiss and how it had affected her. The sooner she put it from her mind, the sooner her peace of mind would be restored.

The outside passengers climbed aboard, the coachman did his ritual inspection and they were off again at a canter, trying to make up for lost time. But there seemed to be little hope of that; the further north they went, the worse the weather became with high winds and driving rain and they were soon reduced to a walk. Helen began to wonder how much of the Captain's teasing had been been true and how much invented. She could see nothing from the window, but a curtain of water. The travellers on the roof, she realised, must be suffering dreadfully.

'Captain, could we not ask the coachman to stop and invite some of the outside passengers to come inside?' Her concern for them overcame her reluctance to address the man beside her. 'They must be wet and frozen up there.' Then to the little man. 'You would not object, sir, would you?'

'I doubt the coachman will want to pull up on this incline,' he said, which was as near as he dare go to refusing altogether. 'He will never get the horses going again.'

'Then we could ask him to stop when we get to the top. I think it is shameful for us to sit here in the dry with seats to spare when they are being soaked.'

'It is what they paid for,' he said. 'To ride outside and risk the elements. They may not wish to spend the extra.'

'Goodness, sir, I am not asking you to give up your seat, simply to ask others in out of the wet. Where is your humanity?'

Duncan groaned inwardly. She was at it again, trying to rule other people, imposing her will and not taking kindly to being denied. He could not deny her. There was nothing wrong with her humanity; she had demonstrated it enough in the last four days.

'It is a question of common practice,' the man said. 'Outside passengers are outside passengers and those who choose to travel inside do so because they do not wish to consort with their inferiors and they pay for the privilege.'

'I never heard anything so top-lofty.'

'And you, if I may say so, miss, are rag-mannered and impertinent.'

Duncan who had been enjoying the exchange, decided it had gone far enough. 'Sir, Miss Sadler asked out of the goodness of her kind heart, if we might share the coach with others less fortunate. I think it is very considerate of her and I, for one, am happy to comply.'

'But I am not.'

'You, sir, are outnumbered.' And with that he put his head out of the window and shouted into the teeth of the gale. 'Coachman, would you be so kind as to stop a moment?'

The coachman, thinking one of his inside passengers had been taken ill, pulled the horses up so quickly, they reared and then shuddered to a halt. 'What's amiss?'

Duncan opened the door and jumped down. 'Nothing is amiss. Miss Sadler would like to invite two or three of your outside passengers in out of the wet. You have no objection, have you?'

'None.' He grinned, though the rain was dripping off his hat brim and his shoulder cape was soaked. 'You can take pity on me too, if you like.'

Duncan smiled back at him and looked up at the passengers huddled on the roof. 'You, you and you,' he said, pointing to a wizened old man in a brown coat and a felt hat tied on with string, a little old lady wrapped in a black cloak and a lad of about fourteen in nothing more than trousers and short jacket who was shivering so violently he was shaking the vehicle. 'You can ride inside if you've a mind to. Nothing extra to pay.' He turned to the coachman. 'That's right, isn't it, Mr Grinley?'

'It's all the same to me.'

In no time at all the three selected passengers were seated inside, loud in their thanks to the kind gentleman.

'Don't thank me,' he said, as they moved off again. 'Thank the lady.'

'Then I do so with all my heart,' the old man said. 'My wife is fair frozen.'

'Poor dear,' Helen said, removing her mantle. 'Here, you have this, it's warm and dry. I don't need it, truly I don't.' She slipped the old woman's cloak from her shoulders and wrapped the mantle round her, then took the tiny wrinkled hands in her own and rubbed them gently. 'You'll soon be warm again. Such dreadful weather to have to travel in.'

'Yes, and like to get worse,' the man said, rubbing his own gnarled hands up and down his thighs to try and restore some feeling to them. 'It was fair enough, though cold, when we set out yesterday to visit my brother and go to the Preston horse fair, but today its seems that winter has come early. I shouldn't be surprised if it snowed afore the week is out.'

'Poppycock!' exclaimed the man with the wart on his nose. 'It is only a bit of rain.'

'Then I suggest you go and sit on the roof and try it,' Helen snapped, and returned to her task of reviving the old lady.

Duncan, watching her at work, was filled with an

aching longing to have her hold his hands like that and look at him with the compassion she was showing the old lady. But to him she was coolly impersonal and it was all his own fault. How to put it right he did not know.

On the hilly roads they needed to change horses more frequently and that was not always easily accomplished; the smooth, practised changeovers of the coaching inns of the south were no more and everything was chaotic, made worse by the weather. Even getting down from the coach and going into an inn for refreshment meant dashing through a downpour. And without her mantle, Helen was cold to the bone by the time they reached Kendal and was glad when she learned the coach was going no further that night.

'It is too dangerous to travel over Shap Fell in the dark,' the guard told them. 'Specially in this weather. We'll set off again as soon as it's light.'

Duncan, afraid that Helen might catch a chill, did what he had done all along, saw to her trunk, arranged for a room for her and ordered a bath and hot water to be taken up to it, though he knew he must draw the line at settling her bill. It was not that he could not afford it, nor that he did not want to pay but simply because she would fly up in the boughs if he suggested it; she had done so on a previous occasion and that was before he had been foolish enough to insult her with that kiss.

'Captain,' she said, summoning all her dignity. 'I am perfectly capable of ordering such things for myself. I wish you would go away.'

'Do you?' he asked softly.

She could not bring herself to look him in the eye.
'Yes.'

'Then I will not burden you with my presence.' He
delved into his bag and produced a small jar, handing
it to her with a smile. 'Use this after your bath, you
may find it efficacious.'

She took it, looking down at it with a puzzled little
frown until she realised it contained ointment, guaran-
teed to kill fleas and soothe their bites, so it said on
the label. She was astonished that he had even noticed
her discomfort when she had made every effort to hide
it and even more surprised that he had diagnosed the
trouble. She felt like dashing the jar to the floor and
castigating him for his impertinence but the sensible,
practical side of her told her it would be foolish.
'Thank you, Captain.'

She turned and climbed the stairs, leaving him to
join a crowd of men in the taproom. Let him play cards
if he wanted to, what had it to do with her? She was
well rid of him.

The room she had been given was large and beauti-
fully furnished, unmarred by a single speck of dust,
with pristine linen on the bed, a bath on the rug before
a glowing fire filled almost to the brim with steaming
water, soap and fluffy towels on the rail by the wash
stand. The chambermaid was moving about, making
sure everything was just as it should be.

'The gentleman said I was to stay and help you
undress, miss,' she said.

If the girl had not mentioned the Captain, Helen
would have been grateful for the offer, as it was, she
decided he took too much upon himself. 'It was kind
of him to think of it,' she said. 'But I can manage very

well, thank you.' She found a coin for the girl. 'I should like a tray brought up in half an hour, some soup, I think, and a little chicken and vegetables, whatever you have to hand. And hot chocolate.'

'Very good, miss.' The girl bobbed and went out, shutting the door carefully behind her. Helen stood and looked about her. It was almost like home, with Daisy in attendance and everything done exactly as she liked it. Would those days ever come again? She sighed and began slowly undressing.

The bath was hot and scented and she sat and soaped herself, examining the bites which had caused so much irritation. She must have caught the fleas at that run-down old tavern, though they could equally well have come from any one of her fellow passengers. It was one of the hazards of travelling by public coach.

Another was meeting people like Captain Blair, handsome, thoughtful, kind and completely unscrupulous. She had never had to deal with men like him before and had no idea how to handle him. He simply refused to be handled. Every put-down was met with a smile which set her quivering as if she hadn't a bone in her body, every attempt at haughty disdain, which was the normal way for a young lady to let it be known a gentleman's attentions were not welcome, was simply ignored. He persisted in helping her, almost as if he had been paid to do so, which, of course, was nonsense.

It would not have been so bad if she had really been as capable and independent as she pretended to be, or even if she had not begun the whole thing by telling a lie. To him she was Miss Sadler, lady's companion, and Miss Sadler she had to remain. To admit to anything else now would just be inviting more mockery. Young ladies who pretended to be what they were not, simply did not deserve to be treated as ladies.

He would never have dared to kiss Miss Sanghurst like that and he would never have had the presumption to offer Miss Sanghurst flea ointment. She smiled suddenly. Miss Sanghurst had every right to be offended, but Miss Sadler had not and Miss Sadler had liked being held so securely in his arms and being kissed. Not that she would ever admit it to him.

She climbed out of the bath and towelled herself dry, before smearing herself with the ointment. She had just taken her nightdress from her small portmanteau and slipped into it when a second maid arrived with her meal on a tray. She found her reticule among the discarded clothes on the bed and fished inside for a sixpence. The girl pocketed it, then dragged the bath out onto the landing, where Helen could hear her shouting down the stairs for someone to help her with it.

Helen guessed the room was the best the inn had to offer and she was sure she had been given it on the Captain's orders, but she wished sometimes, he would not be so careful of her; the best was also the most expensive. She sat on the bed, noticing how soft the mattress was, and tipped out her reticule. The little cascade of coins and paper money was pitifully small, just enough to pay for her night's lodging and a meal later the next day.

She had brought what she thought was sufficient for her needs on the journey, arranging for her next month's allowance to be paid into a bank in Killearn, still many miles, even days, ahead of her. Never before had she been obliged to count her money so carefully and she had not realised how fast it was disappearing.

Her generosity towards the little urchin, whose fare had cost her five shillings; her stubborn insistence on stopping every night, her own fares and tips to the chambermaids and the men who carried her trunk, besides those to the coachmen and guards, had taken every bit of eight pounds on top of the seven pounds' refund she had been given in Northampton.

Everyone who had provided even the smallest service had expected to be paid, and though on several occasions the Captain had offered to stand buff for her, she had refused and must continue to do so. She could not stop him looking after her baggage and giving orders on her behalf—after all, it had made a big difference to her comfort—but the last thing she wanted was to be even more beholden to him. Mr Benstead had written to her guardian asking him to arrange to have her met and she prayed he would fetch her quickly or she would end up penniless.

She went down to the dining-room next morning in good time to enjoy a leisurely breakfast, intending that it would be the last meal she had until they stopped that evening. And then she would travel on through the night to Glasgow. Wondering what her uninvited escort would do about it made her smile. Would he forgo the pleasures of food, bed and the card table to remain glued to her side, or decide to leave her to her own devices? For all she knew, he might already have done so. Perhaps another coachman had not been so faint-hearted about going over the fell in the dark and taken the Captain on. The thought that she might now be completely alone filled her with a kind of panic. There had already been so many hazards and so many pitfalls to catch the unwary, who was to say there would not be more? Uninvited or not, she needed him.

When she saw him at the breakfast table, tucking into ham and eggs, she heaved a huge sigh of relief. Her pride would not let her show it, nor would she deign to sit with him. She moved towards a table on the other side of the room, although she had to pass him on the way.

'Good morning, Miss Sadler.' He greeted her cheerfully, as if he had done nothing wrong at all.

'Good morning.' Her voice was clipped.

He grabbed her hand as she went to pass him. 'Where are you going?'

'To have my breakfast. Over there.'

'Oh, so I am still banished, is that it? I am not to be allowed the pleasure of your company?'

She tried to pull herself from his grasp, but he would not release her. 'Captain Blair, will you please let go of my arm?'

'Yes, if you promise to forgive me for my dreadful lapse and have breakfast with me.'

'I do not see why I should.'

'And I do not see why you should not. I am penitent, as you see.' She saw nothing of the sort but she had ceased to struggle from his grip. 'We have come a long way together and there is still a long way to go and being at odds with each other will not help to pass the time pleasantly.'

He smiled. 'I promise to behave. I will not kiss you again unless you wish it. Come, share my breakfast.

There is too much for me and it would be a shame to waste it.'

Pure economics decided her, or at least that is what she told herself it was, as she relented and sat opposite him.

'Good,' he said. 'We have twenty minutes before the coach leaves. Mr Grinley tells me he is not going to risk Shap Fell. Someone arrived during the night with news of a landslide blocking the road, so he has decided to go the longer route through Windermere and Grasmere to Penrith. With luck we should reach Carlisle by nightfall.'

'Carlisle, is that all? I had hoped we might get as far as Glasgow.'

'You are becoming impatient to arrive?'

'Naturally, I am. And I collect you were in haste when we left London. Has that changed?'

'No, but we can only go at the pace conditions allow.'

'And the further we go, the worse they become. I am surprised you did not think of hiring a horse and riding.'

'Oh, I did think of it, but I decided against it.'

'You must be regretting that decision.'

'Not at all,' he said cheerfully. 'I would have missed so much.'

She smiled, choosing to misunderstand him. 'Yes, I had no idea the journey would be so full of incident.'

'More than usually so,' he said with a hint of amusement in his voice. 'But then you must admit that you have been the instigator of most of it.'

'I do not remember ordering the rain, nor a broken wheel, nor. . .' She stopped. She *had* held the coach up while she argued about the boy; she *had* insisted on staying with Tom and Dorothy; she *had* released the deserter. Rain and broken wheels were nothing to that. 'I promise from now on, not to do a single thing to hold us up,' she said.

'Then I suggest you finish your breakfast and pay your reckoning, because I heard the horses being put in the traces and the guard directing the stowage of the baggage.'

She did as he suggested, paid her fare as far as Carlisle and a few minutes later took her place in the coach, only to discover that she and Captain Blair were the only inside passengers.

'Where are the others?' she asked, looking round in something close to panic.

'Perhaps they did not want to be taken out of their way,' he said. 'Or they thought the road would be cleared soon and they would beat us to it.'

'Do you think they will?'

'No. By all accounts the fall was a big one.'

'Is there no way round it?'

'Not on that stretch of road, it is hazardous at the best of times. No, Mr Grinley is in the right of it.'

Miles and miles to go with no company but the Captain and if he were to try to kiss her again. . . She did not know if she dare go on, but if she stayed and waited for another coach, it would mean more delay and that meant more expense. She was in a cleft stick.

Before she could come to a decision the coachman and driver took their places and, with a toot on the horn, they moved off. Now she would have to sit beside him for hours in silence or try to make polite conversation when all the time they must both be thinking about that kiss. What a simpleton she had been to allow it to happen, but it had felt so right at the time she had not given a thought to the consequences.

But perhaps he would not be thinking of it, perhaps he kissed young women at every available opportunity and forgot it afterwards as of no consequence. Her best plan was to pretend it had never happened.

'There is one advantage of coming this way,' he said, as they headed for Windermere. 'We shall see a little of the Lakes. I think they are one of the most beautiful parts of England, almost to be compared with Scotland for scenery.'

'You know the area?'

'I had an aunt who lived in Grasmere. My brother and I stayed with her occasionally when we were children. She died while I was abroad.' He paused. 'Have you been here before, Miss Sadler?'

'Not I am afraid I have not. I have never travelled further north than Peterborough.'

'The Fens. Very flat round there, I understand.' No wonder she had seemed so bewildered, so ingenuous; it was a new experience for her. It made him admire her all the more for her courage.

'Yes, very different from all these hills, but it has its own charm. You can see for miles and it only seems a stone's throw, and the skies are huge, riven with clouds tinged with pink and mauve. There are a great many waterways too; almost everything is conducted by water.' She laughed suddenly. 'Much easier and smoother than being shaken about in a coach on some of these roads.'

'You do not like hilly country?'

'Oh, yes, in a different way. The light and shade on the grey rocks and the green of the fells as the clouds move across the sun makes it seem they are forever changing. In the Fens the sky is the focal point, here it is the hills.'

'And the Lakes,' he said. 'We shall see Windermere soon.'

She realised suddenly that she was completely at ease with him; her earlier stiffness had gone, as if, having accepted the inevitable, she might as well enjoy it. And because there was plenty of room in the coach, he was not pressed so close to her. She did not have to think about his thigh against her, his elbow nudging her side, nor worry that she might accidentally move and find herself in his arms. No, better not to think of that at all. She took refuge in talking, chattering like a magpie about nothing at all.

The northernmost tip of Windermere was glimpsed as they stopped at Ambleside for a change of horses; now that the rain had stopped the sun was shining on its rippling water and showing the myriads of boats in sharp relief. On the opposite side she could see what looked like a castle and a wood. A little to the right the heather-covered hills rose, purple and grey, dotted with the white of sheep. 'Oh, it is beautiful!' she exclaimed, leaning forward in her seat to see the better.

'Yes, when the sun is shining,' he said laconically. 'It has a reputation for being wet, you know.'

She laughed. 'Oh, I know it looked very different yesterday when it was raining, but isn't that the beauty of England? The weather and the seasons change everything. It is impossible to be bored by it.'

'You do not mind the rain?'

'No, for I know the sun will shine again.'

'What a wonderful philosophy for life,' he said, smiling at her. She enhanced whatever setting she was in. Just now she was making the weak sun stronger, dull colours bright, simply by being there.

'Is it?' she asked, surprised that she could have said anything so profound. But it was true, wasn't it? If her life was going through a rainy patch, then perhaps she could look forward to the sun in days to come. Sitting here beside him, enclosed in the little world of a stagecoach, enjoying the scenery, talking amiably, she had almost managed to forget how she came to be here and where she was going.

'Tell me about Scotland,' she said. 'Is it like this?'

'Scotland,' he mused. 'I suppose it is, but more so. The lochs are like the lakes, but deeper, and the fells are nothing to the mountains of the Highlands. Sometimes the snow never leaves the top of them, you know. And there is a grandeur, a wildness, which is impossible to describe. You have to feel it.'

'Perhaps that feeling is only for those who are born and bred there, not for those who come to it late in life,' she said a little wistfully.

'Not necessarily. You will love it, I am sure.' He hoped that would turn out to be true, that she would be happy with her new employers in spite of their off-hand treatment of her. They should have arranged for her to be escorted; it was almost as if they did not care if she reached them or not. Surely, if it were James, he would have had more thought for her? 'I believe I heard you say you were going to Killearn?'

'Yes. Do you know it?'

'Very well. Where in Killearn do you go?'

She was tempted to tell him everything, to explain about her father and the money and the unknown guardian, but then, realising her insecurity, he might take it as a signal he could behave badly again, and she wanted to keep everything on the same pleasant, impersonal level. But most of all she did not want to confess that she had lied; he had said he hated pretence and deception, more than she hated gambling, and though she longed to confide in him, she could not do it. 'I do not know exactly, I am being met in Glasgow.'

'But you do know the name of your employer?'

Now, she was in a fix. If he knew Killearn as he said he did, then he would also know of the Earl of Strathrowan. 'Yes, I know his name.'

'Let me guess. Is it Macgowan?'

'How did you come to that conclusion?'

'Lord and Lady Macgowan have a young son who is in need of instruction. I can think of no one else, not among anyone of rank, that is. Unless. . .' He paused suddenly. 'There are the Strathrowans. . .'

Her heart began to beat in her throat and she felt the colour suffusing her face. What had her mother always told her? Be sure your sins will find you out. How could she possibly have known at the outset that Captain Blair would be familiar with Killearn? How big was the place? Was it big enough to hide in? But then, she would not be included in any social gatherings the family might go to and a mere captain was hardly likely to attend them either.

'Who said I was going to anyone of rank, Captain? Surely such a family would have arranged a chaperone for me?'

'Yes, of course they would.'

'Then you have your answer, Captain.'

It was highly unsatisfactory, but she obviously did not want to tell him any more and he was beginning to wonder if she had any employment to go to at all. But then, why mention Killearn? It was not a great town; few people from south of the border had ever heard of it. She was either being forced to make the trip against her will or she was being very clever and he wished he knew which it was. And he was a complete noddicock for letting it bother him.

He decided to change the subject and began a discourse on the relative merits of Glasgow and Edinburgh and the difficulties of travelling to the very north where there were few roads and riding was the best way to get about and where, until recently, packhorses were still the accepted way of transporting goods.

'But we are progressing,' he said, as they stopped for one of the many changes of horses. 'Telford and McAdam are both Scotsmen. Telford, in particular, has built over a thousand miles of road, connecting all the sizeable towns, and bridged over a thousand rivers.' He smiled. 'Like the fen country, we have a great many waterways too, Miss Sadler.'

Relieved to be talking generalities again, she encouraged him to go on, soaking up the facts he told her, descriptions of people and places, the local customs, until they arrived at the Crown in Penrith where the horses were changed for the last eighteen miles to Carlisle.

The road ran over very rough country and she was shaken about like a rattle in a drum, musing ruefully that when the coach was full there was less room to be thrown about, though whether the close proximity of her fellow passengers and Captain Blair in particular was preferable she did not know. And to add to her discomfort, the sunshine of the morning had turned to rain again and her feet and fingers were frozen. She was glad when they sighted the walls and towers of Carlisle and a few minutes later turned into the yard of the Crown and Mitre and drew to a stop.

It was then she was dismayed to learn that this was a scheduled stopping place and the coach was going no further that night. 'No, miss,' the guard told her, as she gave him the usual tip, before going into the inn. 'The coach don't move no more until five in the morning. Me and Joe Grinley, we're off back to Manchester, you'll have a new driver and guard tomorrow.'

Now she was really in trouble. For a foolish minute she thought of sleeping in the coach until it left again but she knew that would not be allowed. Besides, the Captain already had hold of her elbow and was guiding her indoors out of the rain, and issuing his usual orders. He had a way of making people take notice, of jumping to do his bidding at once and a that without a single complaint. She concluded he was not short of funds. But she was.

She sat through a meal she had no appetite for, wondering what would happen when the innkeeper discovered she had no money to pay for it, or for her room, which was even now being made ready for her. What did one do in such circumstances? Ask for time to pay? Pretend you had been robbed? Borrow? Captain Blair would lend her money if she asked him, but on one thing she was determined; she would not confide her dilemma to her unsolicited escort. Although it was still only six in the evening, she

excused herself, saying she was very tired and was
going to bed if they were to make an early start in the
morning.

'Of course.' He rose. 'I will go and make sure your
room is ready.'

She went and waited in the vestibule, so wrapped up
in her problem, she was unaware of what was going on
around her. She would have to offer her brooch as
payment. But her brooch was worth a great deal more
than a single night's bed and board and she needed
money for Glasgow as well; she had no idea how long
she would have to wait there, and without the benefit
of Captain Blair's assistance.

She would have to sell the trinket. But where? She
looked around a little wildly. Whom should she ask?
Through an open door she caught sight of the coachman enjoying a pipe of tobacco with his guard. The
room was full of smoke and there were no ladies
present, but she felt she had no choice. She went to
the door. 'Mr Grinley,' she called softly, not daring to
enter the male sanctum. 'May I speak to you?'

He excused himself from his fellows and joined her.
'Yes, miss, what can I do for you?'

'Is there anywhere nearby where I can sell a piece
of jewellery?'

'Jewellery?' he queried in surprise. 'Do you mean to
say you are that low in the stirrups. . .'

'Not yet, but this journey has been fraught with
delay, and I may yet have need of more funds before I
reach its end.'

'Why not ask the Captain? I'll wager he'll stand
buff.'

'No.' She spoke more sharply than she intended,

making him smile. 'He need know nothing about it. If you do not know where I may dispose of some jewellery, then tell me who might. And do not say the Captain,' she added fiercely as he opened his mouth. 'I want you to promise you will say nothing of it to him.'

'If you say so, miss,' he agreed. 'There's a pawnshop about two streets away. It's not difficult to find. Come, I'll point the way.'

She accompanied him to the door and listened carefully to his instructions, then she returned to the vestibule to find Captain Blair had returned from his errand.

'Your room is at the top of the stairs and facing the front,' he said. 'Your trunk and hot water have been taken up.'

'Thank you. I will bid you goodnight, then.'

'Goodnight, Miss Sadler. I have asked the chambermaid to call you in good time to have breakfast before the coach leaves.'

'That is very kind of you.'

'Think no more of it.' He paused, wondering why she looked so distracted. Her eyes were bright and her cheeks more than usually pink. Surely she did not think he was going to kiss her again? Much as he would have liked to, he would not risk it a second time. 'The talk is that the weather is set to become still colder and may even snow,' he said. 'You would be wise to wrap up as warmly as possible tomorrow. I believe extra undergarments are more efficacious than top clothes for maintaining warmth.'

She stared at him in shocked disbelief, unable to answer him. That he had been insolent enough to mention her underwear at all was more than enough, but she was suddenly confronted with a memory of her first night on the road. She had been wearing two layers of underwear and someone had helped her to bed; she remembered gentle hands and a soft voice. They had belonged to the Captain! Without a word, she turned from him and fled up the stairs to her room, banging the door behind her and flinging herself on the bed.

How could he? How could he humiliate her like that? She had forgiven him for that kiss, but how could she forgive him for that? She lay on the bed, shaking with mortification, imagining his hands on her clothes, undoing the tiny buttons, touching her flesh. She had been irredeemably compromised long before he had kissed her. How could she go on? But there was no way back. And she still had the hotel bill to pay the next morning.

Pulling herself together, she rose and went to the mirror to tidy her face and hair, replaced her bonnet, put her cloak about her shoulders and left the room. watching carefully for Captain Blair as she made her way down the stairs and out onto the street.

Joe Grinley, sucking thoughtfully on his pipe, was wondering how he could let Captain Blair know what Miss Sadler planned without breaking his promise to her, when he caught sight of her slight figure in its all-enveloping black cloak passing the window.

'Captain,' he said, addressing the man sitting morosely on the other side of the hearth with a quart of ale in front of him and his chin sunk on his chest. 'I do not know if you are interested, but that there little lady has just gone out into the street.'

Duncan, who had been brooding over his asinine stupidity, lifted startled eyes to the coachman. 'What did you say?'

'I said Miss Sadler has just gone out. I wonder where she is off to at this time o' night?'

The young man abandoned his ale and flew out of the door, 'like a bat out o' hell,' the coachman was heard to say.

Helen was just disappearing round the corner as Duncan emerged from the inn. He hurried after her. What was the silly chit up to now? he asked himself. Surely he had not driven her to do something silly, she was much more level-headed than that and was more inclined to ring a peal over him than take flight. He resisted the impulse to run after her and demand to know where she was going; such an action would put him into even deeper hot water. He walked slowly behind her, ready to dodge out of sight if she should look back, but she was intent on her errand and marched steadfastly forward.

He watched her enter a building over which hung the three balls of a pawnbroker. He crept closer, though he dare not enter. He stood and peered in through the grimy window and saw her hand something over to the man who sat on a stool at a high table. He could see the man's lips moving but could not make out what was said and then the man offered her money, some paper, some coin. She hesitated, then took it and turned to leave. Duncan hid round the side of the shop and watched her walk back the way she had come. So that was it! She had run out of blunt. Poor child; as if she did not have enough to contend with.

He went into the shop. The pawnbroker was still sitting on the stool with a magnifying glass in his hand, examining the piece of jewellery Helen had just sold him. 'How much do you want for that?' Duncan demanded, pointing to the brooch.

'This?' The man turned it over in his hand. 'Fine piece, this.'

'I am sure it is. How much?'

'Two hundred pounds.'

'Two hundred! Are you run mad?'

''Tis worth every penny.'

'Never mind how much it's worth, how much did you give the lady?'

'What's it to you how much I give her?'

'She is my wife.' He grabbed the man by his collar, almost pulling him off the stool. 'How much did you give her? I want the truth, or you'll rue the day you ever tried to gull me.'

'Twenty quineas.'

Duncan released the man and took a purse from his tail pocket. 'Here's the twenty and five more for your trouble. That's a fair profit, wouldn't you say?' He slammed the money on the table, making both it and its owner jump. 'The pin, if you please.'

Silently the man handed it over. Duncan put it into his purse and returned it to his pocket. 'I bid you good day, sir.'

It was not until he was safely in his room at the inn that he took the brooch out to examine it. He had had it in his hand before very briefly when he confiscated it from the little pickpocket but he had assumed it was paste. But pawnbrokers did not give twenty guineas for imitation jewellery, nor were they generous even for the real thing. A careful look at it soon established that the gems were real and the gold eighteen-carat. Two hundred pounds was perhaps its true value.

But how did a little nobody like Miss Sadler come to own such a piece? Was it hers to sell in the first place? If she had stolen it and was running from justice, why wear it so openly? And why wait until now to dispose of it? Unless she thought someone was after her. Was that the reason for her continually changing coaches; to foil her pursuers? But that was nonsense, a thief would be quiet as a mouse, try to blend in with her surroundings, not draw attention to herself. Miss Sadler had a knack of making herself noticed.

He smiled to himself. This latest fantasy of his was every bit as wide of the mark as his idea that she was a princess. As soon as the opportunity presented itself he would grill her, find out, once and for all, where she was going and why, and how she came to be in possession of such a valuable piece of jewellery. If she could offer him a satisfactory explanation, then he would return it to her. If not. . . He refused to dwell on the alternative.

With the money in her hand—far less than she thought the brooch had been worth—Helen hurried back to her room at the inn and went to bed. At least she could pay for her night's stay now and no one the wiser. Mr Grinley was off back to Manchester the next morning and in any case he had promised not to say anything.

She woke next morning to find the rain had turned to sleet and in spite of her undiminished fury with

Captain Blair, she decided to take his advice and wear extra clothing. As soon as she was dressed she went downstairs to be told the coach was just leaving; there would be a stop for breakfast at Gretna Green. She hurried to join the other passengers in the yard, determined to behave with the dignity she should have maintained from the first; the cool politeness of a lady of quality. She would make it clear to him that such familiarity was not to be tolerated. The trouble was that it was all too late, much too late.

She was not given the opportunity to put her resolve into practice because the Captain was nowhere to be seen. Nor had he put in an appearance when it was time to leave. Telling herself that she would not mind if she never saw him again did no good at all; she found herself watching the inn door for his tall figure to appear, searching the people milling about the yard for a tanned face and curling brown hair, listening for that warm voice, even if it was teasing her. She did not want to go on without him.

The nearer she came to her destination, the more nervous and apprehensive she grew. She needed a friend to see her to the end, someone to turn to if things went badly wrong. For all his over-familiarity, for all his insolence, the Captain had been considerate and helpful and protective. And could she honestly say she had not encouraged his impertinence by allowing him to help her, even dictate to her? It had all started with that young urchin; she should have left well alone.

'All aboard!' the new guard called, as the coachman who was to take them the rest of the way took up the reins and climbed onto the box.

She took her seat, hardly noticing the other passengers, knowing only that she felt miserably alone and more afraid of the future than ever before.

It was exactly five o'clock and the coach had begun to move, when the door was flung open and Captain Blair climbed aboard. Helen was so relieved, she forgot she was supposed to be angry with him, and gave him a fleeting smile as she wished him good morning.

It began to snow in earnest as they toiled up hill and down dale, with the coachman urging the horses on, unwilling to risk being bogged down. None of the other passengers, three men and a woman, was inclined for conversation and apart from a greeting and trivial comments on the weather and the advisability of staying at home if you didn't have to travel, nothing of any importance was said.

Duncan, conscious of the brooch in his purse and dwelling on what he might have to say to Helen when he was alone with her, said not a word, though when he would be given the opportunity to interrogate her he did not know. After his dreadful error of the night before, he doubted she would allow him anywhere near her. Why could he not have held his tongue, or at least chosen his words more carefully? It just proved he had been too long a soldier.

She had said she was being met in Glasgow and he might learn more if he saw who met her. But that did not ring true either because no one could possibly know when to expect her after all the delays.

He glanced at her as the coach stopped on the brow of a hill and the guard climbed down to put a drag on the rear wheel. She was staring straight ahead looking very depressed and he longed to comfort her, to tell her he did not care who she was or what she had done;

he wanted only to see her smile, to laugh with her, to hold her... He stopped his errant thoughts; that was what had caused the trouble between them in the first place and telling himself she had asked for it, did not console him at all.

An hour later they crossed the border into Scotland and drew up at the Gretna Hotel. Helen stepped down before Duncan could emerge and help her and hurried into the inn ahead of him. After the poor supper she had had the night before, she was hungry and knowing she now had more than ample money to pay for her breakfast, she was determined to enjoy it. She crossed the threshold of the dining room and then stopped so suddenly that Duncan, immediately behind her, almost fell over her. She ignored his apology, because sitting at a table near the window, laughing at her obvious amazement, were Tom and Dorothy.

CHAPTER NINE

'WHAT are you doing here?' Helen asked, hurrying over to where they sat. 'What happened? I thought you were going to your aunt's.'

'We did but she wasn't at home,' Dorothy said, as Tom rose to greet her. 'Would you believe the house was all shut up? We were told she had gone to Bath, of all the things to do in the middle of winter. We were at a stand.'

'Sit down and we will tell you all about it,' Tom said, drawing out a chair for Helen. It was then that she realised Duncan was right behind her and was pulling up a fourth chair. There was nothing she could do but sit down beside him with a good grace. Now was not the time to tell them that she and the Captain had had a falling out.

'There was nowhere we could stay in Derby,' Dorothy went on. 'And even if Papa had thought of looking for us there, I did not want it to be like that, with us unmarried and no one to persuade him to allow it. I had been counting on Aunt Sophia.'

'There was nothing for it, but to revert to our original plan,' Tom put in.

'But how did you get here ahead of us?'

'We came post chaise.'

'Over Shap Fell?' Duncan queried. 'We heard there had been a landslip.'

'So there was. We came by way of Appleby and I

can tell you the terrain was infernally rough. We were lucky to have a very light vehicle and good horses. Those we picked up at Kendal were top-of-the-trees prime cattle.'

'The best in the country, so I've heard,' Duncan said. 'They need to be with the work they have to do.'

'But how did you get here, if Shap Fell was closed?' Dorothy asked.

'Oh, we came by way of the Lakes,' Helen said. 'Windermere and Grasmere and Ullswater. It was beautiful country and I am glad we made the detour.' She paused. 'Does that mean you are married now?'

'Not yet, we only arrived a few moments before you. You cannot imagine how delighted I was when I saw you getting down from the coach. Now we can have a proper ceremony and you can be witnesses. You will, won't you? Both of you? You have no idea how much it will mean to me, to have friends to see us married instead of strangers. Do say yes.'

'Of course we will,' Helen said without even bothering to consult Captain Blair. Let him refuse if he dare!

Duncan smiled and said nothing, knowing it would make no difference if he did. He had to stay; he had not yet spoken to her about the brooch.

'The truth is, I am not sure how we go about it,' Tom said. Then, to Duncan, 'I believe we have to find the blacksmith.'

Duncan laughed. 'Blacksmith, landlord or toll-keeper, it is all the same. All you have to do is declare, before witnesses, your willingness to marry, no banns, no licence, no parson.'

'And that is legal?'

'Yes, as legal as being married in church.'

'It doesn't seem right to me,' Helen murmured. 'Not without a priest. After all, you are making a sacred vow and it should be done before God.'

'Oh, please do not put obstacles in our way,' Dorothy cried. 'I shall die of shame if we cannot be married at once.'

'Why not see the parson?' Duncan said. 'I am sure a proper ceremony can be arranged.'

Dorothy clapped her hands with delight. 'There! You see how much we need you.'

The men went off to make the arrangements and Helen accompanied Dorothy up to a private room Tom had bespoken for her to help her dress. That was the reason for the pink gauze gown with the rose satin slip and the rosebuds, Helen decided, as Dorothy took it from her portmanteau and shook it out.

'It's very creased,' Helen said. 'Shall I ask a chambermaid to press it? We could have hot water and towels brought up too. After all that travelling, I, for one, feel very grubby.'

An hour and a half later all four stood in the little church as the parson, still rubbing sleep from his eyes, began the marriage service.

Helen found the words of the service very moving and the shy responses of the young couple made her yearn for the kind of love they had for each other. But who would love her now, penniless, unchaperoned, thoroughly compromised by the Captain's behaviour? A tiny bit foxed she had been that first night, too tired and unwell to know what she was doing. If Captain Blair had been a true gentleman, he would not have taken advantage of her.

No, she scolded herself, she could not entirely blame him; she had wanted to be accepted as one of the lower orders, had lied to achieve it, and she had no cause for complaint when she was all too successful. Right from the first she and Captain Blair had behaved with the easy familiarity of old friends, something which would have taken months to achieve in her former life, if they had ever met at all.

She could not understand it. Did losing all your money make you a different person? Was she no longer the properly brought up daughter of a peer simply because she was almost penniless? She risked a glance at the man at her side. He was looking very serious, his brown eyes fixed on Tom and Dorothy, but he was the most handsome man she had ever met.

One searching look from those remarkable eyes and she found herself shaking, one touch and she melted like wax running down a candle. And the thought of parting from him filled her with panic. It was simply no good trying to be angry with him, she loved him. The discovery was too much for her; the tears started to roll slowly down her cold cheeks and she could do nothing to stop them.

Duncan, hearing the faint indrawing of her breath, turned to look at her and was surprised to see her tears. The disdainful, the haughty, the cool Miss Sadler was weeping, and she was no longer disdainful or haughty or even cool, though her cheeks were pinched with cold. Something had touched a soft spot to make her cry and he longed to comfort her. He half lifted a hand towards her but thought better of it and dropped it back to his side.

'I now declare you man and wife.' The parson's

words broke in on his thoughts. Man and wife. Duncan Blair and Helen Sadler. Could it, would it work? But he did not know if that was her real name. Did it matter? And she was not a gentlewoman, not of the aristocracy, not someone of whom his father would approve. Did that matter either? She was probably a liar, might even be a thief. Was that important to him? No, he told himself, the only thing that mattered was that he loved her.

Why he loved her, he could not say, except that his whole mind was concentrated on her, on everything she did and said, every nuance of her speech, every fleeting expression which crossed her piquant face. His body ached to hold her in his arms, to rouse her from her underlying sadness to ecstasy, to make her happy. He knew he was a fool but he could not help it.

'Oh, I am so happy for you!' Helen brushed the tears from her cheeks with the back of her gloved hand and moved forward to embrace Dorothy. 'May you have all the happiness in the world.'

'Not all,' said Duncan wryly. 'We need some of it.'

'Yes,' Dorothy said, beaming round at everyone. 'I wish you both happy too.'

Duncan felt tempted to ask Helen to become his wife there and then, but she had deliberately turned from him to offer her congratulations to Tom and he knew she would not accept him in her present mood.

'Come back to the hotel,' Tom said. 'We have a wedding breakfast laid out in a private parlour, just for the four of us.'

'Oh, but we would be intruding,' Helen demurred. If she spent any more time with Duncan, pretending in front of Tom and Dorothy that there was nothing wrong, she would give herself away. 'I am sure you want to be by yourselves.'

'No, no, we have plenty of time for that, all our lives,' Dorothy said, making Duncan smile. Having obtained her heart's desire, the chit was frightened of what came next. He did not think Helen would be afraid, her response to his kiss had told him that. There was fire beneath that cool exterior, fire and depths he had as yet no knowledge of. But she could cry too... Why had she been crying? He must know.

He grinned at Tom. 'You stopped us having breakfast if you recall. Miss Sadler and I have eaten nothing since supper last night and I, for one, am extremely hungry.'

Helen silently followed as Tom and Dorothy led the way back to the hotel. The coach had gone on to Glasgow without them and there was nothing to do before another one came along with spare seats, and she, too, was hungry. But if Captain Blair thought he could come up sweet once more, he had better think again.

They were halfway through the meal and drinking a toast to the newly weds when a commotion outside heralded the arrival of an unscheduled carriage. Helen became dimly aware of the ostlers calling out and horses neighing and a voice, loud and insistent. 'Where are they?' A moment later the door was flung open and a tall man with greying hair stood on the threshold. His top hat and well-cut frockcoat were covered in mud splashed from horses' hooves and the ends of his muslin cravat, once pristine and carefully tied, were drooping.

Dorothy, who had her back to the door, heard it crash back and turned to look. 'Papa!'

'I'll give you Papa,' he said, striding forward and stopping in front of the quartet. 'What do you think you are about, child? Your poor Mama is distraught and I have had to leave important negotiations to come chasing after you. I pray God it is not too late. You will never take if this escapade gets out, you know that don't you? No one will have you. And as for this scapegrace....' He pointed at Tom. 'I've a mind to thrash you within an inch of your life. Now, get out of my daughter's life. We will concoct some tale. Dorothy has been staying with her Aunt Sophia, that will do.'

'Aunt Sophia is from home,' Dorothy said, as if that were the most important point to pick up in the whole tirade. 'We went there.'

'You went to see your aunt?' He stared at her in surprise. 'Why do that?'

'To wait for you. We thought Aunt Sophia would help us to persuade you.'

'I never heard such a fribble. My sister would no more condone this than I would.'

'Then I am glad she was not at home. Tom and I are man and wife now. There is nothing you can do about it.'

All the fight seemed to go out of him. He sank into a vacant chair at an adjoining table and stared at her for a long time. She reached out and took Tom's hand. 'It was done properly by the parson, with witnesses.'

'When?'

'An hour ago.'

'Then you have not...' He stopped. 'The marriage has not been...'

'Consummated?' queried Tom, guessing what was in his mind. 'No, sir, it has not. But that doesn't make it any less of a marriage. Unless Dorothy wants it, there will be no annulment.'

'Certainly not!' Dorothy said, finding a new courage now that she had the ring on her finger. 'Tom, how could you think I would want that?'

'Then married we are and married we remain, to the end of our days.'

She smiled at her father. 'Papa, please accept it. There is no way you can undo it and I do so want you to be happy for me.'

Mr Carstairs looked at Duncan and Helen. 'And am I to assume, sir, that you were party to this? You helped take my child from me.'

'Mrs Thurborn is not a child,' Duncan said, making Dorothy giggle at the sound of her new name and almost proving Mr Carstairs' point. If Arabella had not been faint-hearted when he suggested it all those years ago, they would have been married in like manner. It took real conviction to go through with a runaway marriage and Arabella, in spite of her protestations, had not been sure enough of her love to defy her father. For the first time he was glad of that. Now, he realised, fate had had something else in mind for him.

'The Captain and Helen were our chaperones and witnesses,' Tom put in.

'Captain?'

'Captain Duncan Blair of the Prince of Wales's Own Hussars, at your service, sir,' Duncan said, inclining his head.

'And this?' He turned towards Helen.

'Mrs Blair,' Duncan said before Helen could reply herself. 'My lady wife.'

Helen drew her breath in sharply. How dare he! How dare he be so presumptuous! 'Mr Carstairs. . .' she began.

'Tom wanted to do everything aboveboard,' Duncan went on. 'He told us of his plans right from the first and as my wife and I were already making arrangements to come to Scotland, we agreed to chaperone the young couple.'

'It seems a bit smoky to me,' Mr Carstairs said, not altogether convinced. 'Where does Sophia come into it?'

Duncan shrugged and looked at Tom; he had done his best and now it was up to the young man.

'Dorothy wanted someone from her family at her side,' Tom said. 'We thought that if Miss Carstairs could persuade you to see things our way, there would be no necessity to come all the way to Scotland. As she was not there. . .' He smiled at the older man. 'We had no choice. Captain and Mrs Blair could not delay their journey and they would not leave us unchaperoned. You do see how it came about. . .'

'Oh, what's done is done, I suppose,' Mr Carstairs said, making Dorothy fly across and put her arms round him.

'Oh, Papa, I knew you would come round.'

He disentangled himself from her. 'But I still have words to say to that young man. In private, I think. After that, I shall be hungry as a hunter.' He looked at the food left on the table. 'I'll have some of the capon and that game pie.' He rose and Tom followed him to the other side of the room, where they were deep in conversation for several minutes.

'Captain Blair, I must thank you for what you did for us,' Dorothy said. 'I am sure that telling Papa we had a married couple to chaperone us all the way made all the difference.' She giggled suddenly. 'What a good fibber you are, Captain Blair. I do not know how you kept a straight face. And you, too, Helen.'

'Oh, Miss Sadler is a master when it comes to hummery,' Duncan said laconically, looking not at Dorothy but at Helen as he spoke.

Helen had no answer to that, but it reinforced her conviction that he suspected her of telling untruths. Could he possibly know her real name? Oh, how she wished she had never started the deception! Scott's verse came to her mind: 'Oh, what a tangled web we weave, When first we practise to deceive.' She, who had always been honest as the day, had woven a web of deceit which was going to enmesh her totally unless she could rid herself of the ubiquitous Captain before they reached Glasgow. It was enough to make her dear mother turn in her grave.

Mr Carstairs and Tom shook hands and returned to the rest of the party. 'Food,' Mr Carstairs said. 'Then back to Derby. Sophia will be back by now. She will have to be a conspirator whether she wills it or not.' He sat down and helped himself to food while the others, who had already eaten their fill, sat and watched.

'The weather is not good, sir,' Duncan said. 'I advise you not to delay your return.'

'No, you are right.' Reluctantly he put down his knife and fork and stood up. 'Come, Tom. Come,

Dorothy. My carriage is outside. I ordered the horses before I came in.'

Duncan and Helen followed them out to the yard where a roomy private carriage with good springs and padded seats stood with a pair of top-class horses already in the traces. A liveried driver sat on the box, reins and whip in his hands. Helen embraced Dorothy. 'I wish you happy, my dear, and all the luck in the world.'

'And you,' Dorothy said, then added in a whisper, 'don't let him get away, whatever you do. You were made for each other.' Then she skipped away and got into the coach, while the men shook hands. Helen stood beside Duncan and watched them go, her smile stiff on her face. As soon as they were lost to view she turned from him without speaking and made her way back into the inn.

'Miss Sadler.' He hurried after her. 'We must talk.'

'I have nothing to say to you.'

'No? But I have something to say to you.' He put a hand on her arm. 'At least hear me out.'

She shrugged him off. 'Why should I? You have behaved abominably and you know it.'

'By introducing you as my wife? If I had not done so, what do you think Mr Carstairs would have said? What would he have done? An unmarried couple as escort would hardly be considered suitable chaperones. And your reputation. . .'

She did not need him to tell her that her reputation had been thoroughly compromised and wondered what the Earl of Strathrowan might say if he learned about it. 'It is in shreds already because of you, Captain

Blair,' she said. 'I did not ask for your escort or your protection. I should have been better off without it.'

'If you truly believe that you are deceiving yourself as well as me,' he said, taking her elbow and guiding her firmly back to the private parlour where the innkeeper was clearing away the remains of their meal. 'Leave us,' he commanded, then to Helen, as the man disappeared, 'Sit down.'

He was so much taller than she was and she hated having to crane her neck to look up at him; it gave him the advantage. She sat down suddenly, as if her knees would no longer support her, but she managed to sound cool. 'I am seated, Captain Blair, but I tell you now, I am not accustomed to being treated with such arrogance. I'll allow that telling Mr Carstairs I was your wife was perhaps for the best, and it was not that I objected to, and you know it.'

He drew a chair up and sat facing her. 'You are complaining that I kissed you?'

'Yes. And that first night in Northampton. . .'

'What about it? I did no more than I would have done for any drinking companion who was a little cut over the head, I carried you to bed and loosened your clothing, no more, though I admit I should not have alluded to it afterwards and for that I apologise.'

'Drinking companion!' She sprang to her feet, anger making her green eyes glitter like emeralds and her cheeks scarlet. 'Is that how you think of me?'

He laughed; she was even more beautiful when angry. 'No, I do not usually kiss drinking companions.'

'No, but I expect you kiss ladies at every opportunity.'

'Now that is something which I confess has been puzzling me.'

'What has?' she asked, taken by surprise.

'Whether you are a lady or no. A lady would never travel alone and even a lady's companion would have an escort. I cannot imagine any responsible employer expecting you to make the journey unaccompanied. . .'

'No doubt he has his reasons.'

'He? Not she?'

'Both,' she said quickly.

He noticed the slip. 'You know,' he said gently, 'you are either a great simpleton or a great deceiver and to be honest I do not really care for either.'

'Then why insist on staying with me?'

He smiled ruefully. 'That, too, is something that has been baffling me. It might be plain curiosity, but I think it is more than that. I do not wish to see you in a bumblebath, you are too beautiful to languish in gaol. . .'

'Gaol?' She was startled.

He took the brooch from his purse and laid it on the table among the dirty plates with their congealing food, where it winked incongruously up at them. 'Is this yours?'

She gasped. 'Where did you get it?'

'I bought it from the man you sold it to.'

'Why? How did you know I had sold it?'

'I followed you to the shop. Now, are you going to tell me where you got it?'

'It was mine to sell if I wished. I have had it ever since my seventeenth birthday. My papa gave it to me.' Tears stood in her eyes, making him hate himself. 'I did not want to sell it, but I needed the money. I thought I had enough to last me until we reached Glasgow, but what with one thing and another. . .'

'You could not pay for your board and lodgings?'

'No.'

He sank on his haunches beside her chair and covered her hands with his own. 'Oh, my dear, I am so sorry. But why did you not tell me of your difficulties? I could have paid your bills, given you money. You did not need to sell your most precious possession.'

'It is not my most precious possession. I still have my mother's betrothal ring but if there is no one to meet me in Glasgow, then that will have to go too.'

'No, it will not.' He put the brooch in her hand and gently closed her fingers over it. 'Take it back, my dear, with my compliments.'

She gave a cracked laugh. 'And what will I have to pay for it? Another kiss? Perhaps something more?' She put the pin back on the table. 'No, Captain Blair, the price is too high.'

He smiled. 'You have not heard it yet.'

She sighed. 'No doubt you are going to tell me.'

'Do you think you will be happy with your new family? What is it you are going to be, a governess or a companion?'

'I truly don't know until I get there. It was all arranged for me.'

'Good God!' He could not suppress his astonishment and his admiration for her courage. That she was now telling the truth, he did not doubt. 'I think you are too young to be a governess or a companion. . .'

She was about to give him another set-down but decided against it. 'I am four-and-twenty.' She smiled ruefully. 'Not quite at my last prayers, but very close to it.'

'Nonsense!' he said, concealing his surprise. He had taken her for nineteen or twenty at the most. 'Why is someone as beautiful as you are still single?'

'Because that is what I choose to be, Captain.'

'Then you are not going to Scotland to be married?' he queried. 'There is no impatient bridegroom waiting for you?'

'Of course not.'

'What manner of man might he be, the man to capture your hand?' he went on. 'No doubt he would need to have a title and a fortune, so that you would never have to sell any of your possessions again.'

'Wealth would not be a consideration,' she said, wondering where his questions were leading. 'I may be poor, but I am not mercenary. To me love and fidelity are the foremost requisites on both sides. They are more important than riches and definitely more important than a man's consequence in Society. I could not marry a man who did not love me and whom I did not love. My papa and mama adored each other. Papa was inconsolable when Mama died. It changed him. He was never the same afterwards.' Her voice had taken on a wistful note which was mixed with a kind of brittleness.

'And now you are quite alone?'

'Yes, but not as helpless as you would like to believe, Captain.'

'Oh, I do not think you are helpless, Miss Sadler. What will you do if word gets out about this little misadventure?'

'Misadventure! Is that what you call it? But why should anything be said about it?'

'Dorothy or Tom have only to drop a hint when they return to London. . .'

'Captain, we are a long way from London and I cannot think that any of my one-time friends or acquaintances have the least interest in my doings. I need consider only my own conscience and that is clear.'

'All the same. . .' He paused, taking her hand again. 'We could be married. Here. Today.'

She looked up at him and was nearly undone. If he had asked her in any other circumstances, if she had a dowry, if her father had not been a suicide, if he had said he loved her, she might have said yes. She would have said yes because she loved him.

As it was she stiffened her back and looked back at him with unblinking green eyes. 'Captain, have you run mad? We are complete strangers. You know nothing about me and I know nothing of you.' He opened his mouth to say something, but she stood up and went on. 'And that is how it will stay. Now, I am going to see if there is another coach to Glasgow today. The sooner we reach there, the sooner you may give up your self-appointed task of looking after me.'

'Oh, but I know a great deal about you,' he murmured to her departing back. 'You have shown me yourself with everyone we have met, everybody you have spoken to, fellow travellers, coachmen, innkeepers. You have demonstrated a huge concern for your fellow human beings and sympathy for their sufferings. You have shown a generous spirit and great courage, pride and humility in equal measure, a wide knowledge and wider intelligence, and a refusal to be beaten which is little short of obstinacy, traits far away and above what is necessary for a little schoolma'am or a lady's companion, though they could be the attributes of a loving wife.'

Love. She would not marry where that was lacking. But he had enough for both of them and he should have told her so instead of making it sound like a cold-blooded contract to get her out of a hobble. Sighing, he followed her and discovered there was a coach about to leave for Glasgow and little Miss Sadler was issuing orders about the stowing of her luggage. He smiled and went to her aid. Once that was done, he handed her in and took his place beside her in silence.

The coach was full both inside and out and everyone was talking about the prospects of severe weather and expressing their hope that they would reach their destinations before the roads became impassable, telling each other tales of blizzards and people getting lost and houses being covered, of horses floundering and coaches getting stuck fast, each story more improbable than the last.

But Helen hardly heard them. Captain Blair had made her immune to tall stories and she was more concerned with what lay in wait at the end of her journey. Now the Captain had put the idea in her head that no good employer would allow a young lady to travel alone, she could not shift it. The Earl was not her employer but her guardian; surely that should have made him more caring, not less? Had he been reluctant to take responsibility for her and hoped she would not attempt the journey at all?

She might, after all, have been better off accepting

Captain Blair's offer. But what did she know of him, apart from the fact that he was a soldier and a second son? She did not think he was without funds and she knew he could be kind and generous, that on many issues they agreed, that he could be a staunch ally and probably a fearsome enemy. He could be domineering too, and he was a card-player, but she knew nothing of his family, nor of his home. Did he live at home or in the saddle on some campaign or other? If she married him, would she be a camp follower? She shivered suddenly.

'You are cold?' His soft voice right against her ear startled her.

'No.'

'But you shivered.'

'Thoughts, Captain Blair, only thoughts.'

'A penny for them.'

'They are worthless, sir, still quite worthless.' She turned away from him and looked out of the window. The steady rain had turned to sleet, melting as it touched the road, but it was enough to make visibility poor and they slowed to a walk.

'I think not.' His voice was insistent. 'I'll wager you were thinking about the future, about what lies ahead of you, and wondering which is worse, a position you don't know about with a family you have never met, or being a soldier's wife. Am I correct?'

He was right, dreadfully right but she would never admit it. 'No. You would lose your bet, Captain, and serve you right too. And you know how much I loathe gambling.'

'That was not gambling, it was a certainty, and saying "I'll wager" is merely a figure of speech.'

'I know that, but you do play cards, you admitted it, and you said you always win.'

'Surely a game of cards to pass the time and a small bet on the outcome to enliven the interest, does not make me an out and out villain?'

'No. But it is a beginning, the start of the dreadful slide downhill to penury. . .'

'You have perhaps some experience of that? Is that why. . .?'

'No, it is not,' she snapped.

'Then why this aversion?'

'I could not marry a gambler and that is all there is to it.'

He laughed suddenly. 'No wonder you have never married if your requirements are so particular. I enjoy a hand of cards but I am not what you call a gambling man and I would not mind if I never had another wager, but I'll be blowed if I'd allow a woman to dictate to me on the matter.'

'Then it is just as well I refused you, isn't it?'

'It is indeed,' he said, with a grim smile. Which was not at all what he had meant to say.

They remained silent throughout the remainder of the journey, though there were a thousand questions she wanted to ask him, a thousand thoughts buzzing in her head, none of them coherent. Her fear of the perils of the road was nothing compared with her apprehension at what lay ahead of her.

They stopped frequently for a change of horses, sometimes being allowed down to take some refreshment, sometimes having food and drink brought out for them to consume on the way. No one wanted to be delayed a second longer than was necessary and they all gazed at the sky, gloomily expecting the worst or optimistically forecasting a change for the better, depending on their temperaments.

They passed through Sanquar at a brisk trot, then on to the Elvanfoot Inn and up across the moors to Douglas Dale, where they stopped at what the coachman proudly told them was the biggest and busiest hostelry in Scotland. Here the horses were changed and they were allowed half an hour for a meal. Then on again to Knowknock and Hamilton where the horses were changed for the last time and, with the smell of home in their nostrils, made a final burst of speed through wooded countryside and clattered into a town which could only be Glasgow itself.

It was late at night, but the place was still busy, with lights showing in many of the shops and people on the cobbled streets, some wrapped up well against the bitter weather, others poorly clad and shivering. For once, Helen was too absorbed in her own concerns to worry about them.

The guard gave a blast on his horn as they turned into Gallowgate and two minutes later they pulled up in the yard of the Old Saracen's Head.

'Here we are, safe and sound,' Helen heard someone say and they all tumbled out, one after the other, clapping their hands to their sides and stamping their feet while their baggage was taken down, and then hurrying into the inn for warmth, food and possibly a bed.

Helen, conscious that the Captain was still with her, hurried in ahead of him, anxious to make enquiries about being met before he could overhear.

'Someone from the Earl,' the innkeeper repeated

when she cornered him in the back parlour. 'No, there's been no one.'

'Are you sure? It might have been any time in the last three days.'

'Nay, I'd know if there had, lass, the Earl is well known to us and we'd have been told if he was expecting anyone. Besides, he's been ill, not entertaining visitors, you see.'

'Ill? How ill?' This was something she had not considered.

'Bad, I think, but he pulled through, though he's no been out since.'

'But he is expecting me. Is there a coach to Killearn?'

'Not this side of Saturday, miss, and only if the weather improves.'

'I shall have to stay here then and hope someone comes for me. Have you a room? A single room?'

'I think I can find ye one, miss, but are ye sure ye've not made a mistake? It is the Earl who's expecting ye?'

'Yes. And please, could you show me up to my room at once? I am very cold and tired.'

'Yes, miss. If someone were to come from the Earl, who shall I say is waiting? Not that I think they will, there'll be nothin' moving' on the roads taenight.'

'Miss Sanghurst. Miss Helen Sanghurst. My trunk is in the hall; it is engraved with the letters H and S intertwined. Would you have it brought up?'

'Of course, miss. Follow me.'

He led her through a door on the far side of the room, so that when Duncan came in two minutes later she was nowhere to be seen. And neither was the innkeeper, who knew Captain Duncan Blair very well indeed and would have wondered why she was looking for a messenger from the Earl when his son had come in on the same coach.

Having discovered from one of the servants that the young lady had retired to her room, Duncan ordered a room for himself and went to bed. There was nothing to be done until the morning. Now he was almost home he began to wonder what might be in store for him. He prayed he would find his father well and in good spirits. After India, the damp climate of Scotland got into his bones, he said, and the mists which gathered on the hills filled him with aches and pains. Perhaps it had been no more than a chill and he would find him hale and hearty.

Duncan was up, dressed and out before dawn. The snow and sleet had stopped but the wind was whipping up slate-grey clouds from the north and he knew there was more to come. The sooner they were on their way the better; he had no intention of waiting until Saturday for a coach. They had come so far and he was not going to be baulked at the last hurdle. Miss Sadler wanted to go to Killearn and to Killearn they would both go.

He wrapped his cloak around him and pulled his hat firmly on his head as he set off into the centre of the town, where he knew there was a coachbuilder. An hour later he returned to the Old Saracen's Head with a stout box-like carriage pulled by two small but sturdy ponies, one of which was ridden by a postboy, who was not a boy at all, but an ancient Highlander, as tough as they came.

Leaving the equipage in the care of an ostler, he strode into the inn just as Helen came down the stairs, muffled in a cloak and with her bonnet tied on with a scarf. Seeing him she hesitated with her hand on the rail and then lifted her chin and came down the last few steps. 'Good morning, Captain Blair.'

'Ma'am.' He made a perfunctory leg. 'Have you had breakfast?'

'Yes, in my room.'

'Good, we have no time to waste.' He stepped forward to take her elbow. 'Come along.'

She pulled herself away just as the innkeeper came through from the back regions of the house. He looked up at them and smiled. 'So you found each other then?'

'Yes,' they answered in unison, each thinking that the other had been making enquiries.

'Ye'll be leaving at once, then?'

'Yes, at once,' Duncan said. 'Please have the lady's trunk brought down and put in the chaise in the yard.'

'Verra good, Captain.'

'And make up a hamper of food and a bottle of wine.'

'Aye, sir, and shall I be fetchin' a hot brick for the lady's feet?'

'Good idea. Yes, please.'

The man disappeared and Helen turned on Duncan. 'Just what are you about, Captain?'

'We are going the rest of the way by chaise.'

'The rest of the way?'

'To Killearn. That is where you want to go, is it not?'

'Yes, but. . .'

'No buts. Unless you want to be stuck in a strange town for the rest of the winter?'

'No, I do not, but I am told there is a coach on Saturday.'

'Three days away. I, for one, am not prepared to wait that long.'

'And I would rather do that than spend another minute in your company.' Oh, why was she snapping at him? The reason she did not want his company had nothing to do with his behaviour, not if she were honest with herself. It was all to do with being Helen Sanghurst, not Helen Sadler, and the shame she felt.

'And what if it snows so hard nothing can move? You could be here for weeks.'

She craned her neck to look past him into the street as someone opened the door. 'It has stopped snowing.'

'That is just the lull before the storm. Ask anyone. Ask that waiter over there.' He saw her hesitation and his voice softened. 'Please let bygones be bygones, Miss Sadler. I would not, for the world, have upset you. I apologise most humbly and I promise you that I will deliver you safely to wherever you have to go and nothing more.' He smiled crookedly and encompassed the inn with his hand. 'Better the devil you know. . .'

She could not risk being stuck; even if she sold her pin again and her mother's ring, she would not be paid their true worth and whatever they fetched would not last long. And a busy inn with all kinds of people coming and going, and where several virile men were employed who would not see her as a gentlewoman, was not a pleasing prospect. He was right; she would be better to trust herself to the devil she knew.

'Very well,' she said.

In no time at all, she was tucked into the corner of the coach all wrapped round with rugs and a hot brick at her feet. The Captain climbed in beside her and the ancient postboy mounted the nearside horse and they were away.

Out of the town they went at a steady trot, then along the north bank of the Clyde where Helen could see the spars and rigging of a myriad of ships lying at anchor there. A short rest at Dumbarton, more for the benefit of the ponies than the humans, then on again northwards in blinding snow, so that there was nothing to see of the distant mountains and even trees and cottages a few yards from the track were blurred.

'Can the old man see the road?' Helen asked.

'He knows it blindfold.'

'He might just as well be blindfold,' Helen said. 'I never realised that Scotland could be so bleak.'

'Anywhere would be bleak in a blizzard,' he said. 'You should see it in summer when the mountains are clothed in green and purple and the burns are tumbling crystal clear over the rocks; with deep, deep lochs reflecting the clouds, heather and coltsfoot and dog daisies carpeting the slopes and the yellow of gorse stark against a sky, blue as forget-me-nots. Sheep are scattered over the hillsides, grouse and woodcock nest in the grass and the rivers are full of fish. If anywhere on earth is heaven it is here, in summer.'

'You must love it very much.'

'I do.'

'How could you bear to leave it to go into the army?'

'I had little choice. I was sent by my papa.'

'Why?'

'Oh, he had his reasons.'

'Tell me.'

He grinned, half shame-faced. 'I fell in love.'

'You?' She resisted the impulse to laugh.

'It was what you might call puppy love,' he said, smiling a little at himself. 'It was considered unsuitable and I was sent away to get over it.'

'And did you?'

'Yes,' he said and meant it. 'I recovered.'

'But you never married?'

'I never found anyone else to engage my heart. There was a war on too, you remember.'

'And now are you going home for good?'

'I might be. It depends. I heard my father was ill.'

'And you were hurrying to his side! Oh, dear, all those delays and most of them caused by me. Oh, why did you stay with me, you could have gone on?'

'No, I could not. Something told me I had to look after you, an inner voice, my conscience, if you like. . .'

'Your conscience?'

'Conscience or heart, I am not sure which.'

They had been going slower and slower while they talked and now had come to a stop. He put his head out of the window. 'Hamish, what's amiss?'

It was no more than a short step for the man to get off the pony because the poor beast was up to its belly in snow. The rider struggled in driving snow to the door of the coach. 'I've lost the road, Captain. And the poor brutes is all but done for.'

'How far are we from home?'

'Six or seven miles, mebbe a wee bit more.'

'We could try and walk,' Helen said.

'Or ride.' Duncan stroked his chin. 'Hamish on one and you and I on the other.'

'Ye'd never mek it,' Hamish said bluntly. 'The pony'll niver carry the both of ye and the lass will freeze. Ye ride and I'll walk.' He floundered back to the ponies, only to find one of them had caught its foot in a hidden pothole and was so lame, it could not be ridden and indeed could not be expected to pull the carriage any further.

'How long d'you think it will take you to fetch help?'

'I canna say, Captain. There's auld Bailey's place nearby, if I c'n find it.'

'Then take the good pony. We will wait here.'

He was out of sight in a few yards. Helen was very afraid for him. How could he possibly find his way when there was nothing to see but a few trees and white and more white?

'If the snow eases, he'll be able to see the mountains,' Duncan said, returning to sit beside her. 'He knows their shapes and the shapes of all the rocks, and every twist and turn of every burn. He'll find his way.' But he was less confident than he sounded.

The waiting stretched from minutes to hours and there seemed no let-up in the snow. Everywhere was blanketed and as silent as the grave. Helen's feet and fingers soon became so numb that she could not feel them, and when Duncan fetched out the food and wine and encouraged her to eat she shook so much that could hardly put the food to her mouth and spilt the drink.

'This is what comes of giving that old lady your cloak,' he said. 'As if we did not have enough to contend with, you have caught a chill.'

'She needed it more than I did. I am not ill, just sleepy, so very, very sleepy. . .'

'No!' he commanded, shaking her. 'You must not go to sleep. Whatever happens, you must stay awake.'

'Sleep,' she mumbled. 'Let me sleep.'

'No! Talk to me. Say whatever comes into your head.'

'How long will we be stuck here, do you think?' Her voice was hardly more than a sigh and he had to bend his head to hear her.

'I do not know.'

'Shall we die here, do you think? Will they find us frozen in each other's arms?' Her lips flickered into a tiny smile. 'Oh, that will give the tabbies something to talk about, won't it?' Her voice faded to almost nothing and her head lolled. 'On top of everything else. . .'

He had a small flask of brandy and put it to her lips. 'Miss Sadler—Helen, my darling, stay awake—please.'

'Not Sadler,' she murmured, choking on the fiery liquid. 'Sanghurst. Helen Sanghurst.'

Sanghurst! Where had he heard that name? 'It doesn't matter,' he said, enfolding her in his arms, rocking her. 'Nothing matters now except keeping you awake.'

'If you only knew the truth. . .'

'It is not important.'

'Yes, it is. I lied.'

'About being a companion?'

'Yes.'

'And about where you are going?'

'No, that is true. Going to Killearn. Going to the Earl of Strathrowan. Papa made him my guardian. . .' She could not keep her eyes open and her voice was becoming fainter and fainter. She was no longer cold, could feel nothing, except an urgent desire for sleep.

Strathrowan! His own father was her guardian! That was why he felt instinctively he had to look after her; she was Lord Sanghurst's daughter and he had met her before, long ago in India when he was hardly out of petticoats and she was a baby.

'Helen, wake up!' He shook her almost savagely and then crushed her to him. 'Helen, you must not go to sleep, you must not. I love you. I need you. We will be married. . .'

But she was slumbering and did not hear him.

CHAPTER TEN

DUNCAN lay down beside Helen along the seat, wrapping the rugs round them both, holding her close,
trying to warm her with his own body, talking and
shaking her alternately, making her groan and protest,
but he could not let her slip away. He told her of his
home at Strathrowan, of his brother and sister-in-law
and his nephew and niece. He told her she would be
made welcome and everyone would love her.

He talked about India, knowing she would not
remember it. He did not recall much himself, except
the journey home, though it had not been home to him
then; he had never been to Scotland. His father had
not expected to inherit, being a second son, and had
gone out to the sub-continent to make his fortune. In
that he had succeeded, marrying the daughter of a
nabob and siring two sons, before his wife had died
giving birth to a still-born daughter.

Duncan had been ten and his brother fifteen when
their father learned that his father and brother were
both dead and he had become the Earl of Strathrowan.
Home they had come to Scotland, home to the mountains and glens of Killearn, which Duncan had come to
love and still loved even after the affair with Arabella
had sent him far from it.

He barely remembered Lord Sanghurst, who had
left India two or three years before they did, but he
had heard of him since. He had been a well-known

figure, something in government, a consort of the
Prince Regent, though when George became King, he
had fallen from favour. He had been a rake and an
inveterate gambler, who would bet on raindrops on
the window pane if he happened to be confined indoors
because of inclement weather.

Duncan's father, who had once called him friend,
had long since ceased to stand buff for him, saying that
Sanghurst's gambling had killed his wife and would
ruin his daughter if he were not stopped and while
people continued to allow him to owe them money, he
would never change. When he was in favour at Court,
he had been allowed endless credit, but after his fall
from grace the dunners closed in on him. In the end he
had taken the coward's way out and shot himself. It
had been the talk of the *ton*, even in Vienna. Poor,
dear Helen, no wonder she hated gambling.

'We will be married,' he repeated again and again,
though whether she heard or understood what he said,
he did not know. 'I promise never to gamble, never
even to mention the word "wager" if it upsets you so.
I am a second son, but I have a good annuity from my
maternal grandmother, besides my captain's pay. I can
do better. I'll join the Diplomatic Corps. They say I
am a good negotiator...' On and on he went, hardly
drawing breath, trying to make her answer, to say
something, anything, just to let him know she was
conscious. But she had not spoken for some time now
and he was afraid...

Helen could hear a voice, quiet, urgent, ragged-edged,
but she could not understand the words; she knew only
that as long as the voice was there, she was safe from

harm. Then through the mist which surrounded her brain and refused to let her think, she heard other sounds, dogs barking, a horse neighing, more voices. Momentarily she knew that whatever had been keeping her warm was gone and icy air fanned her face, then she was being carried.

She moaned a little and heard the voice again, clear as day. 'Thank God, she's alive.' And then she was lying in something which was carrying her over the snow and the warmth and the soft voice were with her again and she sighed in contentment and slept and this time no one tried to shake her into wakefulness.

When she woke she was in a bed. It had all been a dream, a nightmare of epic proportions. Soon Daisy would come with hot water and chocolate to drink. She would lay out her clothes, chattering about the day, whether it was fine or wet and whether she would need stout boots or light shoes if she was going out walking. She turned her head towards the light. The curtains were drawn back and sunshine filled the room.

But the curtains were unfamiliar and the room was different. It was huge, with a large four-poster bed in which she was almost lost, a big wardrobe and several smaller chests and a long mirror. There was a thick blue and pink carpet on the floor and a fire burning in the grate. She moved again and a face came into focus, a finely-drawn face, surrounded by curls of golden hair. 'Who are you? Where am I?'

The vision smiled. 'I am Viscountess Blair, my dear. Margaret to you. And you are safe at home.'

'Blair?' Her heart began to thump uncontrollably. It had not been a dream, it had been real. Captain Blair had brought her here. But why? 'Viscountess?' she queried. 'You are Captain Blair's wife?'

Lady Blair laughed lightly. 'No, I am his sister-in-law. He is unmarried, did he not tell you?'

'Oh, yes, I remember now.' The Captain had asked her to marry him and she had refused him, but that was before she had confessed. She had confessed, hadn't she? That wasn't part of her dream? 'He looked after me and saved my life.'

'Yes, I believe he did. Old Hamish McFaddern came to us through the blizzard and guided my husband, that's the Viscount, and some of the servants with a pony and sled back to where he had left you. You were only half a dozen miles away. If the snow had held back for an hour or so longer, you would have been safe home long before. Duncan blames himself, of course, and he has been very anxious about you.'

'I am deeply indebted to him.'

'We are all truly sorry. You should not have had to face that journey alone but. . .'

'How long have I been lying here?'

'Three weeks.'

'As long as that?' she asked, surprised that three weeks of her life should have disappeared without trace. 'When do you think I might get up?'

'As soon as you feel strong enough. There is no hurry.'

'But I have to go.' She lifted herself on her elbow.

'Go? Go where?'

'To Killearn. To the Earl of Strathrowan, he is expecting me.'

'But that is exactly where you are. Did Duncan not tell you?'

'I am at Killearn?' It was unbelievable. What had the Captain told her? 'I heard a voice, but I was so sleepy, I am not at all sure what was said. Oh, I am so confused.'

'It is little wonder, my dear, but it is simple enough. The Earl of Strathrowan is my father-in-law and Duncan's father. We sent for Duncan to come home because the Earl was ill and we thought it was high time he left off his wandering. When Papa-in-law heard from Mr Benstead about you, he wrote to Duncan at his London club, knowing he was on his way, and asked him to look out for you and bring you to us. . .'

'He knew who I was all along?' No wonder he said he hated pretence. He had given her the opportunity to tell the truth and she had let it go. How could she have been so stupid?

'No,' Margaret said. 'That was the strange thing about it. He was so anxious to come home, he did not go to his club and he never received the letter. It was all a most extraordinary coincidence that he should meet you as he did.'

'And I delayed him with my foolishness. The Earl. . .'

Margaret smiled. 'Fortunately, Papa-in-law made a full recovery, though he has to be careful not to exert himself.'

This was almost too much to digest at once and Helen fell back on the pillow, trying to understand what it all meant. Was this truly her home now? It seemed her fears about not being welcome had been groundless. But had that changed anything? She was still a pauper, still the deceiver. 'Is Captain Blair still here?'

'Of course.'

'Will he be returning to Europe now that he knows the Earl is well?'

'I do not know. We would like him to stay here, of course, but the decision will be his. It is time he put the past behind him.'

'The past? There was some trouble?'

'He did not tell you about it?'

'No, though he did say something about falling in love and being sent away to get over it. He called it puppy love.'

Margaret smiled. 'He *was* very young, but that is not to say he did not feel very deeply about it. And what made it worse was that Arabella married his boyhood friend and became Lady Macgowan. Papa-in-law blamed himself. He said he was wrong to have sent him away, he should have let the affair run its course, instead of which I believe Duncan brooded over it and that fastened his attachment even more.'

'Why did his lordship object?'

'He thought the match was unsuitable. Second son or no, Duncan was expected to marry someone from a good family with a worthwhile dowry. Second sons cannot entirely rule out the possibility of inheriting — after all, the Earl himself was a second son — and they must take that into consideration when choosing a wife. Arabella Novello's father had come over from Italy before the war; nothing much was known of him, except that he had made a great deal of money in commerce. The irony of it was that the Macgowans were not so particular; their estate was facing ruin and Mr Novello's money brought it to rights. Arabella is now Lady Macgowan.'

'The poor man,' Helen murmured. So that was why he had seemed a little bitter. Indigestion indeed!

'Yes, but after all that, James is dead. He died just over a year ago in a fall in the mountains.'

'Oh. Do you think. . .?' Helen could not bring herself to ask and yet she needed desperately to know. 'Will they. . .?'

Margaret smiled and stood up. 'Who knows? As soon as Arabella heard he was home, she came over by sled to see him. She has been three times already.' She leaned over and straightened the coverlet. 'I should not be prattling on about it, you know. Please don't tell Duncan I spoke of it, he is still very sensitive on the subject.'

'No, I won't.'

'Good. Now I am going to tell Papa you are well on the way to recovery. Tomorrow you will be able to dress and come downstairs. Flora shall look after you. She is young, but my own maid has trained her and I think she will do you very well.'

She left and Helen lay back among the pillows, still unable to believe she had arrived. That it was also the home of Captain Blair was almost incredible. All those lies, her false name, her occupation, the story of the nabob's widow, must all be telling against her now. Unless Captain Blair had said nothing of it. He had certainly not told his sister-in-law of his proposal to her or she would not have mentioned Lady Macgowan.

Surely, if he had meant it, he would have said something to his family, he would not have let them assume he would take up his old love again. And the lady in question was obviously intent on renewing the courtship. And this time it seemed the Earl would not stand in their way. What had she told him in her half-conscious state? She hadn't admitted to being in love with him, had she? Oh, why must she fall in love for the first time in her life with someone whose affections were engaged elsewhere?

She looked up as she heard a soft knock on the door and before she could call out, Duncan had put his head round it, grinning cheerfully. 'May I come in?'

She tried to ignore the pounding of her heart and smiled at him. 'Of course.'

He strode into the room, even more handsome than she remembered him. He wore a well-fitting frockcoat in deep blue superfine, pantaloon trousers in soft doeskin strapped under his foot inside soft kid pumps. His yellow and blue striped kerseymere waistcoat framed a neckcloth of starched muslin. He sat on the side of the bed and took her hand in his, his expression one of gentle concern. 'How are you?'

'Better, thank you.' She tried to smile, but though her lips responded her eyes remained bleak. 'I must thank you for saving my life and to ask your forgiveness for deceiving you about who I was.'

'Why did you?'

'Pride, I suppose. I did not want anyone to know that Lord Sanghurst's daughter was penniless and I did not think Lord Strathrowan truly wanted the encumbrance of a ward he had not seen since she was a baby and, if I had to earn my living, then the sooner I became used to the idea the better. I thought travelling incognito would give me a good idea of what that might be like.'

'And you had no notion of who I was?'

'No.'

'Would it had made any difference if you had? Would you have behaved any differently?'

'No, I do not think so.'

He smiled. 'I am glad about that. It is Miss Helen Sadler I came to appreciate for her humanity, to admire for her courage. . .'

She drew her breath in sharply; she could not let him go on, it was twisting the knife in the wound. 'Miss Sadler does not exist, Captain.'

'"What's in a name? A rose by any other name would smell as sweet."'

'Quoting Shakespeare at me does not change anything, Captain Blair. I am still an imposter, a deceiver.'

'You are too hard on yourself. And I am not entirely blameless. Can you forgive me for my lapses from good manners?'

She smiled, remembering that embrace in the woods when she had realised how wonderful it was to be kissed by him; she could hardly reproach him for it. 'Yes, please forget it, I have.'

'Have you?' he queried softly, his warm brown eyes searching hers. 'Have you also forgotten I asked you to marry me?'

'You asked Miss Sadler. And Miss Sadler refused.'

'You have just said she does not exist. What about Miss Sanghurst? Would she refuse?'

He was testing her, trying to find out if she expected him to repeat his offer. He would be in a hubble if she did. 'Yes. Miss Helen Sanghurst and the son of the Earl of Strathrowan are strangers to each other.'

'I am persuaded you do not mean that, not after all we've been through.'

'That is precisely the point. We were two people

thrown together on a coach journey, a journey which took seven days, that is all. . .'

'But packed with incident.'

She smiled wryly, though she felt more like crying. Somehow or other she had to harden her heart, at least until she found out more about Arabella. If what Margaret said was true, then there was no future for her with Captain Duncan Blair. 'That is just it. If there had not been so many misadventures, if we had never met Tom and Dorothy, if we had never witnessed their wedding, if we had not been stuck in the snow, you would not have given me a second thought. . .'

'Fustian!'

'You think you have compromised me, that it was acceptable to carry Miss Sadler to her bed, to take her unawares and kiss her, but not Miss Sanghurst, the daughter of your father's friend. Now you feel you must do the honourable. . .'

'Bunkum! Did you not hear a word I said to you when we were alone together in the snow?'

She had heard only a distant, soothing voice, the words had been lost on her, but she could hardly ask him to repeat them now. 'Said *in extremis*, Captain. I am persuaded you have already regretted your rash proposal. If you are worried that I will hold you to your offer, please be easy. I understand, truly I do.'

'It's more than I do.'

She could not explain, not without betraying Margaret's confidence. 'Captain, I am still very tired. . .'

He released her hand and rose at once. 'I beg pardon. I had not meant to tire you.' His words were clipped. 'I will leave you to rest.' With that he bowed and left the room, closing the door with a firm click.

She was as prickly as a hedgehog, he could tell it from the stiff way she smiled at him and the way she held her chin, as if holding her head up was all that mattered. He cursed her father for his unfeeling selfishness, for leaving her so vulnerable. Her pride was all she had to fight with and he wished with all his heart she would realise that she did not need to fight him, that he understood because he loved her. But he also respected her and because of that, he would try to be patient.

The following day Flora came to help Helen to dress ready to go downstairs. All her clothes were mourning black and there was little to choose between them, but she picked out a warm merino wool, relieving the drabness of the colour with a white shawl of fine silk. Looking in the mirror, she realised she had lost weight and her eyes were overbright in a very pale face. 'You could do with a little carmine on your cheeks, miss,' the maid said, standing behind her, hairbrush in hand. 'And if you wear your hair down, with little curls about your face, so, it will make it look fuller.' She teased out a curl or two as she spoke.

Helen smiled at the girl in the glass. 'It will make me look like a schoolgirl.'

'And where's the harm in that? They will be falling over themselves to take care of you.'

Her toilette complete, Helen stood up and slipped her feet into black satin slippers. 'What now?'

'I'm to take you to the library, miss. His lordship is waiting for you.'

Helen took a deep breath and followed the girl down a beautiful carved oak staircase, lined on one side with portraits, to a vestibule whose vaulted ceiling reached the whole height of the building. Several doors opened from it, no doubt leading to the rest of the house. The maid conducted her to one, knocked and ushered her in.

The man who stood by the hearth was an older version of Duncan. He had the same firm features and his hair curled in much the same way about his ears, although it was greying about the temples. Though very thin, he was tall and upright, impeccably dressed for country living in a check cloth jacket, breeches and topboots. He greeted her warmly and invited her to be seated. She perched herself on the edge of the sofa, her back straight and her hands in her lap. He sat down beside her and took her hand. 'You are recovered from your ordeal?'

'Yes, thank you, my lord.'

'Good. I am only sorry it happened. You should not have been obliged to make your own way here. I can only say I was not in plump currant or I would not have been so foolish as to rely on a letter reaching my son. I hope you will forgive me.'

'It is of no consequence,' she said. 'After all, it is many years since you and my father last saw each other and you could not be expected to be overjoyed at finding yourself guardian to an impoverished nobody.'

'My dear child, you must not think of yourself like that. You are most welcome. This is your home now and you must look on us as your family. Think of Andrew and Duncan as your brothers. They already regard you as the dear sister they never had.'

So, the Captain had not told his father of his

proposal and that proved he had never seriously meant it. She had been right to refuse him.

'I shall make you a decent allowance, so that you can buy any little frippery that takes your fancy,' the Earl went on, before she could find anything to say on the subject of brothers. 'When the roads are free of snow, you will be able to go to Glasgow or Edinburgh, the shops there are as good as those in London, you will see.'

'But, my lord, I have an allowance sufficient for my needs. . .'

'That! Your lawyer has written to me of that. It will hardly purchase one new bonnet a year.' He smiled and patted the small hand which lay in his own. 'I cannot have my friends saying I treat my ward worse than my own children, can I? It is selfish of me to want my neighbours to think well of me, but there it is.'

'Thank you, my lord,' she said, not in the least deceived but loving him for his thoughtfulness, a thoughtfulness Duncan had inherited. He had demonstrated it on the journey from London when he did not even know who she was. But that was all it was, solicitude for her helplessness, even his unconsidered proposal was only an extension of that. At the time he had not known that Lady Macgowan was free.

'Now, you must make the acquaintance of the rest of the family. Duncan has gone out, I am afraid, but the others are gathered in the morning room to meet you.'

The Viscount, when they were introduced, was equally attentive towards her and Margaret was already like a sister to her, making her feel at home, chattering about fashions and what Helen could wear when she came out of black gloves, telling her how she ran the household. The house was not a house at all, but a real castle, with thick stone walls, turrets and winding stairs.

The two children, Robert, who was eight and Caroline, a very pretty six-year-old, were curious about her, but had obviously been told not to pester her, for they were as polite as two boisterous children could possibly be. In no time Helen had become part of the family and was happier than she had been for years, except for the lingering desire for Duncan which she could not suppress however hard she tried. It was made worse when she saw Arabella Macgowan for the first time.

Christmas had come and gone, and it was the last day of 1820. There was to be a joyous celebration to herald in the new year; Hogmanay, the Scots called it. Everyone from miles around arrived by sled drawn by sturdy little Highland ponies, to dine and play parlour games. Helen, halfway down the stairs, saw Lady Macgowan arrive and knew at once who she was and any hope that Duncan's love for her might have cooled over the years, vanished.

She was beautiful. She was much taller than Helen, with a curvaceous figure which was almost voluptuous. She had even features, blue eyes and a rich red mouth, which spread into a smile as she she caught sight of Duncan, resplendent in his blue uniform, standing to receive the guests. Neither was she in mourning as Helen was. Her cloak was taken from her and she was revealed in a gown of azure gauze over a deep blue satin slip. It had puffed sleeves and a very low neckline which revealed the curve of her breasts, between which nestled a diamond and silver pendant. She held out both lace-gloved hands to Duncan, who moved forward to greet her, taking her hands in both his own and appraising her from her crown of golden hair, dressed á la Grecque and threaded with deep blue ribbon, down to her dainty feet in matching satin slippers. They murmured a few words to each other which Helen was too far away to hear, but whatever was said, they smiled at each other before Arabella turned towards a servant who was carrying a small boy. Duncan took the child and, laughing, threw him into the air, making him giggle and grab his hair with pudgy fists.

'Ouch!' Duncan removed the hand and set the boy down. 'Run and find Robert, Jimmy. He is in the small parlour playing with his toy soldiers.'

The child ran off, obviously very familiar with the layout of the castle, and Duncan offered his arm to escort the lady into the large salon to join the other guests.

The intimate scene made Helen want to fly back to her room, to stay there until everyone had gone home, but her pride came to her rescue and she continued down the stairs to be met at the bottom by the Earl, his handsome figure enhanced by the Blair kilt, complete with the sash fastened over his shoulder with a huge silver brooch. The full sleeves of his white shirt ended in a fall of lace over his hands. He offered her his arm. 'Come, Helen, do not look so nervous. We are going to enjoy ourselves.'

He led her into the large reception room where a piper was playing, and introduced her to a great many people, including Lady Macgowan, who smiled and asked her how she did, while appraising her from head to foot and making her feel even smaller than she really was. The Earl moved on, taking Helen with him. She smiled and chatted inconsequentially to everyone she met, trying not to let her hurt show.

Andrew went out just before midnight carrying a lump of coal in order to return and knock at the great iron-studded front door as the clock struck the hour. They sang 'Auld Lang Syne' and everyone kissed everyone else. Duncan, she noticed, stood looking at Lady Macgowan just a little too long before he kissed her and whispered something which made her laugh, before moving away to join the rest of the company in a Highland reel, his feet and arms working rhythmically to the sound of the bagpipes played by a ghillie in Highland dress.

Helen, not knowing the intricate steps, sat and watched, marvelling at the energy of the dancers. At the end of it, to encouragement from everyone, Andrew and Duncan took two swords down from their place on the wall and laid them crossed on the floor and as the bagpipes began another tune, they danced over them, placing their feet so exactly that they were only inches from the blades but never touched them. 'Better than drawing them in anger, don't you agree?' said a voice at Helen's elbow.

She turned to find Lady Macgowan at her side. 'Yes, indeed.'

'They grew up together, Andrew, Duncan and my husband. James and Duncan fell out over me, you know. There was a sword fight. That's how Duncan got that scar on the back of his hand. I'll wager you thought he had earned it in the war.'

'I didn't think about it at all.'

'No?' She laughed lightly. 'How strange. Perhaps you found other things to talk about on your journey to Scotland.'

There was more to the lady's conversation than appeared on the surface and it set Helen's hackles rising. 'The discourse was very general among all the passengers,' she said coolly. 'And there were other incidents. . .'

'Yes, quite. I have been told of those, but I would not wish you to be under any misapprehension. Duncan was sent away because he loved me. His father was too top-lofty to consider an heiress outside his own narrow circle. After he went, I was forced into marriage with James. Now James is dead, the boot is on the other foot. I have the title and a great deal of money. The Earl will no longer stand in our way.'

'Then may I wish you happy.' Helen forced a stiff smile.

'Thank you. I am so glad we had this little talk.'

Helen wanted to escape, to run away, anywhere where she could give vent to her misery alone, but the dance had ended and Duncan was bearing down on them, a broad smile on his handsome features. He stopped before them.

'Helen. I wish the new year will bring you everything you could hope for, your heart's desire.'

'Thank you, Captain Blair.'

'And will you not wish me the same?' The voice was soft, the voice she had heard in her frozen delirium, the voice of the siren.

'Yes, of course.' Oh, let her be strong, let her be resolute. 'I wish you happy, always.'

'Oh, Margaret is playing a waltz,' Arabella broke in before he could say any more. 'Come along, Duncan, you used to dance this very well. Show me you have not forgotten.' And with that she took his hand and dragged him into the centre of the room, where he put his arm about her waist and they began to move gracefully round the room, her blue skirt swishing about his pantaloon-clad thighs, her eyes lifted to his.

'Why did you do that?' he demanded.

'Do what, Duncan, dear?'

'Drag me away from Miss Sanghurst. Anyone would think you are jealous.'

'Jealous! Of that little black mouse! You were always the jealous one, as I recall.'

'That was a long time ago. We have both grown up since then.'

'But you have not forgotten me, have you? We can start again and this time your papa will not be so stubborn.'

'I am glad he was.'

'Why yes, as you say, we have both grown up, we are not so easily swayed by what other people expect of us. James is dead.'

'I know and I am very sorry.'

'Do not be, because I am not.'

'You can't mean that?'

'Yes, I do. I wish you had killed him when you took that sword to him. We would not have wasted all these years.'

'They were not wasted. And the only thing I regret is that I fell out with James.'

Although he continued to dance, a faraway look had come into his eyes, as if he had been transported in time and was young again, a lonely ten-year-old boy, wandering over the hills and moors of his new home. It was hardly surprising that he and James, who lived on the neighbouring estate and was the same age, should meet and become friends. They had grown up together, fished and hunted together, went off to school together, and later, when the opportunity arose, attended social gatherings together in Glasgow and Edinburgh, meeting young ladies of their own class, flirting a little and afterwards comparing notes.

But when, at eighteen, Duncan had fallen in love with Arabella, James had been neglected in his pursuit of her, a pursuit which caused some amusement to the older generation who waited for it all to blow over. When it did not, the Earl had purchased Duncan a commission in the Prince of Wales's regiment and sent him away to get over it. Duncan had accepted that he was far too young to think of marriage and once he realised there was no help for it, he had not minded going. With James's connivance, he and Arabella had managed a few minutes of privacy in which to say goodbye. Their parting had been tearful on her part and grim on his, but she had reassured him with kisses and promises. 'They can lock me up in a tower for ever, I will marry no one but you,' she had said.

'Then I will scale that tower, inch by inch, to reach you,' he had replied, with all the confidence of an eighteen-year-old unused to letting obstacles get in the way of his heart's desire.

He might not have been so complacent if he had known that the war would drag on for years, years in which he had written to her at least once a week and hoarded up her replies to be read over and over again whenever the fighting died down and he had a few minutes to spare.

When the advance took them deeper and deeper into Spain and then over the mountains into France itself, the letters became less frequent, but that was hardly surprising, he had told himself, it would be a miracle if they managed to follow him at the pace of the advance and Wellington's diplomatic bags had more important things to carry than love letters. Not for a moment did he doubt Arabella's fidelity. If only he had questioned it, the final humiliation might have been easier to bear.

He had received a head wound in the last days of the fighting and found himself on a ship coming home, home to Arabella, waiting in her fantasy tower for her lover to return and claim her. But it was his fantasy, not hers.

She was already married to James, had been for three years, even while writing to him of her constancy, James his boyhood friend, James who knew exactly how he felt about her. Duncan had challenged him to a duel, but fortunately his father put a stop to it before any lasting damage could be done, but he had regretted it ever since. 'You, my dear Arabella, were not worth the loss of James's friendship and the last thing I want is to begin all over again.' He smiled as he spoke and no one, glancing at them from a distance, would have guessed that they were quarrelling.

Helen could not bear to look at them and turned away. She found a seat in a corner, half hidden behind a potted palm, but she was not there long before Andrew found her and asked her to dance. Her protests that, being in mourning, she ought not to, were brushed aside and she was whirled into the middle of the floor. He danced well, but how she wished it was Duncan and not Andrew who was holding her. She kept a fixed smile on her face, but her heart was breaking.

Any hope she might have had that Duncan had forgotten his first love, and would propose again, had faded to nothing. Oh, if only she had the wherewithal to be independent, she could go away, make a life for herself, become the lady's companion she had pretended to be. By the time the party broke up, just before dawn, she had made up her mind. She would not stay.

She watched the weather carefully in the ensuing days, waiting for a thaw, waiting for the roads to be opened, so that she could begin planning an escape. But they remained obstinately frozen and the longer she stayed, the more firmly she became entrenched in her life with the Strathrowans.

She loved the people, loved exploring the castle and finding delightful hidden nooks, watching the birds pecking in the snow for the scraps put out for them, turning her eyes to the mountains where, every now and again, she glimpsed a stag, standing on a crag, antlers outlined against the sky. She knew the men would go out stalking it, but refused to dwell on it. How could she walk away and leave all this? But she must. Sooner or later, Duncan would marry Arabella and she could not bear to be there when he brought his bride home.

* * *

It was the second week of February when she woke to the sound of water dripping off the eaves. She slipped from her bed and went to the window, pulling back the heavy curtains and looking out on the sight of a few blackened shrubs in the garden below her appearing above a layer of snow. The paths had already been cleared by the outdoor servants and she could see the nodding heads of snowdrops peeping through the ground near the terrace. For the first time she could see its shape, the steps from the lawn up to the higher level, the outlines of the borders. It was thawing fast and time to think about leaving.

But before she could make any plans at all, Margaret came to her room one morning before breakfast, to tell her a visitor had arrived in a hired chaise all the way from London to see her. 'He says his name is Benstead,' she said. 'Do you wish to receive him?'

'Benstead?' Helen repeated, then as realisation dawned, 'Goodness, he was Papa's lawyer. What can he want with me?'

'Come down and you will see. I'll send Flora to you. Hurry up, do. I am consumed with curiosity.'

Margaret was no more curious than she was, Helen thought, as the maid came in with hot water and towels and began to lay out her clothes, half-mourning now, a lilac satin over a white slip decorated with white ruching and silk violets. Half an hour later, she went downstairs to find the little lawyer in the anteroom, gazing out of the window at the dripping trees. He turned when he heard the rustle of silk behind him. 'Miss Sanghurst, your obedient.' He made a rheumaticky leg. 'I hope I find you well?'

'Very well, sir. But what has brought you here? The journey must have been quite dreadful.'

'The winter has not been too severe in England, Miss Sanghurst. I did not realise it had been so hard in Scotland until I crossed the border. I came post-haste as soon as I could.'

'Why? Is something wrong?'

'Wrong, my dear Miss Sanghurst? Oh, dear, no, quite the reverse. Your papa's cargo arrived safely in dock.'

'His cargo?' She was mystified.

'Yes, you remember him saying all would be well when his ship came in. Well, it has. It did. A fine cargo of spices and rich silks from the Orient, all highly sought after. I have been able to dispose of everything very profitably. Lord Sanghurst's debts are all paid and there is a surplus over expenditure which is yours. I came to appraise you of it and to await your instructions.'

He smiled slowly. She had come on a lot since he had last seen her; she had a new poise as if she had grown up from child to woman, which was a foolish thought because she had been a grown woman when she left. 'It will provide a good dowry, not top of the trees, you understand, but enough...'

It was a moment or two before the news could sink in, before she realised that it could make a great deal of difference to her life. 'It was very kind of you to come all this way to tell me of my good fortune,' she said, so solemnly he wondered if she was pleased by the news at all. 'Is the money entirely mine, to do with as I please?'

'Yes, subject to your guardian's agreement. According to your late father's will, his lordship has the last word on any decision you may make until you marry, or if you do not, until your thirtieth birthday.'

'Will the money buy an annuity?'

'Yes, but why do you need that?'

'I mean to leave here and live independently.'

'My goodness, Miss Sanghurst, you do surprise me. Have they not treated you kindly? I gained the impression from Lady Blair that you were thought of as one of the family.'

'So I am, no one could have been kinder, but that is half the trouble. They are too kind and I am too dependent. I would like to live quietly on my own with Daisy for a companion. Do you think she would come?'

'I am sure she would, but I do not understand why it is necessary.'

'My reasons are private, Mr Benstead. Do you think you could rent a cottage in the Lakes for me? Ambleside, perhaps.'

'Of course, but I must speak to the Earl first.' He looked at her, trying to divine her reasons from the expression on her face. She had smiled at him and expressed pleasure at seeing him, but she was not happy. He could not blame her surroundings, which were nothing short of luxurious; he could only surmise it was a man who had put the bleak look in her eyes; it was even worse than when he had told her about her father's gambling debts.

Who had put it there? Lady Blair had told him, in the few minutes conversation they had had, that Captain Blair had met with Miss Sanghurst on the journey and escorted her to Killearn in appalling weather conditions and she had been very ill as a result, though now fully recovered. If that young man was responsible for her unhappiness, then he must be brought to book over it. He had been offered hospitality for the night and he would contrive, in that time, to speak to Captain Blair as well as the Earl.

'Miss Sanghurst wishes to leave here?' queried Duncan when Mr Benstead begged a few words in private after everyone else had retired. They were sitting in the library enjoying a glass of brandy beside the dying fire. 'Are you sure you have not misunderstood?'

'Oh, I am sure. She asked me to find her a cottage in the Lakes and send for her maid to join her. She said she meant to live quietly alone.'

'Cork-brained ninny!'

'Really, sir, I see no call to insult me.'

'I do not insult you. I am cursing myself for a cow-handed clunch. Did she say why?'

'No. She said her reasons were private. I deduced from that that there was a man in the picture. . .'

'Yes.' He sighed. 'I had better tell you the whole, you may have good advice, for I have not been able to make her see reason.'

'Women are not renowned for their aptitude in deduction, Captain. They think with their hearts.'

'And Helen's heart? What is that telling her?'

'She feels she has to flee from a situation she cannot deal with. I am sure you understand.'

Duncan looked up in surprise. 'Did she tell you that?'

'Naturally she did not. I surmised it. I also surmised it had something to do with you.'

'I made a cake of myself, Mr Benstead.' He smiled crookedly and went on to tell the lawyer of all the incidents on the journey to Scotland. 'I have put myself utterly beyond her touch,' he finished. 'She is convinced I offered her marriage to salve my conscience and will not believe I want to marry her because I cannot contemplate life without her.'

'Is that all?'

'All? Is it not enough?'

'Perhaps she will come about. She cannot leave without the Earl's consent.'

'You do not know Miss Sanghurst very well if you think coercion will serve,' Duncan said gloomily.

'Captain Blair, are you a gambling man?'

Duncan looked across at him, taken aback by the question. Was it a trick? 'If you are alluding to Miss Sanghurst's unhappy experience with the late Lord Sanghurst. . .'

'Not at all. I meant are you prepared to take a gamble on Miss Sanghurst admitting what her heart is telling her? I have a plan. It might work.'

'Then, for the love of God, let me hear it.'

CHAPTER ELEVEN

Mr Benstead left next day to execute Helen's orders and she settled down to wait for his return and the arrival of Daisy. She told herself that life in a cottage by Lake Windermere was exactly what she wanted, that in the peace and solitude there her heart would mend. Duncan had accepted that she was leaving, just as his father had done, expressing his regret and saying that, of course, she must do as she pleased. It had all been too easy, which just went to show what they really thought of her. Only Andrew and Margaret continued to try and persuade her to stay, but then they did not know the reason she could not.

She tried to fill her days so that she did not have time to think. She read a great deal, borrowing books from the his lordship's extensive library, walking on the lower slopes around the castle, getting her feet wet and smiling enigmatically when Margaret or Duncan scolded her. Sometimes Duncan accompanied her, striding beside her with a sporting gun under his arm which he never used, and his dog scampering about in the heather sniffing for rabbits.

'Will you miss all this?' he asked one day, using his arm to encompass the view. They were on the top of a knoll which overlooked the castle, standing in the shelter of its valley. In the distance was the gleam of a large expanse of water and further in the distance, the mountains, still snow-capped.

'Yes,' she admitted. 'It is lovely.' Then half-smiling, so that he would not know what she really felt, 'But the Lakes are also beautiful.'

'Yes, I collect you saying that when we passed through.'

She wished she had not reminded him of that journey, especially that section when they had been at peace with each other, when the first faint glimmering of her love for him had made itself felt. Every time she looked at his firm profile, every time he spoke to her in that soft, sensuous voice, the voice which had kept her from dying, she felt herself crumble a little more. 'I shall miss the people too, everyone has been very good to me, the Earl and Margaret especially. She has been like a sister to me.'

He stifled the retort that she did not have to leave and instead commented that with her capacity for making friends, she would not long be alone. 'But you must be careful,' he added. 'You have a penchant for falling into a hobble.'

'Daisy will see that I don't.' She forced herself to laugh. 'At any rate, she will not scold me like you do. Or tell me what I ought or ought not to do.'

'How dull,' he said wryly. 'Do you mean to have no adventures at all?'

'None. I shall spend my time in good works, reading and walking over the fells.'

'But that is what you have been doing here. No one has prevented you.'

There was no answer to that and she remained silent for a time, watching the dog chasing after a stick he had thrown for it. It came running back, its tail wagging, dropping the stick at their feet. 'Good dog,' he said, bending to pat its head.

'I think I will buy a puppy for company,' she said.

'A puppy?'

'Why not?'

'Why not indeed.' He smiled, this time with genuine pleasure. 'But you do not need to buy one. One of the retriever bitches has had pups; Robbie, here, is the sire. Come, I will choose one for you.' And with that he turned and set off back to the castle, leading her down the winding track to the road and over the drawbridge to the stable block, followed by the faithful dog.

The kennels were at the far side of the yard. He opened the door and disappeared inside. A few moments later he emerged with a soft, sandy-coloured bundle. 'Here,' he said, putting the puppy into her arms. 'He's yours.'

She cuddled the puppy, rubbing her cold cheek along its soft fur. It responded by licking her ear, making her laugh. It was the first time he had really seen her laugh since she arrived, and it made his heart ache to hold her, to reassure her, but he held back, watching her. 'He's been weaned, though he hasn't a name yet. I think the handler calls him number three because he was the third of the litter.'

'Oh, how unfortunate for him to be called by a number. Are you sure you want to give him to me? Will the Earl mind?'

'Yes to the first and no to the second. Keep him. Let him remind you of me, when you are walking in the hills of Cumbria.'

'Thank you.' She turned and fled, dashing across the

yard, in at one of the side doors, along the corridor and up the stairs to her room. She just managed to shut the door behind her before her tears overwhelmed her.

She sat for a long time on the bed, nursing the puppy, with tears streaming down her face onto his head. 'Oh, Pup,' she whispered. 'Why couldn't Papa's ship come in before he died? There would have been no suicide, no stigma, no dreadful gossip about his cowardice, and I would have had my dowry and Miss Sadler, the deceiver, need never have been invented. I would have been acceptable in Captain Blair's eyes. And the Earl's.' She chose to overlook the inescapable fact that if her father had not died and left her penniless she would never have been making the trip to Scotland at all, might never have met the Honourable Captain Duncan Blair, never been com-promised by him, never kissed, never seen him dancing with Lady Macgowan. Her ladyship was the real prob-lem, though strangely she had not been visiting since the New Year. Had they quarrelled? She refused to allow herself even that small hope.

The puppy was licking her face, doing a good job of mopping up her tears. 'You don't care who I am, do you, Pup? Names are unimportant.' She smiled down at him, a crooked rueful smile, weakened by crying. 'You do understand, don't you? I have only my pride.'

She put the puppy down on the bed, where it snuffled round and round to make itself comfortable before settling down to watch her with a baleful eye. She washed and changed for supper, taking great care with her appearance. The skin around her eyes was puffed and red, but a little discreet maquillage hid that.

She dressed in a white crepe gown over a delicate lilac slip. A mauve velvet ribbon outlined the high waist and was also threaded through the hem and tied in a series of tiny bows with floating ends. The same ribbon was threaded through her dark hair.

Flora, who had come to help her, expressed herself satisfied. 'Beautiful, Miss Sanghurst, truly beautiful. Just wait until ye go tae London with the Viscount and Lady Blair in the summer, I ken ye will be a great success. Not that London has anything to beat Edinburgh,' she added. 'You should ask Mr Duncan tae take ye there.'

'Thank you, Flora, that will be all,' she said, rather more stiffly than she intended. There would be no summer in London with Margaret, no trip to the Scottish capital with Captain Blair. Nothing. She put her feet into mauve satin slippers and picked up her fan. 'Look after Pup for me, will you? I imagine he is hungry.' With that she took a deep breath to steady herself and went down to the drawing-room where everyone was gathering before supper.

'Helen, how charming you look,' Margaret said, ignoring the evidence of the tears. 'Isn't that so, Duncan?'

'Yes indeed,' he agreed. 'She will be quite wasted in Cumbria.'

'Then persuade her not to go.'

'She would not listen,' he said with a smile as he offered her his arm to take her into supper. 'Is that not so, princess?'

Helen laid her fingers on his arm and even that small touch nearly overset her again. Forcing her trembling limbs to obey her, she walked beside him into the dining room.

'Princess?' Margaret queried, as they took their places at the table. 'Why do you call Helen that?'

He laughed, a slightly mocking laugh. 'Because when I first met her, she would not tell me who she was or where she was going and when I suggested she was a princess in disguise, she asked me how I had guessed.'

'He did not really believe that, did he?' Margaret asked Helen.

'No, of course not. He was roasting me.'

'And he is still doing it. Duncan, I think it is very uncivil of you.'

'Oh, Miss Sadler does not mind, Miss Sadler is an altogether more agreeable person than Miss Sanghurst.'

'Duncan,' his father remonstrated with him. 'I think you should not tease Helen. She will think you have taken a dislike to her and wish her to be gone and that is not true. It is certainly not true on my part. I am her guardian and pleased to be her guardian until she marries. This is her home and she is more than welcome to stay.'

'And I second that,' Margaret put in, looking from Duncan to Helen and wondering what had passed between them on that long journey from London. What was going on now? They were both Friday-faced, refusing to look at each other. 'Helen is like a sister to me and I do not want to part with her. You should be persuading her to stay, not driving her away.'

'Oh, I am not driving her away, she is old enough to know her own mind,' he said. 'She has told me so often, and I would not, for the world, hold her against her will.'

Helen sprang to her feet, fresh tears flowing down her cheeks. 'Stop it! Please stop it.' Then to the Earl, 'Please excuse me.' She pushed back her chair and fled back to her room.

'I do not know what manners they teach in the army these days,' Andrew said. 'But I never thought to see a brother of mine behave so abominably towards a lady.'

'Yes, Duncan,' his father said. 'Whatever game you are playing, you have taken it too far. I suggest you try and make amends.'

Duncan, seeing Helen run from the room in tears, knew his father was right and he had overplayed his hand. He excused himself and followed her up to her room, where he knocked on the door and called her name.

'Go away.' The voice was muffled.

'No. Helen, I am sorry.' He rattled the door but she had locked it. 'Please let me in. I must speak to you.'

'To deal out more of the same, I suppose. I have had enough of your mockery. Keep away from me.'

'I was not mocking you, rather myself for making such a mull of things. I am sorry if you thought I was. Please let me in.'

'No.'

In desperation he put his muscular shoulder to the door and burst it open. She was pulling clothes from the wardrobe and throwing them into her trunk.

'How dare you!' She turned to face him, though she could hardly see him for tears. 'Captain Blair, I insist you leave me.'

'No.' He forced himself to smile, though the sight of her nearly undid him. 'You are evidently going on a journey.'

'So, what if I am? You knew that anyway. I am simply bringing it forward.'

'Why?'

'I have my reasons.'

'Which you will not tell me.' His voice softened. 'Why can't you talk to me? Why can't you tell me what is wrong? Surely we are not still strangers?'

'Strangers?'

'Miss Helen Sanghurst and the son of the Earl of Strathrowan are strangers, that's what you said. It was your reason for refusing my offer of marriage, wasn't it? And if you insist on leaving, we shall never have the opportunity to remedy that.'

'Not strangers,' she said, so distressed she did not take in the significance of what he was saying. 'Brother and sister.'

He was astounded. 'Wherever did you get that idea?'

'That is how your father said I should think of you. He said you and Andrew considered me the sister you never had.'

'When did he say that?'

'When I first met him. You did not tell him you had asked me to marry you, did you? He would not have said that if you had. You knew he would not approve.'

'Why should he disapprove?'

'Because even second sons are expected to marry someone of consequence. They never know when they might inherit and if they never do, they need a good dowry.'

'I never heard anything so cork-brained. I am sure my father did not tell you that.'

'No, Margaret did, but it makes no difference because she also told me the Earl has set his heart on putting right the wrong he did you when he sent you away and. . .'

'He did me no wrong. On the contrary, he did me a favour and I have told him so. It gave me time. . .'

'What difference does that make? I am persuaded you are not one to change your mind with the wind.'

'Indeed, I am not.'

'Then I will not embarrass you by staying. I shall do very well in Cumbria.'

He sighed heavily. 'Very well, if you insist, but you will need an escort.'

'No, I am perfectly able. . .'

'You said that before and look what happened. Do you think I could let you go alone, knowing you would fall into a scrape before you had covered half a mile?'

'That is no longer your concern.'

'No? I think it is. I think it is very much my concern. If you do not allow me to accompany you, then I must follow on behind like the puppy I gave you.'

'Follow?'

'I cannot let you go. I shall continue to follow you and look after you until you recognise the fact that your life and mine are indivisible.'

She stopped with a petticoat in her hand and stared at him. 'But you can't. . .'

'Why ever not?'

'Lady Macgowan. . .'

'What has she to do with it?'

'Everything. Isn't that what we have been talking

about? Goodness, you fought a duel with your best friend over her and it is obvious. . .'

'Not to me it is not. What has she been telling you?'

'It was not only her, Margaret did too. Now that Lord Macgowan is dead. . .'

'You thought we were going to take up where we left off?' He laughed suddenly and joyfully. 'Oh, my darling Helen, Arabella cannot hold a candle to you. She is a selfish, scheming woman who wants to keep her cake and eat it too. I am glad my father sent me away, very glad indeed. I am afraid I told her so, when she was here for Hogmanay.'

'You did?' She could hardly believe it.

'Yes.' He stepped forward and took her shoulders in his hands. 'Now I am asking you again. Will you marry me?'

'Why?'

'Why? For no reason, for every reason, because my life is empty without you, because I love you. How many more reasons do you want? The only way you will be rid of me, is if you tell me you do not care for me and never will.'

She simply stared at him with her mouth open.

'Go on,' he urged. 'Say it. Say, "Duncan Blair, I do not love you. I will never love you."'

She dropped the petticoat on the floor and silently stared at him.

'Are you going to speak?'

She shook her head.

He took her face into his hands, tipping it up so that he could look into her eyes. Tears glistened on her lashes and he hated himself for causing her unhappiness. 'I am sorry for the Turkish treatment, my love. I wanted you to change your mind about marrying me. I wanted you to see that we belong together and instead of that I nearly drove you away. Will you forgive me?'

She found her voice at last, but it was so weak he had to listen hard to hear it. 'If you had decided against Lady Macgowan, why didn't you ask me again after Mr Benstead had been instead of letting me think you would let me go?'

He smiled. 'And risk another put-down? I do not think, even then, you were ready to admit the truth.'

'And what is that?'

'That we love each other, that it is of no consequence at all who we are, princess or lady's maid, common soldier or aristocrat, it makes no difference.'

'And Papa? The manner of his death. . .'

'Good heavens, you did not think I considered that, did you?'

She nodded.

'I think your father was wiser than you have given him credit for,' he said slowly. 'He made my father your guardian because he knew that if you came to Scotland you would be sure to meet me and he hoped we would make a match of it. It was his last gamble.'

She knew he was only saying that to make her feel better about her father and she loved him all the more for it.

'It was mine too,' he said. 'I gambled on making you accept the truth and it nearly finished me.'

She laughed. 'It was no greater than the risk I took, especially as I did not know I was taking it. But are you sure. . .?'

His answer was to lower his mouth to hers in a kiss

which went on for a very long time and drove all their doubts away.

'Helen.' It was Margaret's soft voice which made them draw apart.

'In here,' Duncan said, raising his head reluctantly, then, as his sister-in-law appeared beside the broken door, 'I have breached the defences. Miss Sanghurst has capitulated. You may congratulate me.'

'Oh, indeed I do.' She hurried to embrace them both. 'I never thought to see you wed, Duncan, you have taken a prodigious time coming to it.'

'But I had to wait to meet my match, didn't I?' he said, smiling at Helen. Then, turning to his sister-in-law, 'And I intend to have words with you later. . .'

'Why, what have I done?'

'Duncan, please,' Helen said. 'Margaret did not know, did not understand. There is no need. . .'

He smiled. 'You are right, my darling. No recriminations. I am too happy. Let us go down and tell the others. We must celebrate.'

Which they did, to everyone's satisfaction.

Historical Romance™

Coming next month

HIS LORDSHIP'S DILEMMA
Meg Alexander
A REGENCY NOVEL

When the Bath seminary closed, Miss Elinor Temple had
no choice but to take Hester Winton to her guardian. Their
arrival in the midst of Marcus, Lord Rokeby's entertaining
guests—which Elinor dubbed an orgy!—was not greeted
with good grace. Marcus equally had no choice, though he
insisted upon employing Elinor as Hester's duenna. Two
things became clear to Elinor—Hester's guardianship
owed rather more to family feuding than goodwill, and
Marcus was not averse to flirting with herself! But it really
wouldn't do to allow her own feelings to become
engaged…

AN AFFAIR OF HONOUR
Paula Marshall
LONDON 1920s

Clare Windham had jilted her fiancé without explanation
and been ostracised for it. What malign stroke of fate had
brought the past back to haunt her in the shape of Ralph
Schuyler? It seemed her life was in danger, and Ralph was
trying to save her—but who could tell with this secretive
man, no matter how attractive he was to her…? Ralph
walked a fine line, and the more he learned of Clare's
integrity, the more he knew that, when all the danger was
past, she might never forgive him.

SINGLE LETTER SWITCH

A year's supply of Mills & Boon Presents™ novels— absolutely FREE!

Would you like to win a year's supply of passionate compelling and provocative romances? Well, you can and the're free! Simply complete the grid below and send it to us by 31st May 1997. The first five correct entries picked after the closing date will win a year's supply of Mills & Boon Presents™ novels (six books every month—worth over £150). What could be easier?

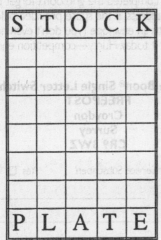

S	T	O	C	K
P	L	A	T	E

Clues:

A   To pile up
B   To ease off or a reduction
C   A dark colour
D   Empty or missing
E   A piece of wood
F   Common abbreviation for an aircraft

Please turn over for details of how to enter ☞

How to enter...

There are two five letter words provided in the grid overleaf. The first one being STOCK the other PLATE. All you have to do is write down the words that are missing by changing just one letter at a time to form a new word and eventually change the word STOCK into PLATE. You only have eight chances but we have supplied you with clues as to what each one is. Good Luck!

When you have completed the grid don't forget to fill in your name and address in the space provided below and pop this page into an envelope (you don't even need a stamp) and post it today. Hurry—competition ends 31st May 1997.

Mills & Boon® Single Letter Switch
FREEPOST
Croydon
Surrey
CR9 3WZ

Are you a Reader Service Subscriber?   Yes ❏   No ❏

Ms/Mrs/Miss/Mr _____

Address _____

_____

_____ Postcode _____

One application per household.

C6K